D1489050

A TIGHT LIE

A TIGHT LIE

Don Dahler

Minotaur Books ⋈ New York

A THOMAS DUNNE BOOK FOR MINOTAUR BOOKS.
An imprint of St. Martin's Publishing Group.

A TIGHT LIE. Copyright © 2009 by Don Dahler. All rights reserved. Printed in the United States of America. For information, address St. Martin's Press, 175 Fifth Avenue, New York, N.Y. 10010.

www.thomasdunnebooks.com
www.minotaurbooks.com

Library of Congress Cataloging-in-Publication Data

Dahler, Don.
    A tight lie / Don Dahler.—1st ed.
      p. cm.
    ISBN-13: 978-0-312-38350-3
    ISBN-10: 0-312-38350-9
    1.   Golf Stories.   I.   Title
    PS3604.A345T54 2009
    813'.6—dc22

                                    2008034140
First Edition: March 2009

10   9   8   7   6   5   4   3   2   1

For Mom,
who taught me
pages are wings

ACKNOWLEDGMENTS

It was Nathaniel Hawthorne who said, "Easy reading is damn hard writing." I like that a man who wrote about puritanical New England would curse when describing his vocation. And boy, do I know what he means.

I wanted *A Tight Lie* to be, first and foremost, an easy read. I envisioned it a yarn, told to a good friend by the guy who lived it, with empties littering the table and the barman sweeping up the peanut shells around them while leaning in to catch all the details.

To that end, I have employed some unorthodox methods of punctuation and grammar in an attempt to replicate the experience of a storytelling. And so, my first acknowledgment must go to you, the reader, for picking up this book, cracking the spine, and, I hope, stepping into the first page even if, at first, the visual terrain seems somewhat unfamiliar.

You would have no such opportunity if certain people didn't believe in this project, believe in these characters on its pages, believe in me.

Claudia Cross of Sterling Lord Literistic is an agent who cares passionately about her clients and works tirelessly and creatively to develop and place their literary babies in the right hands. Her enthusiasm over the initial manuscript for this novel breathed a sustaining life into it, even when I secretly questioned my own quirky creation. For a writer to be included in the impressive family of authors Sterling Lord Literistic represents is an honor in itself.

Peter Wolverton of Thomas Dunne Books was the first publisher Claudia thought of when she read my novel, not only because he has a keen eye for mysteries and thrillers, but he is, as I am, a hopeless addict—of golf. There is no cure for this curse, only constant self-abuse. We share that pain. Peter is also, as they say in the business, a writer's editor: gentle but clear-thinking, open-minded, and attentive. And, like a good border collie, Peter shepherded me around faulty logic, inconsistencies, and clichés.

My thanks to Katie Gilligan for lending us her sharp eyes and perceptive sense of human behavior, and to Helen Chin for keeping my *i*'s dotted and *t*'s crossed, as well as making sure we were historically accurate with the sports statistics. Joan Thomas read the first version of the manuscript with enthusiasm and a million terrifically helpful questions. Writing a mystery is not unlike strolling through a minefield, where a misplaced (or missing) clue can be an author's undoing. It takes a village to raise a child; it takes a team of smart editors and proofreaders to keep from insulting a reader's intelligence.

Like most writers, I have a folder of yellowing rejection letters from editors collected over the years, and millions of thoughts and words that are buried in the crypts of unpublished pages. Were it not for dear friends and family members who read our efforts when no one else will, who tell us as tactfully as possible when something doesn't work, and who unflaggingly push us to continue on despite said yellowing letters and unpublished pages, I daresay the publishing industry would cease to exist. For me, the stalwart cheerleader of my literary dreams was Giselle Fernandez, who never doubted and always, always, encouraged. My most heartfelt thanks to you, my friend.

My mother, Barbara Dahler, used to haul us all off to the library every week, where we checked out the maximum number of books allowed. I don't remember ever turning one in unread. Such was the gift of joy for reading and love of books Mom gave to me, the most precious gift: a thirsting mind. Her world of history and fantasy and imagination was perfectly countered by my father's more granite view of life on this earth.

She made me a romantic; he made me tough. In reality, the former trait doesn't survive long without the latter. Thank you for that, Dad.

And finally, to Katie, Callie, and Jack, I save my deepest gratitude. For these wonderful days of laughter and surprises. For the ceaseless adventure of being a family. For your patience when I absolutely had to be at the computer hacking through countless rewrites; for your understanding when I was off in some dangerous place for that other career; for giving me a beautifully clear lens through which I can see the world anew. Nothing in this life gives my heart a thrill more than your sweet faces. I love you.

A TIGHT LIE

CHAPTER ONE

I found out later it was just about the time I spanked an eight-iron to the edge of the number twelve green at the Bob Hope Classic that someone plunged an ordinary table knife into her heart. Six times. That was after whoever the killer was beat her bloody with a Krups cappuccino machine. Her naked body was discovered lying in her own gore in the kitchen of her moderately expensive Santa Monica beachfront apartment, and the medical examiner later determined she'd had rough sex, or been forcibly raped, shortly before she was killed.

It takes a very angry or very psychotic human being to kill another of his species up close with a knife. Try shoving your ginsu into an uncooked chicken if you don't believe me. Gristle and bone are tough and unyielding. So how much angrier, or psychotic, does a person have to be to do that with a dinner knife? A round-nosed, unsharpened, serrated-edged, stainless-steel dinner knife.

Six times.

That, my friend, is rage.

She was a pretty girl, an erstwhile actress and part-time waitress, who was better at rising through the social strata of the movie industry on the arms of various important men than she was at learning her craft and landing roles. Girls like her are cannon fodder for that business, like Russian peasants at the siege of Leningrad getting crushed by German Panzers. And yet somehow, year after year, more and more keep running to the front. Thousands of eager little beavers, maybe hundreds of thousands for all I know, 99.999 percent of whom never make a dime as actresses. I guess they keep coming because every once in a while, a Gwyneth or Julia or Halle manages to rise above the clamoring fray and live a fairy-tale life of money, magazine covers, gossip columns, mansions, and equally famous boyfriends/husbands/lovers.

Come to think of it, in terms of the odds against making it big and being a household name, it's not that much different from my line of work.

She was a pretty girl with an appealing little laugh, a nice little story of making her way from Bumpkin, Illinois, or someplace, all the way to Hollywood, and an earnest little head full of dreams.

Dreams.

The crack cocaine of the unaccomplished.

She was a pretty girl who, like dozens of others that same day around this sometimes violent nation of ours, was in a position to be murdered primarily *because* she was a pretty girl. Occupational hazard.

And while I was trying to close a two-stroke deficit to make the cut on a Friday afternoon on a typical Southern California winter day so crisp and clear it actually hurt your eyes to look up and watch the flight of the ball against the blue, someone who was very, very angry with this particular pretty girl plunged an ordinary dinner knife into her pretty chest. Six times.

Her name was Holly Ann Cramer.

I didn't know her well, although I ran into her a few times at various parties in the Los Angeles area. Holly would've been a remarkable beauty anywhere on earth except Hollywood. She was, there, just another exquisite tulip in the vast fields of Holland. Sandy blond hair. Slim hips, full lips, perky tips. Brown eyes still unguarded and friendly, which was more a reflection of her limited time in LaLaLand than any realization of her limited chances of success. I recall her being nice to stand near. She smelled like summer.

Had she not been dating a guy I knew, I might've even made an effort to connect. But Los Angeles is Holland and the tulips are aplenty, and I've never been one to try to horn in on another guy's squeeze. Not that I even could've in this case. The guy she was dating happened to be the current Savior of the City, a multimillionaire stud-puppy athlete who was supposed to bring the hapless L.A. Dodgers back to their formerly formidable winning ways.

I first met Joniel Baker at a pro-am charity tournament. I was the pro, he was the am. Although that day it would've been hard to know the difference. Joniel is one of these natural athletes you really just have to hate. He's gifted at all sports, period. Took up golf three years ago and already has a gorgeous, effortless, loopy swing similar to the one he used to get on base two hundred times last season. There are guys on the tour who would kill for a swing like that. He's a long-ball hitter with good extension and only a little wild off the tee at times. Easy, consistent iron play. If not for his heavy hands around the greens he would be a scratch player.

As it was, we won the tourney handily, grinned while we took a half-million-dollar check from the tournament sponsor, and handed it over to the nice lady from the Red Cross, and pocketed five grand each from a side bet with Phil Mickelson and his clarinet-playing amateur partner. Which really, really bugged Lefty.

Over beers at his enviable estate near San Diego he challenged Joniel to a double-or-nothing free-throw shootout on his home all-weather composite-surfaced basketball court he was so damn proud of, and Joniel sank fifty-two in a row to take another five k from our host. Phil plays everything like he plays golf: with full-out balls-to-the-wall confidence. As a result, up until the last few years he famously lost tournaments he should've won, but he always looked like he had a lot of fun doing it. Still, who in their right mind would go up against a former collegiate two-sporter in a game of horse? If Joniel had a few more inches coming out of UNLV, University of Nevada, Las Vegas, he would've been drafted by the NBA, too. But God love him, Lefty thinks he can beat anybody if he just tries hard enough, so he talks trash with Joniel and convinces him to have a shoot-out. What a wonderful lunatic. Ten grand is nothing to the Masters champ these days, but his pretty wife, Amy, didn't look exactly overjoyed.

Back in the desert oasis called La Quinta, about a hundred and fifty miles away from where Holly lay sprawled on the Saltillo tile with a knife protruding from her chest and every last wisp of dignity and light and promise and dreams vanishing to wherever such things go, I chipped in from a foot off the green for a birdie three. Six more holes to make one more birdie and live to play another day and maybe even finish in the real money, although that was something I refuse to let enter my mind during a match. Nothing dims your focus like thoughts of winning. You tighten up, start to overthink every shot, and the putts . . . God, the putts . . . like some force field surrounds the cup. I don't know how the other guys do it, but when I feel those *I'm-playing-great-today-jeez-what-if-this-is-it?* thoughts start to well up from my gut, I pull out the big guns. The really big guns.

Pamela Anderson's breasts.

I picture those impossibly round, impossibly high, impossibly fake globes, and my heart rate lowers, my hands steady, and my mind empties of extraneous crap like wondering if I'm going to win, and how much money would that be after taxes and my caddie Kenny's cut, and who'll interview me on the Golf Channel. Works every time.

Try it. I bet you just glazed over for a second and thought about her enormous breasts, even if you're a woman. Know why? Because we've all seen them. It's a fact. Every single person in the Western world has at some time or another seen Pamela Anderson's tits. And maybe because they're so familiar to me, pictorially speaking, of course, they act as a sort of hypnotic talisman, or sacred religious relic, or . . . juvenile erotic distraction. Probably the last.

The thirteenth hole was a downhill par-three with a tricky little swale just behind the cup that, if you hit the slightest bit long, would take your ball and run it all the way down to a bitch of a bunker. I know: That's what happened to me here the day before. I had asked Kenny for my eight-iron; he squinted the way he does when he's not sure that's the right club, but he couldn't argue with the distance. I smacked an easy, smooth, pretty little shot that landed four feet short of the flag, bounced past it, and ended up a good twenty yards away in a steep-sided sand trap. I walked away with a miserable double bogey.

I'm not by any means the biggest guy on tour, just a hair over six feet, but like most of the younger generation of players, I work hard at conditioning. That pays off in distance, with every club in the bag. Most of the time that's a good thing. Sometimes, I have to remind myself to dial it back a bit. So this time, lesson learned, I reached for the nine, aimed a little left of the green, swung a little firmer than usual, and let the club face cut through the ball. It started left then floated in a wide curve and plopped on the fringe in front of the green, slowly rolling to a stop seven feet from the cup. I smelled my birdie.

Oh, if it were only so easy.

I two-putted, of course. Then got a bogey on number fourteen, birdied the fifteenth to put me back just below the expected cut line, and made a tidy pair of recovery shots from the trees and a greenside bunker on the sixteenth to save par.

The seventeenth was a dogleg left par-five, 581 yards, with a water hazard in play to the right. It set up well for my swing, and knowing that, I tried to uncork a long drive.

Within a split second of contact, the crucial data imparted by ball meeting club face had traveled up the shaft to my fingertips and from there to my suddenly not-so-happy brain. I watched as the little white pill took off straight, then swooped wide left and buried itself among the top reaches of the lovely palm trees massed along the friendly green shores of the fairway. Golf is such a forgiving game.

A communal gasp rose from the modest gallery that surrounded the tee box, and I'm pretty sure I heard John Daly, who was playing in my group, snicker. Like he's never sent one on a tour of the real estate. In the history of professional golf there has never been a guy who's blown more chances, on the course and off. I resisted the urge to shoot him a glance and tried instead to affect a nonchalant raise of the eyebrows. That was really hard to do at that particular moment. Instead, I probably looked like I was about to strangle a Taiwanese orphan.

Kenny took the driver from my hands.

Take a breath, Huckleberry. You're fine.

Okay, yes, that's really my name. So my dad was obviously a big Mark Twain fan. That or he was a sadist. He deliberately didn't give me a middle name so I had few options growing up except to run or fight. Huckleberry Doyle. A schoolyard bully's wet dream of a name. Kenny and my dad always use the full thing. Pretty much everyone else just calls me Huck. If you haven't heard of me, well, it's probably because I'm one of many professional golfers who makes an adequate living playing the game we love, but who has yet to win a major tournament. I came out of college as the next big thing, U.S. Amateur Champion, ready to take the golf world by storm. Didn't quite happen that way. I had a few good showings at minor tournaments early in my career and even a posted top-ten finish at the PGA Championship two years ago, but in reality I'm what they call a *scuffler*. I'm usually found in the bottom half of the pack, picking up some show-up money and freebies, driving around in the courtesy cars, living the outwardly glamorous life of a professional golfer, but secretly making barely enough to keep my tour card. It's the small tournaments that put money in the bank for us. Like a pool-hall hustler trying for a title, for some reason we have a better chance to clean up as long as the big stakes aren't on the table.

I have no idea why Kenny stays with me. His income is tied to mine.

I managed a slight smile.

That thing looked like it had someplace else it wanted to go.

He flashed the barest of winks as he brushed by me, which, in the spare, nothing-wasted lexicon of Kennyspeak, meant, *Don't sweat it: It's not as bad as it looks.*

After five years of this weird partnership that is golfer and caddie, I have learned to trust this man implicitly, most of the time without question. Most of the time, he's right. But when we've disagreed and I've gone with my club selection or putting line or whatever, his average rises to about 100 percent. The tactical mistakes I've made in tournaments came from disregarding his advice. Oh, I hit crappy shots, and miss putts, and shank and scull and chili-dip as much as most other pros, but those things are part of the operational aspects of this battle against psyche and physics we call golf. Ken Czwikowski can't hit a golf ball straight to save his life, but he is a master tactician when it comes to reading distances, the roll of a green, the lift of the wind. He's like the guy from that movie *The Matrix,* Neo, who sees the glowing green binary code streaming down, the underlying structure of the world, how things really *are,* not just how they seem.

If I could bring myself to listen to him *all* the time, hey, I'd be a pretty damn good golfer.

But I'd be lacking a Y chromosome.

This time . . . he was right again, of course. When we rounded the bend I could see my little white Titleist Pro-V1 with the red dot on it lying in the second cut just off the fairway. Somehow the ball had sailed through the gauntlet of palm fronds and tree trunks, inexplicably missing them all, and took a shortcut to the Promised Land. By eliminating a big swath of middle fairway this was the equivalent of a 370-yard drive. I was 211 yards from that big, open, flat green that made this hole the most birdied on the course, and with a solid second shot, I could be looking at putting for eagle.

Pamela Anderson. Pamela Anderson. Pamela Anderson.

We had to wait for Daly and the others who hadn't driven as far to hit their second shots, which I'll admit gave me no small amount of pleasure.

Then Kenny sidles up, tosses a few strands of grass in the air, and watches them float away.

Steady five knots maybe, helping wind.

He consults his notebook, the holy Talmud, which contains all his accumulated knowledge of the golf course. In the week prior to the tournament he walked every inch of La Quinta, measuring distances from fairway bunkers or distinctive trees, marking down how the greens are contoured. Like a lot of veteran caddies, Kenny likes to have all his thoughts and notes and memories from past rounds at hand, so instead of starting a fresh book each year, he keeps adding on to the original one. Damn thing must weigh five pounds with all the new pages over the years.

Deuce and a quarter to the pin, give or take. Not much roll from the sides. Slight movement maybe toward the back of the green, but not a lot. Pretty flat.

Translation: We were looking at a fairly attractive landing zone.

Drop it in front and let it run a bit?

Kenny nodded and put his hand on the seven-iron. I had been thinking about hitting a six and started to reach for it, but this was one of those times when I actually had enough sense to pay attention. Two-hundred-plus yards is a long way to hit a seven-iron, but with a solid strike, the wind coming from behind us, and a good roll, I can make the distance.

Then it struck me, Kenny was also thinking eagle.

Damn. Kenny almost *never* thinks eagle. He's the guy in the stirrups who's usually telling me, *Whoa there, big fella . . . get the safe birdie.*

My gut tightened up. My heart missed a beat. I had to step away from the ball, pretend I was scanning the treetops for signs of nefarious winds, and take yet another little mental walk with the silicone twins. I can't remember the last time I had to do that twice in one tournament, much less twice on one hole.

How're the girls?

Kenny was smiling at me. He knows all my tricks.

Getting sunburned from all the attention today. You thinking what I'm thinking?

I'm not thinking nothing but watching you swing a club and hit a ball like you've done a hundred million times before.

The golf course was absolutely silent. A few spectators had wandered up close and were standing quietly, waiting for my shot. I reached down and plucked a few more strands of grass and tossed them in the air. They lollygagged past me exactly the same way Kenny's had. I took the seven from his outstretched hand and tried to be glib.

How about steak tonight? Feel like a good porterhouse or something?

Sounds good, Huckleberry.

He heaved the big bag onto his shoulder and moved away. I stood behind the ball, pictured my easy swing and the flight path of the ball arching toward the green. I imagined a little door about six feet in front of me that would be the target zone I'd hit through. In my mind's eye I saw the ball roll up onto the green and stop three feet from the hole.

Then I stepped up and tried to replicate everything I'd just seen.

It happened almost exactly as I imagined it would. We got our eagle.

It was one of those precious few thrilling moments in the life of a tour player that makes one think it's actually possible to be really good at this game. I was flying. Full of confidence. Bring on the world. I had this tournament in the bag.

Until the next hole.

I was so damn fired up I plopped my drive on the eighteenth smack into the middle of the pond. Chipped over the green. Two-putted for a double bogey.

We finished one over the cut line, which meant Kenny and I were going home early this weekend.

Such is golf.

CHAPTER TWO

The cell phone was ringing when I opened my clubhouse locker.

Hello?

Huck. It's Joniel, man. We need to talk.

Okay, that was a surprise. The great Joniel Baker calling me. I thought for a second he wanted me to team with him at another tourney or something. Or maybe he was calling to commiserate with my lousy performance, but that wasn't really like him.

Hey, Joniel. Where are you, man? I can barely make you out above that racket. You at a game?

As I strained to hear his garbled voice, my eyes drifted up to the bank of TVs along the far wall. One carried the Golf Channel with David Leadbetter giving some putting lessons; another had a rerun of some World Series game from the past; and the third, well, the third was on some cable news network.

And there was handsome young Mr. Baker wading through a crowd of cameras and reporters and cops, shouting into his tiny designer cell phone. I watched his mouth move as his words came sporadically into my ear.

There was a delay of a few seconds, which made it seem like he was calling from the moon.

—need your help, man! —ing home? You just won't believe what's—

The banner headline written at the bottom of the television screen read,

STAR BALLPLAYER SUSPECT IN GIRLFRIEND'S MURDER.

At the time, I had no idea what Joniel was talking about, or who the girlfriend of the banner headline could be. I'd been on a golf course all day. Frankly, had someone of Joniel's stature not been linked to Holly Ann Cramer's murder, I wouldn't have been seeing it on the national news. People get murdered every day in this country and what does it take to get noticed?

Fame.

Either the murderer, or the murderee, has to be a household name.

That, or be a cute little blond prepubescent beauty queen, or a cute pregnant middle-class white woman.

It helps to be cute and white if you're going to get murdered. That is, if you want anyone other than your immediate family to notice.

What passes for news in this country is pretty selective. Like Albert Einstein said, "It's all relative." Actually, he probably never said that, but he could've.

I mean, come on. Fifty thousand Americans a year die in car accidents, almost as many British citizens were killed during all of World War II from the Luftwaffe's blitz of England. Fifty thousand a year. And yet, that's not news. There's no outrage at that statistic, no organized marches, no celebrity-drenched fund-raisers, because, I guess, we've gotten used to the carnage. We reserve the right to kill ourselves, but panic at the thought that someone or something else might want to do us the same favor. Tens of millions continue to eat themselves into life-shortening obesity. A hundred and fifty thousand complete their slow suicide each year by smoking cigarettes. None of that is news.

But a few people croak from some weird Asian disease and you'd think the world was ending. A couple more unlucky souls get near anthrax-laced letters and all of America rushes out to buy antibiotics. Want to encourage people to get their flu shots? Tell them there's not enough vaccine. People who've never before gotten a flu shot in their lives will wait in line ten hours for one once there's a shortage.

So, okay, I have a lot of time to read newspapers and magazines on airplanes. What the hell else do you think golfers have to talk about when they get together other than sports? We talk news, and politics, and, occasionally, golf. We used to talk about who Tiger was dating, but then he got married and took all the fun out of that.

I'm just saying that murder in and of itself isn't national news; it's local news because, after all, people in Duluth don't care if some Joe Blow in Houston is killed. Murder is only national when a Joniel Baker is mentioned as a suspect.

So there was Joniel, on the TV screen, going into what appeared to be some sort of municipal building, while yelling into his cell phone.

At me.

    . . . said you could help. You got skills. That thing you cleared up back then. Showed talent. You hearin' me, Huck?

    Yeah, Joniel, I hear you. Call me back later when you get some privacy. I'll be waiting. We'll talk then. I'm on a plane home tonight.

    Done, man. Later.

The tall, well-dressed man on the TV screen nodded and snapped shut his phone just before disappearing inside the building. The image then changed to a picture of a woman. A very pretty woman, with sandy blond hair and big brown eyes. Holly's publicity photo, what they call a head shot. That's when I recognized her, and remembered the last time I saw her at that party, where she seemed so nice to stand next to. The news channel put her name up under her smiling face with the subtitle FOUND BRUTALLY MURDERED IN STAR ATHLETE'S APARTMENT.

What murder *isn't* brutal?

I was suddenly very, very sad.

I knew why Joniel was calling me. I just hoped he was smart enough to have called a good attorney already.

I cleaned out my locker and found Kenny in the bar, knocking back a Glenmorangie on the rocks. By taking a swim on the eighteenth, my little Titleist had cost Kenny at least a few thousand dollars, more if we could've finished fairly high up. He always handles it well, but I can't imagine how hard it is to have your financial well-being depend on another guy's golf swing. Especially mine, these days.

I asked for a beer and squeezed in between him and the guy on the stool next to him. The bar was crowded with golfers and caddies and corporate VIPs.

Sorry. Thought we were in the groove. Pulled it or something.

All I could think of to say.

He shrugged.

Nice day of golf, Huckleberry. You made some pretty shots. Pebble Beach is next. You'll be ready for it.

When Kenny speaks in more than one or two sentences he's either drunk or upset. Judging from the pile of little red drink stirs lying next to his glass, I guessed he was both. But the thing about Kenny is, he never shows it. He never raises his voice, gets sloppy or sappy or sarcastic. He just sips his scotch, stares straight ahead, and when he's had enough he bids you a pleasant good-bye and walks ever so poised out the door.

One of these days I'm pretty sure he's going to walk out and keep going, and dump this hack of a pro he had the misfortune of linking up with.

Plane leaves in two hours, Kenny. Want to grab a steak?

No thanks. You go ahead.

Gotta eat something.

I'll grab a sandwich.

Okay. See you at the airport.

Right.

Then my phone rang again. It was my turn to hold it tight to my ear and yell into the mouthpiece until I could make my way out of the noisy bar.

Hello? Hold on, I can't hear you.

It was Joniel again. He was much calmer.

So you know what's up.

It wasn't a question.

Yes. Listen man, you better not say anything else about that over the phone, Joniel, no matter what. I'm no lawyer but I know that much.

I thought you are a lawyer.

No, Joniel. I have a law degree but I'm not licensed. I never took the bar exams. So I can't advise you. Please tell me you got a good attorney.

Yeah, yeah. Just hooked up with someone from Bert's office. I'm on my way to the crib. When can we talk?

That would be Bert Fields, I'm guessing at this point. Lawyer to the stars.

Good choice. He's good. I missed the cut again so I'm heading home in a few hours. How's tomorrow morning?

How's tonight?

I started to object, but it wasn't like I had plans or anything. Or a date or anything. Or anything.

Sure. I'll be over around nine. Want me to bring something to eat?

Naw, man. I got people for that shit. Bring your big brain, that's all.

The phone clicked dead.

I felt Kenny eyeing me from the bar. I pushed my way back inside and he handed me my beer. The guy sitting next to him got up and I took his place. Kenny, who knows me so well, motioned with his glass toward where I'd just been talking on the phone.

You look worried.

I nodded and took a long draw on the Sam Adams.

Guy I know in trouble. Not sure what I can do for him, though. It's a pretty big problem.

You'll do what you always do, Huckleberry. You'll figure it out.

A random thought popped into my mind and I wondered, for the umpteenth time, why there are no beer carts at PGA tournaments. Golf is a game best played with a little buzz. Maybe we wouldn't all take it so damn seriously. Some days I find myself practically running off the eighteenth green just to get that tall cold one.

Yeah, well. I wish I could figure out that hook. I'm coming out of the swing or something.

Kenny chucked me in the ribs.

Let's go have that steak.

Mike Weir, Adam Scott, and a couple of others who'd made it through to the weekend were pushing into the bar as we were leaving. They nodded with little pitying smiles. Not making the cut in golf is like being the victim of a corporate layoff: Everyone feels bad for you, but they breathe a sigh of relief when you've said your good-byes and left the building.

Because it could've been them.

CHAPTER THREE

The flight from the Palm Springs International Airport back to Burbank lasted thirty minutes. Kenny and I parted ways on the tarmac with nods of the head. He keeps all the clubs and gear at his place so the only luggage I had was my carry-on bag that had three dirty pairs of shirts and slacks, and exactly two clean, unused, and neatly folded pairs.

It's a bad week for a professional golfer when you're bringing home clean clothes.

I picked up my old Ford Bronco from valet parking and headed south toward the Santa Monica Mountains, where Joniel's huge modern glass-and-stone showplace jutted out into the void just below Mulholland Drive. I'd left the Bronco's removable hardtop hanging up in my garage as usual and chugged along with car exhaust, the greasy/sweet smell of taco stands, and occasional ocean breezes mixing and swirling and teasing my nostrils. Southern California was made for convertibles. Driving up Coldwater Canyon, the air felt soft and a little cool, and the traffic was unusually light.

One advantage to having a somewhat dented, rusted, vintage truck in this area is I don't have to worry much about it being stolen. There's no stereo visible because I use an iPod and plug it into an amplifier hidden under the driver's seat. The rims are plain and white. No satellite radio, no DVD player, no twelve-way adjustable seats. If a thief ever looked under the hood, however, he might have second thoughts. I had long ago replaced the tired, underpowered 302-cubic-inch engine the Bronco was born with in 1969 with a new fuel-injected, computer-tweaked 351. Like the song goes, ain't no mountain high enough. I like knowing the juice is there when I need it.

There are some great places to live in and around Los Angeles, if you have the money. The Valley is for porn stars and the worker bees who really keep the entertainment industry humming. Los Feliz and the Hollywood Hills are for the funky, artistic types like writers, TV actors, and independent filmmakers. Malibu is home of the has-beens and the up-and-comers. Beverly Hills tends to be populated by the studio executives who want to brush shoulders with the biggest stars. And Hancock Park is for the biggest stars trying to get away from the studio executives.

Joniel lived above it all.

As I neared his house I ran into a traffic jam. Cops were out, directing traffic through the cluster of news vans, satellite trucks, and photographers. Lit by blindingly bright lights, reporters stood hip to hip along Mulholland, speaking earnestly into camera lenses, as wide-eyed tourists, local gawkers, and irate neighbors made their painfully slow way past.

After creeping along at a pace of about two feet a minute, I finally pulled up to the menacing twelve-foot-tall metal gates at the entrance to his driveway, told the cop there I was expected, and pressed a button on the intercom panel, flipping the bird at the fish-eye lens camera. Everyone who's anyone in L.A. has a gated drive.

The gate started with a jerk then smoothly rolled open. All of a sudden, flashbulbs exploded like machine-gun fire, with no letup until the gate drew closed behind me.

Small lanterns illuminated the driveway as it curved downward and to the left, where the enormous house was hidden from view. I smelled oranges and a pungent, sweet flower of some kind. The landscaping was lush and exotic.

He was standing at the end of the drive, out of view of the mass of media, looking just as I'd last seen him: phone to his head, talking emphatically to someone. He flipped shut the phone as I pulled up.

When are you going to get a real ride, man? That thing's trash.

I glanced over at a Ferrari F430 crouched malevolently on the pavement, like a ferocious predator about to spring, one of a half dozen cars he owned worth altogether a few million bucks.

It'll take that sissy-machine in the quarter any day. Just name the time and place.

He made a *phsssh* sound and rolled his eyes.

Yeah, whatever. Man, you help me out of this and I just might give you one of my Italian stallions. Maybe I'll even let you take your pick.

I suddenly got a burning sensation in the pit of my stomach, like when there's a voice-mail message from the IRS, or the girlfriend starts a sentence with the words, *I don't understand, I'm never more than a day or two late. . . .*

I hoped he was kidding. Those cars average about 250k each. That's a lot of help he's wanting.

He motioned skyward with his phone, where a half dozen helicopters vied for position.

Come on inside. They've been hovering overhead all day like vultures waiting for someone to die.

As I peered up through the overhanging tree limbs that shielded us from their telephoto lenses, I thought, *Someone already has.*

We went in through the warehouse-sized garage in which sat a few more shiny candy-colored exotic sports cars, including a sapphire blue Aston Martin convertible—which happens to be my fantasy car—a Cadillac

Escalade, a bright yellow Hummer, and a row of motorcycles on display stands. My Reeboks squeaked against the polished tile floor of the garage. There was not a speck of dust anywhere. Double-glass doors led directly into the game room, where Joniel spent most of his time and where usually, this night excepted, there were a handful of buddies and luscious women hanging out, playing pool or PlayStation.

In fact, of all the times I've been here, I couldn't ever remember Joniel being alone.

To our right, a ten-foot-high wall of glass displayed the entire San Fernando Valley, twinkling with streetlights and headlights. Another wall was filled with large plasma-screen TVs, most of which were featuring either sporting events, porn, or cartoons. I found it momentarily odd that not one was tuned to a news channel. On second thought, maybe not so odd.

Listen, Joniel, before you say anything else you need to understand something . . .

He waved me off.

I know, I know, man. You're not a lawyer . . .

Not just that. Not only am I not a lawyer, but nothing you tell me is protected by attorney-client privilege. What that means is I could be subpoenacd to testify and anything said here can be used as evidence.

He turned around and fixed me with a look.

Evidence? Man, you think I did it. Shit . . .

Look, before we even get into that, I just want to make sure you understand the situation. Call your attorney and ask them if you should be doing this . . .

That was him on the phone just now. He didn't want me to talk to you.

Yeah, see?

But I told him I was going to. I pay him, I call the shots. That simple.

I started to say something like, But you pay him to give you good legal advice, or, But you pay him because you're not a lawyer and this shit you're in is serious. Instead I just asked,

Why?

He made the *phsssh* sound again.

'Cause you're good at finding things out that sometimes even police and lawyers and all can't find out. That little girl that was missing. That dude took everybody's money. You found them. You know people. You know how to work quiet in this business, low-profile shit. Under the radar. No press conferences. Not trying to get famous or nothing. Lawyers, they just want the big case so they can get a show on cable. You got skills and a shut mouth, man, and I need that sort of thing right now.

But Joniel, near as I can tell, and trust me, other than seeing a few news reports on TV, I don't know much about this situation yet, but near as I can tell, you're a murder suspect. That's not some theft or a missing person or a traffic ticket. It's not so easy to fix a murder rap. What in the world do you think I can do to help?

His eyes flashed anger.

Man, what you think? Find who the fuck set me up!

He turned away and let out a long breath. Joniel Baker was famous for never, ever, no matter what, showing emotion. Once last season, a hack minor-league call-up pitcher plinked him two straight times after Joniel went yard in his first at-bat. Now, after the first hit-by-pitch, about 50 percent of all major league sluggers would've at least glared. Not Joniel. After the second thumping, about 99 percent would've stormed the mound and pummeled the little fuck into the dirt. Not Joniel. He just trotted to first base both times, looking like he'd just drawn a walk, like he wasn't sporting two Rawlings tattoos on his arm and thigh.

Maybe, I thought, that reputation was just Joniel Baker the athlete. The performer. Maybe this was Joniel Baker the human being.

Or Joniel Baker the guy with a big ugly secret. Something in my psyche, maybe because my dad was a cop, is always just a little cynical.

He walked over to a large refrigerator, opened it, and got one of those tiny little designer caffeine drinks that cost too much.

Want anything?

Got any vodka?

You know I do. Goose?

Fine.

He pulled a bottle of Grey Goose from the freezer and set it on the bar top. Frost formed instantly on the frozen bottle and a fog of vapor lifted into the warmer air around it like a wraith searching for a new place to haunt.

Help yourself.

I filled the glass halfway and almost drained it with one swallow. The icy liquor sliced into my brain like a bone saw. I filled it up again and sat on one of the big white leather couches. Joniel had returned to his normal composed mien. He was staring at the bank of TV screens, waiting for me to talk.

I realized on the drive up that my overall concern wasn't for Joniel. He had enough money to buy an army of lawyers and private investigators. He'd be fine, so long as he didn't do it. And maybe even if he did.

My concern was that young girl who never did a bad thing to anyone in her short life. The girl who told me a story at someone's party one night, as we sat on the couch and watched the gaggle of adorers hang on every word Joniel was uttering, about trying to save the life of a rabbit she'd found that had been opened up by some wild animal and left for dead. She'd cleaned its wounds, tucked everything back where she thought it went, and sewed the poor thing up with her mother's needle and thread. It died three days later.

Holly was seven at the time. Fifteen or so years later, she still got tears in her eyes while remembering.

A thought formed in my mind as I watched the droplets of condensation meander down the outside of the crystal tumbler. Joniel wanted me to help find out who set him up. If I took that request at face value it meant he really didn't kill Holly. On the other hand, it could be a bullshit way of looking innocent when his lawyers marched me onto the stand to testify that he did, in fact, hire me to find the real killer. I mean, if O. J. Simpson had followed up on his vow never to stop searching for whoever killed his wife, maybe most people wouldn't still be thinking he's a guilty SOB. Instead he spent a lot of time playing a lot of golf. Badly. Every time I think of O.J., I still get pissed off. At the legal system. At that idiotic, vain judge. At those idiotic, vain lawyers. At all the people who chose to sacrifice justice for two people in order to make a straightforward murder case into a statement about racist cops and the persecution of minorities.

Joniel must've gotten tired of all that silence. He turned back to me and changed the subject.

What about that con man you went after, what's his name?

Souther.

Yeah, Souther. Fuckin' thief. Glad I never had dealings with him. You get back that money?

I thought about all the red tape, the plane trips, the legal fees, the myriad bank accounts he'd set up, the dummy corporations, the hours and hours and hours of effort.

Not yet. I haven't given up, though.

I could still picture his smug face when I finally caught up with him. *Congratulations, Huck,* he said. *You won't find a penny.*

He was wrong. I found it all. I just haven't been able to get it away from the crooked bankers and lawyers who help guys like Souther do what they do. Thanks to my testimony he drew a four-year prison sentence for embezzlement and mail fraud. And while he sits in a minimum-security Club Fed, those self-same bankers and lawyers are making damn sure his money, *my* money, is drawing a healthy rate of return.

This is how it went down. Two years ago, a number of high-profile athletes and Hollywood stars got sucked into an investment scheme by a really smart, really slick, really believable con man. This guy, Randy Souther, had all the tools. Harvard Business School degree. Maserati. Mansion in the Palisades. Surrounded by women who made your heart skip a beat just by entering the room. I mean real walking Viagras. He seemingly came out of nowhere but quickly built up a clientele that looked like the guest list at SkyBar, where he also happened to do much of his schmoozing.

And schmooze he could, man. He was passionate and exuberant and could tell you exactly why Kmart was underpriced by at least twenty bucks a share while Boeing was overdue for a fall. He knew the numbers, he knew the corporate structures, hell, he knew the names of the CEO's kids. The folks who signed up with his investment group early were bragging about 80-, 90-, even 150 percent returns on their money.

Souther was lauded in all the L.A. area glossies as a stock-picking genius along the lines of Warren Buffett, but unlike that irascible old Oracle of Omaha, Souther spent money hand over fist. Best of everything. First kid on the block. You get the picture. He was also secretive about his trades because, he said, if other fund managers copied his techniques, the phenomenal returns he was getting would be diluted.

It was a disaster waiting to happen. The numbers on everyone's monthly statements continued climbing up Mount Everest with young, handsome, and dashing Randy Souther in the starring role of Tensing Norgay. The air got so thin up there no one could see the bottom.

Not even me.

I was in it to the tune of six hundred grand. My entire life savings. Everything I'd won and managed not to spend. After eight months, Souther had added another five hundred forty thousand to the balance. It was a heady time. I felt like one smart bastard.

It may surprise you to know that not all professional golfers make millions of dollars a year. It's the hardest thing on earth to get, and priceless to those who do, but a PGA tour card is not a permit to print money. The bottom fourth of qualified players earn barely enough to cover their costs.

The key is making the cut. No cut, no money. Make the cut and you've made a pretty good paycheck, even if you finish dead last on Sunday. String enough of those together and *voilà!*—you're in the middle six figures without ever winning a tournament. As long as you finish the year in the top 125 moneymakers, you get a card to play next year. But we few, we happy few, we band of brothers, are self-employed. Subtract the caddy's share, and agent's cut, and coach's fees, and business manager, and travel expenses, and health insurance, and there are those duffers on tour you might catch a glimpse of on any given Sunday who are hanging on financially by the skin of their teeth. Some familiar names, even. Endorsements help but if you're not a Tiger or Phil or Sergio, there aren't many car companies banging down your door holding checks with lots of zeroes on them. The income from that little shoe company logo on my shirt is just about what a minimum-wage worker makes a year in one of their stores.

But most of us don't play golf to get rich. Most of us play golf because we can't bear the thought of doing anything else. I'd really hate to have to work for a living.

SportsCenter came on one of the big TVs. I watched clips of Tiger and Vijay and Lefty, half holding my breath for the highlight shot of my eagle. Nope. Missed the cut for the second time that day.

It occurred to me, and not for the first time that day, that I didn't really know Joniel all that well. Maybe not even well enough to judge whether he was capable of murder. After all, who of us ever thought the affable rental-car pitchman and former Heisman Trophy winner was before those two young lives were snuffed out with a couple dozen slashes of a really sharp knife? Oops, sorry, he was acquitted of their murders, I know. It was a civil court that found him responsible for their deaths. Big difference.

Joniel and I had hung out at this beautiful mansion occasionally, had a few drinks, run into each other at bars or events, but it's not like we'd ever had a warm and fuzzy moment of deep talk before. But, you know, it really didn't matter at this stage in the game whether I believed Joniel was innocent.

I wanted to know who killed Holly. I'm a sucker for a woman in trouble.

Even if she's dead.

If the Los Angeles Police Department was focusing on Joniel as their lead suspect, or *person of interest* as they now call it to avoid lawsuits from suspects who don't get convicted, then I was pretty sure they weren't looking very hard for anyone else. That's just the way homicide detectives are. They're essentially trained to follow the principle of Occam's razor: the simplest solution is usually the right one. They like to solve the case quickly, get the bad guy off the streets, and pick up the next folder on that huge stack piling up on their desk and start working on it. That's not to say they won't entertain a secondary theory, but in my experience they aren't too eager to cast a wider net when they think the biggest fish is already in the boat. And my experience was growing up watching probably one of the best and certainly one of the worst homicide detectives to ever carry a shield.

I had two weeks before my next tournament. I had the time to look into things. What I didn't have was the money. Thanks to Souther, I was almost broke. Between this year and last, I'd missed three straight cuts and was already sweating whether I'd pull it together in time to keep my card, or whether I'd be headed back to that singularly dreaded torture chamber of self-flagellation known as Qualifying School.

And the season had barely started.

I got up for another vodka. Joniel was getting impatient, sucking at his teeth and flipping in the air one of about a hundred different remote controls that lay around the room. I reached out and caught it in midflip and sat on the table directly in front of him to lay things out.

Here's how it'll work. First, stay off the phone. You're probably already bugged, even if they can't use it in court, just to get leads from you. Even your cell. Digital is almost impossible to tap but don't take the chance. You can conduct normal business and bullshit on it, but anything regarding this case you should use one of your boys to get messages to people or meet them in person. Two, if your lawyer hires me on as a private investigator, then the information I come up with is probably protected by attorney-client privilege. And that includes our conversations.

He looked dubious to say the least.

And you can just call yourself a private investigator? Just like that?

Actually, I *am* a private investigator. I got a license a few years ago. It's nothing in California, really, to get one.

That was the truth. All you have to be is eighteen, have no criminal record, and take a class for a few hours. That's it. I needed a private investigator license to get access to some state records when I was trying to track down Souther. A P.I. license has come in handy a few times since then. It's also gotten me in trouble a few times since then. I was hoping this one wouldn't turn out that way, too.

So, we gotta deal?

He nodded.

I need some cash up front. Expenses.

No problem.

Wanna know how much I cost?

He shook his head.

Naw, man. Send my guy a bill.

All right, question number one. Who hates you enough to frame you
for murder?

Joniel slouched back into the couch and pulled a slender cigar tube out of
his jacket pocket. He clipped and lit the Dunhill, fixing me with a steady
gaze for the first time since I got there.

This thing gonna work, you gotta quit with the bullshit, man. Either
you trust me or you don't.

He sent a cloud of blue smoke toward the ceiling.

That ain't your first question.

CHAPTER FOUR

It was almost midnight by the time I left Joniel's. A wet breeze had moved in off the ocean and the seats of my Ford were covered in dew. I started it up, rolled past the stable of exotic supercars and out the gate. The news crews had disappeared. A scraggly coyote, nonplussed by my headlights, munched on some roadkill in the middle of Mulholland, a sign of how little traffic came by here this time of night.

I paused at the intersection of Coldwater Canyon, debating whether to head home, get some sleep, and start on this puzzle fresh in the morning, or make one last stop. It wasn't that complicated a decision, flip a coin, but I sat there in the Bronco with the big engine rumbling in smooth idle, and let my gaze drift up to the sky. Between wisps of clouds the stars were like salt spilled on black velvet. I thought about what Joniel had said. I thought about how much I didn't know about the case. I thought about Holly.

Under the celestial sea, with my ass and back soaking wet from the seats, and my brain slightly buzzed from a combination of jet lag and really good vodka, it occurred to me that I was way, way over my head. I had no idea where to start. But I knew who would.

I put the car in gear and pulled a U-turn, heading back west, past Joniel's house, toward the angry dark Pacific.

Twelve minutes later I turned into the dirt parking lot of an out-of-the-way bar frequented by Harley-Davidson riders and ex-cops. The guy I wanted to see happened to be both. I spotted his bright blue Fat Boy parked next to a rotting hitching post that looked to have actually been used to tie up horses once upon a century. His Harley bore a distinctive illustration on the gas tank: an ACLU logo with a bullet hole and blood dripping from it.

Inside, the bar smelled of leather, sawdust, body odor, and just a tinge of vomit. Billiard balls clacked in the far corner and a loud hum of conversation waged battle with the southern rock blaring from ceiling speakers.

I recognized three extremely large men hunched over the far corner of the bar. As I made my way over to them I caught some disapproving glances from a few of the regulars. On the back wall of the bar hangs a hand-written sign that reflects the motto of the people who drink here: DAMN TOURISTS NOT WELCOME. And since I wasn't wearing a leather vest, a beard, or a do-rag, nor was I old enough to be a retired member of the Fraternal Order of Police, I must've been a *Damn Tourist.*

The three were in the middle of the kind of drunk, heated, worn-out political argument in which they all agree in principle about the subject but fail to listen long enough to each other to realize they all agree. I caught something about immigration. And taxes. And liberals.

You'd be surprised how their opinions mirrored those of most of the guys in my line of work.

Two of the men were so overweight that the fat on the back of their necks rolled up out of the collar of their shirts, making their heads resemble those little nubs of roots that sprout out of potatoes when you've left them lying around the kitchen too long. Those two were in the familiar blue uniforms of the LAPD, stitches straining against their bulk. The man in the middle wore a T-shirt under a black leather vest with an American eagle emblazoned across his broad back and the motto LIVE FREE OR KILL in flowing script underneath. It strained against his bulk, but unlike his buddies, with the exception of his impressive belly, his mass was almost pure muscle. And a lot of it.

I landed the punch about six inches to the left of his backbone, just about where his kidney would be sitting snug and warm under a layer of beef. It was just a little half pop but I heard the wind go out of him and a mist of beer spewed across the bar to the assortment of bottles stacked against the far wall. He whirled around on the stool, face beet red and glaring, ready to rip off my head. Then recognition set in. He looked me up and down, snorted, and turned back to his beer.

Fuck you want, shitbird?

Well, hello to you, too, Pete. You're losing your touch. Can't hold your liquor. Can't take a punch.

I've taken more punches in my life than you've had pimples. And that's a helluva lot.

His buddies had a good laugh at that one. But they made room for me at the bar next to him. Somehow.

How ya been?

Fuck you care?

You know, you're supposed to keep tearing off those little word-of-the-day calendar pages. I think you're still stuck on the *fuck* day.

He cut his eyes to me. They were bloodshot and yellow, subtly malevolent in the same detached, emotionless way as the caged predators at zoos that pace back and forth, staring at the visitors, just waiting for a chance. Pete was a former cop who'd seen too much, done too much, hated too much, felt the hate of others too much. His eyes were sunken into reddish brown skin laced by dry riverbeds of sun lines. A piece of his left ear was missing from some long-ago battle. When he spoke his breath was sharp as kerosene.

I repeat: What the fuck do you want? Shouldn't you be in some ritzy hotel somewhere having some pretty young groupie polish your putter or kiss your balls or something? Oh, wait, you must've lost again. Only reason you'd be anywhere near the real people.

I looked around in mock amazement.

So that's who these are? The real people? I would've guessed the Village People.

Say that just a little louder. I dare you.

I'd need a megaphone to be heard in here. Listen, this poignant little reunion has been fun, but you got a minute? It's important.

He looked at me hard for a second, then grunted, reached into his pocket, and slapped a twenty on the bar.

What the fuck. Had enough of these assholes anyway.

He mumbled his good-byes to his two cop buddies and we made our way outside. The air was even cooler and fresher than when I remembered it ten minutes earlier. There was a buzzing in my ears from the abuse they'd taken from the loud rock and bull inside.

He propped an ass cheek on the Fat Boy.

So whatcha need, Huckleberry? Money? Advice? Golf tips?

All three, but not from you, thanks anyway. I'm looking into something, a murder investigation. Just some quiet poking around for a friend. Guy accused says he's been set up. I need the full autopsy report and the M.E.'s findings, any drugs in the dead girl's system, any DNA of the perp at the scene, that sort of thing.

You don't ask for much.

And the lead detective. If he's a friend of yours and if he'll share.

He shifted on the seat and scratched at a stain on his jeans, thinking.

So that black ballplayer's your buddy, huh? Trying to do an O.J. for him? Blame someone else?

Nope. Doing it for the girl.

He raised his eyebrows.

Hope she paid you before she was stabbed.

Joniel hired me to find out who's framing him. Can you help?

Sure. He did it. There, wasn't that easy?

And how do you know?

Simple. Same reason dogs lick their sacks. Guys like that can get away with anything. Case solved. It's always the ex, you learn that quick in murder investigations. You owe me a case of beer.

His tone was joking, but his eyes weren't.

Pete wasn't always this way. Sometime, maybe a very long time ago, the world wasn't so literally black and white to him. I almost never rose to the bait anymore.

He just told me he didn't do it.

That was the question Joniel said I should be asking him. So I did. Not that I believed him. Or didn't.

Well, damn then! I'm convinced! Dismiss the jury, judge, case closed! Ya know, usually they just up and admit it. That's what makes our job so easy.

Former job. What do you know about the case?

He may have been drummed off the job a few years ago, but Pete still knew everything that was going on in the area. Connections are the currency of the streets. Twenty-five years as a cop gives you an impressive collection of favors, both owed and owned.

Not much that you don't. Girl was definitely raped. Beaten to hamburger with a coffeemaker, then stabbed a bunch of times. Guy did it thinks he knows how to cover evidence. Coffeemaker and knife were wiped down or he used gloves. And one other thing the reporters don't know. Somebody stuck a bottle of bleach inside her and squeezed.

Jesus.

Yeah. Apartment belongs to your buddy. She lived there for almost a year. Nobody seen coming or going that day but he's evidently been getting it a lot in the off-season. I mean, he's around there a lot when not on the road. His alibi, such as it is, is he was at a strip club at the time she's killed.

That jibed with what else Joniel had told me. He'd been out clubbing and got drunk. Pete was watching me mull all this over.

This Holly Ann Cramer someone you knew?

Yeah.

Pretty girl.

Yeah. Why bleach though?

Pete snorted.

No wonder you ain't a lawyer. Think about it. Guy rapes a girl, realizes he left his so-called genetic material behind, what's he do? Douches it out with Clorox. No more DNA.

Does that really work?

Fuck knows? Don't think the M.E.'s happy about it, though. Listen, that's all I have right now. I hear anything else, I'll give you a call. Same number?

You know it is.

He swung his leg over the bike and hit the starter. The Harley made a grinding noise then growled to life. Pete twisted the throttle, goosing the big engine into ear-shattering blaps before kicking it into gear.

Yeah, well, been so long since I seen it pop up on my caller ID I forget.

I reached over and put my hand on his arm before he could release the clutch. I practically had to yell in his ear to be heard.

Hey, one other thing. Seen Blue lately?

He blinked hard at the mention of the name, like he'd just been slapped. For a second I thought I saw the tough-guy mask slip a millimeter or so. He looked past me at something I knew wasn't there.

Naw. You?

Not for a few weeks. Hey, maybe we should head over there sometime. Pay a visit.

He glanced at the ground, then his gaze moved back in the general direction of mine and settled somewhere around my left ear.

Yeah. Sure thing, sport. Maybe next week. See ya.

He revved the big motor again,

Yeah. See ya. Thanks . . .

and released the clutch.

. . . Dad.

The Fat Boy's tires spat out some gravel before catching. I watched him roar through the pale wash of a streetlight and disappear. I was suddenly very thirsty.

CHAPTER FIVE

I didn't for a second entertain going back into the biker bar. My watch said it was still prime drinking time in other parts of Los Angeles, so I climbed back into the Bronco and made my way to the 405 Freeway. The air was considerably chillier at eighty miles an hour. By the time I took the Century Boulevard exit I was shivering.

Two blocks from the entrance to the Los Angeles Airport, I pulled into a spacious but almost empty parking lot. The few cars that were scattered about looked to be rentals. None was parked anywhere near the others, as if they were all afraid of catching some nasty disease.

The letters on the neon sign mounted to the roof of the squat warehouse-type building were each about four feet high and screamed out in pink and blue that this was an oasis for lonely businessmen far from home. It said ALL NUDE DANCING with three exclamation points and a silhouette of a shapely woman dancing all nude.

I wasn't sure she'd be working here tonight, but it was worth a shot. Or two.

I paid my twenty bucks at the door, made my way past rows of porn and sexual playthings of all persuasions, and ducked through the cheesy strings of colored beads into the dark. The bass notes thumped so hard from the dozen or so speakers it was impossible to discern what song was playing, but then the musical selection doesn't really matter here. It's the rhythm that rules; a steady, loud, insistent sexual pounding.

She wasn't on any of the three stages. Peering around I could see only a few shadows of customers sitting in the outer reaches of light, indistinct like windshield smudges on a rainy night. Except for the brightly multicolored spotlighted stages, these places are always kept almost pitch-black so some illusion of privacy is preserved. Two waitresses in tiny halters and skirts meandered around the tables, looking bored. I caught one's attention with a wave. New girl. Didn't recognize her. She put a napkin down at my table.

What can I getcha?

Absolut. Neat and cold.

No can do. No liquor served in all-nude clubs. It's the law.

She was right. It's the law in California, hence the steep entrance fee. But there were ways around it.

I'm a member. Ask Charlie.

Charlie was the club manager—the tall, scary, black Vin Diesel–type giant seated at the far right of the stage, counting the night's take. As a manager, Charlie was the strong silent type, except if you touched one of his girls or made an ass out of yourself. Then Charlie assumed his other role, that of bouncer. That's the scary part of Charlie. I knew a little about his past, and it was as dark as it gets. The waitress glanced over and caught his eye. He nodded.

Guess you are. Absolut it is.

Lindsey here tonight?

She's coming on center stage soon, I think. Next song.

Great, thanks. Make sure it's really Absolut, not that Smirnoff crap you guys keep in the well, if you don't mind.

She snapped her gum in affirmation and was off, bumping her way like a pinball through the empty chairs toward the service bar. All this without once looking me in the eye. She seemed tired, unhappy, and a little angry. Maybe she gets sick of having men check out her ass and boobs night after night.

So not like Lindsey.

Just as I thought that, the music changed into a steroidal country-western-disco-rap typhoon of sound. A somewhat small but perfectly proportioned long-haired blonde slid into the beam of light on the center stage. She had on white leather chaps, white fringe vest, a pink cowboy hat, and, I had to look hard to make sure, but yep, nothing else on but a matching G-string. Or what these days the lingerie catalogs call a thong.

Lindsey Feller was my sometime high-school sweetheart who at some point in her teens decided she liked it when men looked at her. She figured out early on that they were willing to give her money for the right to do so. When she told me a few months after our graduation from Santa Monica High that she was going into the exotic dancing business, I thought she meant management. I mean, this was a girl who never let me get past the elastic, which was, frankly, why we broke up so many times. It was simply unbearable to be so close to all that deliciousness and not be able to partake of it. But Lindsey had these funny ideas about sex and marriage and purity hammered into that lovely little California sun-streaked head by her fundamentalist Christian parents. So I'd get sick and tired of having blue balls pretty much every night and we'd argue about it and I'd say there were other girls who were more open-minded and she'd say then go be with them and I'd say well okay I will.

The only problem was I'd see her in class the next day in those cheek-hugging faded jeans or at the lineup sitting on her board waiting for a wave all bikinilicious, and my heart would seize up and I'd give in and ask her about what our plans were that night, as if nothing had happened. She always smiled cheerfully and went along, no hard feelings, no need to talk it through. I have no idea why. To this day she finds no irony in the fact that she was still a virgin when we broke up that final time our senior year.

I'm relatively sure she no longer is.

Lindsey whipped her little body around onstage like a feather in a hurricane, somehow managing to keep time with the music while swinging on the pole or strutting across the tiny stage.

My second drink came, then my third. By then Lindsey had lost the hat, the vest, and the chaps. She leaned against the pole with one leg wrapped around it and a thumb hooked in the elastic of her tiny triangle of nylon. Her blue eyes pierced through a cascade of blond hair, smiling at her admirers, knowing what they wanted. What they needed. What they'd sell their lives for.

Then, she gave it to them. In one motion, the pink G-string was off and floating through the air. Two guys leaped out of their seats for it as if it were A-Rod's five-hundredth home run ball. Lindsey dove to her knees and slid pubis-first toward the edge of the stage, head laid back, hair flowing, exquisite breasts shimmering in the beam of heavenly light, naked and exposed as the day she was born. Except for the boots.

Exotic dancing, when it's done well, is a cross between gymnastics and gynecology. But Lindsey somehow makes it seem playful. Not scuzzy and pathetic and sad as this place really is, but like we were all getting ready to skinny-dip, or taking part in a game of strip poker and Lindsey was losing really badly, every hand. And loving every minute of it.

I summoned the surly waitress and switched to vodka tonics to get some H_2O in the system, since I was sweating so much watching my ex-girlfriend writhe and dance and flirt with her anonymous lovers under the hot lights.

Lindsey finished her turn by twirling acrobatically around the brass pole, a move so fluid and graceful it reminded me of the first lick of an ice cream cone, when you run your tongue all the way around the sides.

She curtsied enthusiastically and began collecting the ones and fives and occasional twenty that littered the dance floor. There were maybe a dozen guys in that room, and every one of them threw money on the stage.

Then she stood and smiled into the darkness, scanning the room until she spotted me, saying hi with an almost imperceptible nod. Her light brown skin was glistening with sweat. Under the lights it looked like fine marble; stunningly, perfectly smooth. An art critic could make a career out of studying only that.

She gave the adoring audience one last wave and skipped offstage.

Five minutes later she sat down at my table. She was wearing a shiny red full-length robe that had the club logo embroidered over one breast, and her hair was pulled back in a ponytail.

I'm not really supposed to do this, it's against the rules, so if Charlie comes over I'll have to leave. Howya doin'?

I'm good. Like the cowgirl getup. How'd you come up with that one?

I got tired of the whole princess shtick and saw that movie *Oklahoma!* on TV one night when I couldn't get asleep after work. The musical, ya know? And I always liked horses, remember? The boots are too small, though. They really hurt.

Couldn't tell. You really sold it.

She seemed sincerely pleased that I thought so. As we were talking a drunk wandered over and asked her for a lap dance. Lindsey gracefully demurred but the guy wouldn't give it up. Before I could open my mouth to tell him to crawl back into the shadows, Charlie suddenly appeared at his side. A big hand wrapped around the guy's upper arm. The expression on the poor drunk's face went from dopey lust to pain to anger, then instantly to fear as he whirled around and looked way up, up, up into Charlie's eyes. He didn't say a word, just kind of shrank and shuffled away. Charlie raised an eyebrow at Lindsey.

Five minutes, Charlie, I promise. I'm on break.

He turned and glided back to his piles of money. He moved like a prizefighter. Every guy was eyeing him, glad not to be on his bad side. Me, too.

That is one impressive dude.

Who, Charlie? He's a sweetheart. He's just rough on the outside.

Yeah. And Sherman's March was just a garden tour of the South.

What?

Nothing. You want a drink?

Naw, can't. I've got two more shifts tonight. The girl who was supposed to do them, my friend Tiffany? She bugged out a few nights ago and hasn't been back. Probably stretched out in a resort somewhere. I don't mind. More pay for play, ya know?

She patted my hand. Her nails had little twinkly stars embedded in them.

Haven't seen you in a long time, Huck. Sometimes I think I see you sitting back here in the shadows but you're gone by the time I get off-stage. Hey, aren't you supposed to be at a golf tournament somewhere?

Yeah. Missed the cut. I'm in a rough patch right now, but I'll work through it.

You always do, baby. Seriously, you ever come here without telling me? I swear I've seen someone looks just like you. It would make me happy to know I've got a friend out here.

You've got a thousand friends out here, Lindsey. I always say hi when I come out. It's tough to find the time, you know? Travel, practice, groupies, all that.

I'm not sure she bought the lie but she let it go. This wasn't exactly the best place to talk to her about my little project, but I needed to start arranging the puzzle pieces in my head and Lindsey at some time or another has met just about everybody in the L.A. exotic-dancing scene.

You know a guy named Joniel Baker? Baseball player?

Sure. He why you're here tonight?

Sort of, although seeing you dance always puts a smile on my face.

Her hand moved from the table to my lap.

Used to have a different effect on you. Oh, still does. That's nice.

I have no control over that. Ignore it and it'll go away.

Such a waste.

Now, any sane person listening in on this conversation would think there was some serious fun being proffered, but they'd be wrong. Lindsey is a natural flirt, period. You think you're getting the green light and the next thing you know you're getting T-boned in the intersection by an eighteen-wheeler. Moments like this, I change the subject. Or go take a cold shower. Sometimes I think she does it just to get a rise out of me. The emotional kind, I mean.

Joniel Baker. He ever come in here?

She pulled her hand back onto the table, glanced over at Charlie, who was busy talking on a cell phone, and took a quick hit from my glass.

Yes. Every once in a while. Lots of sports guys do.

When was the last time you saw him here?

She thought for a second.

Actually, come to think of it, two nights ago, I think. Sat with a bunch of his buds through a whole evening. Serious partiers. Only drank Cristal. Threw around a lot of money. He seemed real nice.

How so?

Oh, you know. Just generous. Looked you in the eye sometimes instead of just staring at your hoohoo. Smiled. He has a nice smile. Really good-looking guy. Built.

He get a private dance?

Not from me. One of the other girls took him to the back, I think, I didn't see who. I know he disappeared for a while when I was onstage and then I saw him back in his seat later.

You don't know which girl?

She shook her head.

Hey, wait, Joniel Baker. Yeah, didn't he kill someone? I don't watch the news much but I heard something on the radio. That why you're asking?

He's a suspect in the murder of his girlfriend. I'm just looking into it. He says he's being framed and asked me to help.

Is that a good idea? What if he did it?

Then he goes to trial. I knew the girl. I'd like to find out who killed her.

Lindsey looked closely at me.

You liked her. That's why you're doing this.

I nodded.

You would've, too. She seemed like a nice girl. She sure as hell didn't deserve this. But Joniel hired me to figure things out. So, back to that night. You said he stayed all evening. How late?

I don't know, past two, I think. Did you sleep with her?

No. Did he leave with his crew or alone?

45

Did you want to?

Alone or with his guys, Lindsey?

Don't get pissy. I didn't see him leave. I just noticed when they were all gone. I guess they all left together. Why didn't you sleep with her? You're a cute guy, Huck. You can have any girl you want.

Except one . . .

Because she was dating someone, Lindsey. You girls talk about stuff, did anyone say anything about Joniel leaving with one of the dancers? Maybe the girl he hired for the lap dance?

I didn't hear. Want me to ask around?

Yeah, but quietly. Only girls you can trust. The cops will probably be in here in the next day or two asking the same questions. They're probably making their way down the list of strip clubs. Tell them everything you told me.

That you wanted to sleep with the dead girl?

She can really get my goat if I let her. She leaned over and gave me a kiss as she stood up.

Time for me to get ready for my next performance.

My mind wandered to what that could possibly entail.

Need help spraying on that sparkly stuff?

No, baby. We girls help each other out with that sort of thing. Thanks, though.

They help each other out. The mental image was suddenly vastly improved, and that's saying a lot. I watched her walk back to the stage entrance, her butt moving firmly under the robe. She paused to whisper something in Charlie's ear and he just nodded. Lindsey turned and gave me a small wave. I noticed every other guy in the room was watching her, too. That had to royally piss off the naked brunette wrapped around the pole onstage.

Lindsey's second performance was every bit as inspiring as the first. The drinks kept coming. I lost track of time. Finally I realized the place had pretty much cleared out and the dancers were looking like third-stringers. I waved Surly Waitress over and paid my tab.

I had a little trouble standing up. Goddamn jet lag. I carefully made my way to the door and out into cold Pacific fog, which felt really good on my face. Lindsey's beat-up Corolla was parked where it always was, next to the rear door. I remembered something else I wanted to ask her so decided I'd wait for her. I was leaning against the car with my eyes closed when she came out a few minutes later so I didn't see her at first, but the next thing I know I'm inside her shitty little Toyota and she's driving up La Cienega, jabbering away.

. . . he said I'd make lots of money, like in the six figures, he said. So what do you think?

I tried to rewind the tape in my head but turns out the recorder had been shut off.

Sorry. About what?

About the movie. About acting in a movie. Jesus, haven't you been listening at all? You should cut back on the booze, Huck. You're killing your brain cells.

It's not the booze. It's the travel. I'm just tired. What movie?

An adult feature, he called it. A guy a few weeks ago gave me his card. Some really famous producer. Tiffany introduced us. He offered me a part in his next adult feature.

You mean porn.

I caught sight of her profile in the rhythmic splash of the streetlights. She'd changed into a shapeless gray Mickey Mouse sweatshirt and tan capri pants, and without her costume and stage makeup, she seemed about fifteen.

No, not porn. It's an adult feature. Tiffany says it's a higher class than porn. It's almost like a regular movie.

It's porn, Lindsey. That's just another name for it. Mr. Famous Producer whose name you can't remember is scamming you. Probably just wants to get into your pants. Why would you want to do that, anyway? You're doing okay for money, right?

She scrunched up her nose, which made her then seem about twelve.

Yeah, I'm doin' okay. I'm just trying to, you know, look at the future. Dancing's not really a long-term career, but acting is. Maybe it could lead to real movies, you know, like what Traci Lords did. Like, she made it legit.

Yes, that's true. Out of, oh, maybe a few hundred thousand porn actors over the years who wanted to make it into real movies or TV, one person does it. One. Those are great odds, Lindsey. Go for it. But there's a big difference between dancing and fucking.

She shot me an angry look.

I hate you when you're drunk. You're so sarcastic.

I'm not drunk. Just tired.

Whatever. Jet-lagged my ass. You came from where, Palm Springs? How many time zones is that, exactly? I should've just let you drive yourself home. You'd probably be wrapped around a tree about now. You don't appreciate how much of a friend I really am. You never got that when we were together. I was more than just your girlfriend, I was your friend. And it's *acting*. It's not really fucking.

I closed my eyes and slumped down into the immensely uncomfortable sticky vinyl seat that smelled of old ketchup and hairspray. Somewhere about fifty yards behind my left eye, a headache was lurking with an ax in each hand. I cracked the window to let in some cool air and noticed the street we were on looked unfamiliar.

Yes, I do appreciate you. Thank you for driving me home. But I think you're going the wrong way.

I'm not going the wrong way. I thought I'd make you dinner and sober you up, you jerk. I'm starting to regret it.

The last line was delivered in a pout. I peeled open my eyes a little wider and looked skyward. Orange and pink streaks of light played across lucent clouds.

You mean breakfast. And fucking's fucking.

Sometimes I really should just shut up. It was like we were right back in high school and I instinctively knew the exact right thing to say to spoil things. She remained quiet for a few moments, then sighed wearily and shook her head.

Yeah. Whatever.

CHAPTER SIX

Whoever said vodka doesn't give you a hangover lied.

I awoke with the taste of dog shit in my mouth and boiling hot oatmeal in my skull. I couldn't get my left eye completely open. My cheek rested in a damp spot on the mattress that I was reasonably sure was my own drool and not, unfortunately, the residue of hours and hours of happy lovemaking. This was a safe bet because one, I couldn't remember a thing past Lindsey telling me she was getting into porn while we were in her car and two, I was still fully clothed.

You may think reason one above doesn't qualify as proof since most guys and more than a few women have had drunken sexual encounters they couldn't later recall. But we're talking about a sexual encounter with Lindsey. You wouldn't forget that, no matter how drunk you were.

I slowly rolled over while trying to keep the molten mush inside my brain pan as still as possible. Keeping my eyes closed against the cruel sunlight, I felt across the bed for another warm body. Nothing greeted my hand but pillows and a tangle of sheets and covers. I dared a peek: more flowers, pinks and greens and yellows, but no little sleeping blonde. My stomach flopped again and I forced myself to sit up just in case a dash to the bathroom was imminent, which caused my eyeballs to remain somewhere back on the bed for a few moments longer than my head, giving me exceedingly blurry vision until they whipsawed back into their sockets and things slowly began to clear.

I looked around Lindsey's bedroom. No actual Lindsey there, but Lindsey everywhere, if you know what I mean. Candles on shelves. Stuffed animals on chairs. Clothes piled up next to the closet, awaiting a trip to the Laundromat. Various bottles of makeup and perfume arranged neatly on top of her dresser. Pastel watercolors of horses and kittens on the walls.

Inside every woman is a little girl, I guess. This little girl happens to be only a year younger than I, but sitting there looking at all her stuff I began to feel like a pedophile. This only a few hours after I and a dozen or so strangers could clearly see that, among other things, Lindsey has a close relationship with her bikini waxer.

Other than the high-pitched hissing in my ears that changed tone when I moved my head even just a fraction of an inch, there was absolutely no sound in the little half-duplex Lindsey calls home. I stood carefully and shuffled into the bathroom. More pinks and blues and flowers. More little clear bottles of perfume. I took a whiz, being extra cautious about splash-over, and wandered back into the main room. White couch, matching chairs, old TV on a glass table. That's about all that fit.

The only thing in the whole place that didn't look color-coordinated was a black cargo bag next to the couch. I thought about opening it to see if it held male or female items of clothing, but in a moment of uncharacteristic character, decided it was none of my business.

The shelves on the back wall were full of porcelain figurines, fashion magazines, and sundry knickknacks. Not a single book in sight. A part of my brain began making excuses as to why it really isn't important that a woman be well-read and how there are lots of different kinds of smart.

The note was on the countertop between the kitchenette and main room, which doubled as a dining-room table. It said she'd gone to work an early shift and to make myself at home and to please lock the door on the way out. She signed it with a looping *L* and a little heart. I looked at my watch for the first time since waking up. A quarter to one. I'd slept away half the day. Kenny and my coach, Paul Warren, were expecting me at the practice range in fifteen minutes.

I found Lindsey's phone and started making calls. Kenny doesn't own a cell phone, but I tracked him down at his ex-wife's house, where he still does odd jobs sometimes, out of sheer guilt, I think.

Hey.

Hello, Huckleberry. You sound hungover.

How's Bernie?

His ex-wife's name is Bernice. She hates being called Bernie. Which is the whole point.

Mean and bitter. You're not canceling practice.

It was a statement, not a question.

Hey, who works for whom? I'll cancel if I want. But no, I'm not. I just need a ride.

Fine. No worries.

I gave him Lindsey's address and asked him to bring a clean Polo shirt and some golf shoes. He's got about fifty freebies stacked in his garage, which just happens to be two garages down from where he was trying to get his ex's lawnmower started so sixteen-year-old Kenny Jr.—K.J. to his friends—could mow the yard. Kenny couldn't bear to live with Bernie, but neither could he bear to live too far away from K.J.

I had some time to kill while I waited so I took a peek in the fridge, which had a surprising amount of food in it, mostly fruits and vegetables and what appeared to be different kinds of soy products. Obnoxiously healthy stuff. My fridge tends to contain little more than a few beers, some American cheese slices, and various mold-encrusted condiments. I do most of my dinner preparation with a phone.

Her cabinets, too, were neatly stacked with boxes of organic crackers, Asian noodles, tins of herbal teas, those sorts of fairly unappetizing things. I began to feel fortunate I'd missed out on a home-cooked meal. I heard a car horn toot outside and started to close the cabinet door when my hand bumped a jar of honey and the damn thing fell, exploding on the linoleum floor.

The cleaning supplies were, surprise, under the sink. Here's a little house-keeping tip I then learned: Wiping up honey with a dry paper towel is about as effective as spreading spackle with a toothpick. I stuck my head back under the sink looking for something that would melt the gooey mess, but Lindsey, ever the environmentalist, apparently didn't stock anything stronger than GreenFriendly NonToxic Bio-detergent.

Bio-detergent? That sounded like it couldn't melt a cube of sugar. And why does every eco-friendly product have the most off-putting, self-congratulatory, awkward name in the whole goddamn grocery? If they really wanted to save the environment they'd package the most benign cleansers with the most aggressive names imaginable: StainNUKER! MAX-MELTO laundry detergent! Kitty-Killing Karpet Kleaner! Fool the bastards who simply don't care into thinking they're getting the strongest stuff available.

It's called *marketing*. Not *honesty*.

I peered into the darkness. Then, in the very back of the cabinet, behind the loop of the drain trap and an empty box of sponges . . . all-natural, of course . . . I spotted a plastic jar of nondairy creamer.

Contradictions attract: (a) Lindsey was a health nut; she would never let such sludge down her pretty gullet, (b) it didn't appear she even drank coffee, owing to the fact that there was not a single ground to be found in the whole apartment, nor even a coffeemaker, and (c) the last thing she'd have to worry about is putting on a little weight. The girl was about as heavy as one of my socks.

I popped the lid off. Instead of powdered creamer, the jar contained syringes still in the wrappers, cotton balls, matches, and a flame-blackened tablespoon.

What the fuck . . . ?

Outside, Kenny leaned on the horn, shaking me out of my stupor. I replaced the works, slopped up as much of the honey as a damp dishcloth would remove, scribbled on the same sheet she left for me a thank-you note apologizing for the mess, and pulled the door shut behind me.

Despite what she did for a living, Lindsey's always been very, for lack of a better word, *clean*. She respects her body. She never took drugs while around me, even with all the experimentation I went through in high school. She never drinks more than a few glasses of wine. She eats only stuff that's good for her. She exercises. She's careful.

The cargo bag . . . the drug kit . . . could mean only one thing.

Somebody new was in her life. Somebody I was absolutely certain I wasn't going to like.

Kenny read the frown on my face when I plopped into his Chevy.

Not the look of a man who just got laid.

She's just an old friend. It's nothing.

Right.

Seriously, Kenny. Drop it.

He raised an eyebrow, shrugged, and drove in silence, leaving me to my thoughts. Thing is, even if I could put it into words, I could talk for a day and Kenny would never understand my relationship with this girl. I can't think of anyone who would. Least of all me.

CHAPTER SEVEN

Paul was a good sport about me being half an hour late to practice, considering I'd still have to pay him for the full session.

As usual, he took me through the paces from putting to chipping, up through the irons to the big dog. I pushed my concern for Lindsey into a corner of my brain and focused on my job. Paul watched without comment, making an occasional note in his little book.

His theory, and every good coach has one, is that one's golf game is an organic thing, with each part relating directly to all the other parts. If you're having trouble with your driver, then chances are your long irons are hanging by a thread, and your putter is approaching the valley of the shadow of death. But by the same token, he believes if you can spot a problem and make some minor adjustments, that should have a beneficial ripple effect throughout your game. There are always tiny fixes that can be made to each individual part of your game, but in the World According to Paul Warren, all sins start with a single flaw.

His challenge was to find the disease, not just the symptoms.

After I had hit a dozen shots with each club we took a break on the bench next to the range. My head was still pounding despite the three Excedrins I wolfed down at the pro shop, and I was thirsty as hell. As I sucked from a water bottle, Paul consulted his notes. He spoke like a high school principal.

I saw tape of your last round. You're not swinging exactly the same way today but that might just be due to your condition. Next session I suggest you stay sober the night before. It might give me a better chance to really see your mechanics. But overall, I don't see anything terribly egregious. Mechanically, your takeaway seems to be on a flatter plane than usual so we'll work on that. You're letting your head move forward before impact, which you're countering by opening your left hip a little early.

So, that would explain the pulls, I guess.

That's right. And I think we can fix that pretty easily. But what I really want to work on more is your mental preparation. This last tournament you were actually striking the ball well, all the way through your putts. But when you got into trouble you had a hard time recovering, and that's not like you. You've always been a scrambler, even in college. So I wonder if you're losing focus. Are you doing anything differently before a match?

I thought back to the last few tournaments. Wake up, eat breakfast, go to golf course, play like crap.

Nope. Nothing I can think of.

But it's hard to keep losing, isn't it?

No shit.

Yes, but I've had a few good finishes. I feel like I'm close to making a run.

Really? Are you getting discouraged you haven't yet?

Fuck yes.

No. Just a few lucky rolls and I'll be back in it.

He nodded and made notes in his book, humming under his breath like a shrink chewing on an interesting head case. Why did I hire this guy again? Do I need the fucking psychoanalysis?

All right, we'll drop that line of thinking for now. But I'm going to make a few suggestions about your mental and physical preparations before each tournament. I think you can approach them more like a fighter approaches a prizefight. Gird your loins, so to speak. Get up for the game.

Jesus Christ. Just tell me what I'm doing wrong with my swing, Sigmund.

Sounds good.

Paul ran me through a series of drills and by the time the sun disappeared I felt pretty much back in the groove, hitting my targets and shaping the shots at will. But if tournaments were played on driving ranges, we'd all be Arnold Palmer. Still, it felt good to be striking the ball well again and I could tell Kenny, the ever-silent Kenny, was pleased as well.

We gathered up the gear and headed toward the parking lot. Paul stopped at his black Porsche SUV.

I'll write up a few thoughts about a possible prematch routine you should consider and send them to you. But I think your swing fundamentals look good right now so you should be ready for the next one. Hit the range every day to keep it flowing.

Will do. Thanks, Paul. Any chance of a good-citizen discount for today?

He just smiled and climbed into his eighty-thousand-dollar truck. He was an expensive bastard, but a bastard worth every penny. The electric window whispered open and Paul leaned his head out.

Practice, Huck. Practice and prepare. That's what the very best do. You've got tons of skill. The only thing you lack is that extra little bit of discipline.

Gee, thanks, Mom.

You're right as usual, thanks. You've convinced me.

I thought I heard a snort from Kenny. My coach-slash-psychiatrist waved and pulled away. I stood watching him go, a little poorer as usual when his bill arrives, but hopefully a little wiser. I turned to see Kenny shove the clubs in his trunk and close it.

Up for some dinner, Kenny?

He shook his head.

Can't, thanks. Promised K.J. we'd do something. He's going away for a few weeks.

Got time to take me to pick up the Bronco? I can get a taxi . . .

Naw, we're fine. Hop in.

Traffic was minimal and I pulled into my driveway less than an hour later. The mailbox was full of catalogs and flyers and nothing much else since all my bills go straight to my business manager, Louie, and all my fan mail goes straight to my assistant, Natasha. Just kidding. I don't have an assistant. Mainly because I don't get fan mail.

I dropped my overnight bag inside the front door, switched on the TV, and headed to the kitchen. The light was blinking on my digital message machine. I hit the Play button and reached inside the fridge for a beer.

The machine told me I had fifteen messages. Ten were hang-ups, either telemarketers or someone not wanting to leave their name. Three were from Louie asking me to call him about my financial well-being, which was anything but well and close to not being. One, from earlier today, was from Kenny reminding me we had a practice session scheduled. And the last message, time-stamped just ten minutes before I got home, was from my dad.

He answered on the first ring.

Doyle.

Hi, Pete. You called?

Yeah. Just a sec.

I heard the scrape of a hand being pressed to the phone and the muffled sound of his voice talking to someone. A moment passed and he was back on the phone.

Got a name for you on the Cramer murder. Lead detective. Phillip McIntyre. Good guy, a little tight-assed but all right. You can mention me. Just stay out of his way and don't keep nothin' from him if you get it first.

He read off three sets of numbers for Detective McIntyre.

Got it. Thanks. Anything else you find out?

You payin' me for this? I get a cut of your fee?

Jesus. Forget I asked. Thanks for the name.

I started to hang up but I stopped when I heard his raspy laugh.

Calm your ass down. There is something else. Your buddy Joniqua or Jonto . . .

Joniel.

He knew his damn name. Pete is a huge baseball fan.

. . . whatever, this thing has some serious action with the bookies. Talkin' big-money bets on whether he ever plays again. Vegas has it twelve to one he gets off. Either way this goes, someone's going to make large cash.

People are already betting on whether he's guilty?

People'll bet on anything. Few years ago there was a line on which of Tony Danza's twins would lose their cherry first.

Wait . . . who?

Danza's little girls. From that TV show.

The Olsen twins, you mean?

Yeah, them.

That wasn't Danza's show. That was that other guy's.

Whatever the fuck. Somewhere, some guy cashed in big on that one. There was a pool going, down to the week of the month of the year it happened.

But how did they know? The bookies, I mean. How could they be sure?

It was in the tabloids. Don't you read the newspapers?

The tabloids? You've gotta be kidding. They're not exactly the end-all source of truth.

Naw, but it don't matter. That was the agreed-upon condition—the first of the girls named in a newspaper as having lost her virginity, in an article that also gave some kind of date of when it supposedly happened, that satisfied the line. No gynecological verification necessary.

It doesn't matter if it's not true?

Hell no! Don't matter. The game ain't about what's true, it's about making the right pick. The best horse don't always win the race, that's why you gotta handicap the field.

So by that logic it doesn't matter if Joniel is innocent. The bet is whether or not he's convicted.

Oh, like I told you, he killed her. Who knows with this fucked-up judicial system if they'll convict him, but yeah, that's the bet. And it's getting into big money, so I'm just sayin', watch your ass. With money out there riding like that, what you do or do not find out can seriously affect someone's bank account. You keep poking into this you better damn well have your insurance papers in order, and be sure you spelled my name right.

Rest easy, Pete. I'm leaving you my entire fortune.

Hot damn. That's my boy. Any chance you can score some Lakers tickets for me and the guys?

Sure. How many you need?

Four. No, five. Benny's back from Vegas tomorrow.

A college buddy of mine worked in the Lakers' front office. Pete knew that. Pete went to more games than I did.

I'll see what I can do.

We hung up. I took a sip of beer and wandered back into the living room, trying to decide whether to call up Lindsey and finally ask her out on a real date, or start plugging away on Joniel's case. The TV made the decision for me.

CNN was on. Two people, a nice-looking middle-aged couple, were sitting across a table from the bespectacled suspendered interviewer. The woman was in tears, gripping her husband's hand in both of hers. She was the picture of anguish.

The words at the bottom of the screen said in typical cable news tortured syntax, PARENTS OF STAR ATHLETE'S MURDERED GIRLFRIEND.

I dialed Detective McIntyre's cell phone.

He seemed somewhat distracted but pleasant enough when I dropped Dad's name. There was some kind of hubbub in the background and it sounded like he was standing outside near a highway. I decided the only way I would get anything from this guy is if he felt like he was getting something, too, that's the way it works, so I told him a little of what I'd found out from Lindsey. He paused for a second, and suddenly I could tell I had his full attention.

You were at that strip club, the one near the airport, last night?

Yeah.

And the girl you talked to, the stripper who told you Joniel Baker had been there the night of the murder, you know her?

Yeah, she's an old friend. We went to high school together.

Uh-huh. Did you happen to see her leave the club?

Yes, as a matter of fact. I left with her. She drove me to her house. I was too tired to drive myself home.

He was silent for a beat.

You happen to see her today?

No, not since I fell asleep last night. Why?

A siren passed near where he was standing, drowning out his reply. I had to ask him to repeat it.

I said because, Mr. Doyle, I just so happen to be standing at a murder scene. And by all appearances the attractive but very dead young woman lying in front of me made her living as an exotic dancer. Now, please tell me where we can meet so we can continue this helpful discussion. And don't say Mexico.

CHAPTER EIGHT

It took me fifteen minutes to get there. A half-dozen LAPD cruisers were pulled over on South La Cienega, next to the Hahn Recreation Area. I saw an evidence truck and some unmarked sedans I took to be detectives' vehicles. The news media hadn't turned up en force yet but two helicopters were already buzzing overhead, their gyroscopic telephoto lenses no doubt peering down into the heavy brush to see what they could see.

I put on a grim cop face and flashed my private detective credentials at a bored-looking young officer standing in front of some yellow crime-scene tape that was stretched between two feeble-looking shrubs. He nodded without really looking, so I ducked under the tape and made my way through some bushes to where a group of uniformed and plainclothes cops were milling about. It took me all of two seconds to pick out McIntyre. He was the tall guy in the no-nonsense black suit that had the air of a college professor. He was standing next to a forensic photographer who was taking pictures of the scene.

As I approached him I saw a flash of red on the ground in front of him. A few investigators knelt around the body, momentarily obscuring my view, but between them I could just make out a smallish person covered by a grimy white sheet, some shiny red fabric spilling out at the edges. Only her legs were fully visible from where I stood. They were thin and very pale. Ugly black marks encircled her ankles. Her feet were bare.

I was pretty sure I hadn't taken a breath since leaving the truck. Maybe since hanging up the phone. I just remember some big muscular guy in my head shoving all the terrible possibilities into a corner and not letting me look at them. Somewhere in that corner was a picture of Lindsey, from last night, wearing a red robe. I tried to recall what her feet looked like, but the guy in my head wrestled that thought away, too.

McIntyre was looking at me.

Huck Doyle?

Yeah.

I stuck out my hand. He gave it a cursory pump with an extra-firm grip.

Thank you for coming down. You got here quick.

I don't live very far from here.

I couldn't stop staring at the feet. They were so small.

The coroner's not here yet so we haven't been able to pinpoint the time of death, but given the existence of rigor I estimate she's been here between twelve and seventy-two hours.

The toes were painted pink. The little toes on each foot were so tiny the nails were mere dots. Pink dots.

That's a big spread.

It's an inexact science. Guesswork, really, until the experts have a look. They can tell a lot from the blood so long as it's not all dried up. As I said, the coroner hasn't gotten here yet. Do you need to sit down? You look a little ill.

Bad burrito. You have an ID on her yet?

Not yet. She isn't carrying any. I was hoping you could help with that, if you wouldn't mind.

I felt him looking at me closely, like he was watching for some telltale tic or some slobbery fascination a sicko killer might have. It really is true that lots of foolish criminals return to the scene of the crime. But all I wanted to do was leave, right then. Or yank that sheet off of her face first to make sure it really wasn't Lindsey. But leave, for sure. And rewind the last half hour of my life and tape over the tape. And then find her and make sure she was safe.

Absolutely. Always happy to help the LAPD. Did I mention my dad used to be on the job?

Yes, you did. I know exactly who your father is.

I couldn't tell from his tone if that was a good thing or bad. McIntyre nodded to one of the guys kneeling next to the body and he gently folded the edge of the sheet away from the girl's head. A small cloud of flies lifted away, then quickly settled back down. I saw blond hair spilled onto her face and onto the ground around her. I saw a naked, pale shoulder that had ugly black and red marks on it. I saw a breast peeking out from under one arm.

The crime-scene photographer snapped off another shot. The flash made me jump. McIntyre spoke to his guy next to the body without taking his eyes off me.

Move the hair away from her face.

The investigator waved at the flies, to no real effect, and scooped a handful of hair off the girl's face.

I couldn't speak.

Mr. Doyle? Do you recognize this woman?

I closed my eyes. I was picturing that beautiful face when life still shown from its blue eyes, when that lithe little body danced and twirled onstage, when it wasn't a corpse lying in the dirt with cars whizzing by. I turned away and took a long, deep breath.

Mr. Doyle?

Yeah? Yes, yes. I know her.

Is she Lindsey Feller?

What? No, sorry I . . . No. It's not Lindsey.

Thank God. But I knew who it was.

She worked with Lindsey. At the club. Her name's Tiffany. Probably a stage name. I've seen her there a few times.

I was wobbly with relief. But I didn't want McIntyre to see that. So I stooped down to examine the dirt. He knelt down and joined me.

Thank you. I know that's hard.

Guy named Charlie at the club, the manager, he'll know her real name. I think she's missed a few shifts lately. Lindsey mentioned it.

I looked back. I was relieved I couldn't see her expression.

Any idea how she died?

He glanced over at the body and shrugged.

Not easily. There are signs of trauma, scrapes, and contusions. It appears she was in a struggle. I'm not at liberty to go into it any further.

Sure, I understand. You never know who's a potential suspect.

I learned early on from hanging around with my dad that cops make it a point always to keep some information under wraps, in case a suspect tips his hand by knowing more details about the crime than has been made public.

Yes. That's regrettably true. Since you mentioned it, should you be? A suspect?

McIntyre was obviously the straightforward kind of investigator. We stood just as I heard a vehicle crunching to a stop near us. Through the underbrush I could make out a black sedan. The door opened and an attractive brunette, probably late twenties, early thirties, got out with a medical satchel. She pushed through the wild shrubbery and approached us. She walked nicely for someone with too much education.

We've got company.

Yes, that would be Dr. Judith Filipiano, with the medical examiner's office. On the job for all of two months. You didn't answer my question.

I faced McIntyre, let him get the full monty of facial expressions, eye movement, all the crap they teach cops about how to detect lies. The comely forensics expert politely stopped a few feet away.

No, detective, I'm not your guy. I'm trying to find out who killed Holly Ann Cramer. In the course of my investigation I happened to talk to a young woman who works at the same club as this young woman. I called you to pass along some helpful information, coincidentally at the same time you began investigating this murder. I've told you what I know. If you need anything further from me, you have my numbers. I'll be of any assistance I can.

That little speech wasn't entirely for McIntyre's benefit, and the slight upturn that appeared at the corners of his mouth told me he knew it. I turned and made eye contact with the coroner's investigator.

Hi. Huck Doyle. I'm a private investigator looking into the Cramer murder. That offer extends to your office. Should you have any questions, please call.

I handed her one of my business cards. She slipped it into her jacket pocket without looking at it. I thought I saw a bemused look pass her otherwise professional countenance.

Thank you, I'll remember that. Meanwhile, the fewer unauthorized people walking through this crime scene, the better. I'm sure you understand.

That last line was delivered to McIntyre. He suddenly wasn't smiling anymore. Detectives aren't used to being talked to like that, especially by nice-looking rookie assistant medical examiners.

Mr. Doyle came down to identify the body. He in no way compromised the evidence. He was just leaving.

But she was already past him, kneeling next to Tiffany's body. She quickly snapped on latex gloves and pulled some plastic Baggies out of her black bag. Gently, as if giving the recently retired dancer a manicure, she eased the Baggies over Tiffany's hands. An assistant stooped to help.

I handed McIntyre one of my cards, too.

The deal is, I'll give you whatever I can unless it directly implicates my client. In return, all I ask is the occasional favor, a confirmation here, a phone number there, a name.

He studied the card as if memorizing it, then pocketed it.

That's a novel idea. I'm fairly sure it's against procedure for me to share information with a private individual, especially someone working for a murder suspect. It could potentially jeopardize a prosecution. And by the way, if this goes forward and he's indicted for Ms. Cramer's murder—and I have to tell you, all evidence is pointing toward that—you will be considered a material witness.

Not what I was hoping for. I shrugged.

Good luck. I'm on retainer by his lawyer. Anything I gather is under the umbrella of attorney-client privilege. But, look, believe it or not we're on the same side. If I find out Joniel Baker killed Holly Ann Cramer, I'm not interested in helping him get away with it. I'll just drop the case. Consider that a clue. You don't hear from me, you'll know you're on the right track.

And if I don't hear from you, how do I know it won't be because you got a little too close to the truth and somebody decided to help you disappear?

Damn good question. I hadn't thought of that. So I ignored it.

I might be able to help you. At least give it some consideration.

He looked me over for a second, playing the skeptical-cop bit, I guess, then nodded.

All right, Mr. Doyle. I'll think about it. But if I give you some . . . conditional cooperation, we'll call it, this will not be an all-give-and-no-take arrangement. You *will* share.

Don't worry.

I turned and started to make my way back to the Bronco.

Mr. Doyle?

It was the assistant M.E. I looked back to see her laying the sheet back down onto Tiffany's legs.

Yes?

I do have one question. How well did you know this woman?

Not well at all. I've seen her at the club a few times. She and Lindsey, another dancer there I know, are . . . were . . . friends.

Did you spend any time with her? Ever date her?

Who, Tiffany? No. I told you I barely knew her.

She stood, pulled off her gloves, and motioned to the evidence guys to start loading the deceased onto a gurney.

Because in addition to the recent bruising on her wrists and legs that appear to have happened at or near the time of death since the contusions are fresh but bear no discernable swelling, there is additional ecchymosis which, judging by the faint yellowish color, are between a week or two old. I'm just wondering what might be the context under which you knew her. She was apparently in an abusive or sadomasochistic relationship.

So obviously, to the hotshot new medical examiner babe, I looked like a guy who likes it rough. McIntyre was all ears. I felt mine turn red.

Look, Dr. Filipino . . .

Filip*iano*. Like the musical instrument.

Filipiano. I've been hired to look into a murder which may or may not be connected to this one. Detective McIntyre asked me to come identify the body. As I said, I'll help any way I ethically can.

I thought bringing ethics into it was a nice touch, loaded with caveats, conditions, and cover-your-asses, but she didn't bite.

And I appreciate that. It's just that I just don't quite get why else someone like you would be hanging out at a strip club.

Someone like me?

Oh, shit.

Yes, of course, someone like you. A professional golfer. Why would you choose to frequent such a place? It stands to reason you have a fetish or a girlfriend there.

I have neither. That I know of. I just try to be supportive of my friend's artistic expression. I'm a patron of the arts.

Oh? The art of what?

The art of the strip, of course. But I didn't say that.

McIntyre had taken a whole new interest in me. He moved over closer to us and stood beside the dear doctor Filipiano-like-the-instrument.

You're a professional golfer? What, do you teach at a local country club or something?

She looked at him and laughed. It was an easy, unselfconscious laugh, kind of husky in a Lauren Bacall sort of way, that completely melted my first impression of her as being a stiff prig. Even if she was in the process of humiliating me in front of a potentially key source of information.

No, detective, I'm surprised you don't know this. Huck Doyle is a touring pro. With the PGA. I just saw you play yesterday on the Golf Channel. You had some beautiful shots until things got a bit hairy coming down the stretch.

Yes, well . . .

That eagle was fantastic. I have yet to make two pars in a row, much less a birdie. Tell me, how is it a PGA pro has the time and the inclination to get involved in a murder investigation?

I really wanted to go. This was getting absurd. All golfers are the same; they can talk about the game anytime, anywhere, under any circumstances. But it was not helping bolster my street cred with the good detective. The Golfing P.I.—I could hear the guffaws back in the squad room.

It's a long story.

She opened her satchel, pulled out a set of car keys, and snapped it shut.

Well, my CSIs can finish up here. Can I buy you a coffee?

McIntyre raised an eyebrow. There was a human traffic jam behind him: Tiffany on a gurney, the guys carrying her, some other cops wanting to leave. They all, including Dr. Judith Filipiano, stood waiting for my reply.

Sure. I know a great café. In Timbuktu.

CHAPTER NINE

Or Santa Monica, as the case may be. She followed me to a parking garage next to the Third Street Promenade, a sort of outdoor mall with shops and restaurants and the biggest, most bizarre collection of street performers, homeless bums, and bug-eyed tourists outside of Berkeley. The typical Saturday crowd was in full glory. We found a table in Jinky's Café and ordered legalized drugs in the form of liquidized caffeine. Dr. Filipiano surveyed the scene with an amused expression on her face.

Lively place you've brought me to.

You should get out of the office more often. This is actually a movie set. They're shooting *Return of the Night of the Living Dead.*

She laughed that easy laugh again.

They obviously recruited extras from our morgue.

People will do anything to get into the movies.

We watched the zombies walk by for a moment as I told her about the Promenade and what this area used to look like when I was a kid. Which was, oh, pretty much nothing. My cell phone buzzed twice but I didn't answer it. When it buzzed a third time, I checked the caller ID. It was Joniel.

Excuse me a moment, I have to take this call.

Certainly.

I stepped out of the café and answered the phone.

Hi, Joniel.

'Tsup? 'Bout time you answered the fuckin' phone.

Working your case. How're you holding up?

Considering the word's out they're going to charge me with the bitch's murder any time now, just fine.

I felt my face flush. I knew he was stressed and probably more than a little scared, but still . . .

Her name was Holly, Joniel. It would probably do you well to remember that.

I heard the *phsssh* sound and was expecting a smart-ass reply, but instead his voice came back quieter, maybe even contrite.

Yeah. I hear you. For sure.

I'm in a meeting, Joniel. Trying to get some information. Is there something you needed?

Bert wants to meet you. Tomorrow. He's got some papers for you to sign.

Okay. I know the address. See ya.

The phone clicked off. I pushed the speed dial for Lindsey's phone but voice mail picked up.

Lindsey, Huck. Give me a call. Soon. Bye.

As I went back inside, Dr. Filipiano was looking at me curiously.

Your client?

Yes. Joniel Baker.

So you didn't tell me why you're mixed up in this.

You want the truth, or the better story?

She actually thought about it for a moment.

Why don't you start with the better story. I may not need the truth if it's good enough.

Okay, smart choice. I knew the girl who was killed, I know the guy who's being accused of killing her. My dad's an ex-cop. I learned a lot from watching him work. I have a law degree. And I've always been good at finding things out, so Joniel hired me to help find the murderer.

Assuming he's not it.

Innocent until, last I looked.

Of course. But there's always somebody who's not . . . *innocent* . . . and statistically it's usually the spouse or lover.

You know what Mark Twain said about statistics.

That from a man who lived under a pseudonym. Look, you can't argue with facts.

I can argue with anyone. I told you, my dad was a cop.

Easy laugh. Appraising look. Shake of the head.

I still don't get it. You're a professional golfer, for God's sake. Why in the world would you want to involve yourself in a murder investigation? Why not just let the professionals handle it?

Because sometimes they can't. Or won't.

Well, look, I have nothing but respect for cops. But they don't always get it right and they usually have too many cases to deal with to devote their full attention to each one. I'm just trying to help out a friend. Two friends, actually. I didn't know Holly well but she was a good kid. I have some free time before my next tournament. I find murder investigations a good distraction from the depressing and violent world of the Professional Golf Association.

Okay, I guess that's fair enough. But if I were you I'd probably spend my spare time on a beach somewhere, like Hawaii.

Overrated. Way too beautiful a place to be real. It's obviously a movie set.

Like this one.

The zombies have better tans.

She checked her watch and scooted back her chair to leave. I took out another business card and jotted down my cell number on the back.

Let me give you a better number to reach me. I meant it—if I can do anything to help, just call.

Okay. I need some of Mr. Baker's pubic hairs and maybe a sample of his semen.

Ha ha ha.

She took the card and actually looked at it this time.

So typical, Mr. H. Doyle Investigations. Promise the moon but deliver a lightbulb. I suppose you'll want reciprocity. The kind of deal you were pushing our detective friend for. You scratch my back, that sort of thing.

That was a very pleasant thought.

I've cut back on reciprocity. Doc says it was giving me indigestion. Just a copy of your report is all I need. Joniel's lawyers would be getting it in discovery anyway; it'll just help me to have it as soon as possible.

That shouldn't be a problem.

And maybe the occasional answer to a question or two.

Aha.

Nothing unethical.

No, no, of course not.

We stepped outside and began walking toward the parking garage. A healthy young man fully capable of meaningful employment approached us for a handout. I stared him down without comment but the good and kind doctor fished out a few bucks and handed it to the pathetic lazy ass. She couldn't help notice I rolled my eyes.

You think that was silly.

No, I think that was a wonderfully generous act.

Liar.

Seriously. I'm sure he needs that money badly. To tip the guy who washes his Bentley.

Are you this funny on the tour? You should have your own show.

I am definitely this funny on tour. But it's usually my golf shots that get most people laughing.

By the time we reached the cars, she'd conned me out of a golf lesson and dinner. Okay, I bribed her to have dinner with me by promising a golf lesson, but the end result was the same. She settled into the rich dark imitation leather seats of the government-issued car and started the wimpy six-cylinder engine.

Hey. So you told me the better story about why you're poking your nose in somebody else's business. What's the truth?

I'm broke.

She laughed out loud.

You really are hilarious. I'll call you next week after we finish the autopsy.

CHAPTER TEN

I spent the evening online, boning up on everything I didn't know about Joniel Baker. His life was well documented from the first moment he materialized from the mean streets of Compton to hit three home runs in the Little League World Series, and along the way caught the imagination of sports bookies everywhere. There were 148 search-engine pages of articles about his athletic, financial, and personal lives. And that was just what was public record. I hadn't even started to dig into the secret world of information for sale.

Holly Ann Cramer, on the other hand, had a sum total of thirteen citations to her name. All were recent news accounts of her murder. There were no *Variety* articles about an up-and-coming actress. No Internet Movie Database list of movie credits. No nasty items in the gossip rags.

It was as if she didn't exist, until she ceased to exist.

Before I climbed into bed I called Lindsey again. And again, no answer.

I wasn't going to let myself get worried about my ditzy ex. Yet. Mainly because Lindsey has an impressive history of going on walkabout. She'll just up and disappear for a few days, then turn up all blissed-out about some beach or yoga retreat or dude she discovered and immersed herself in until she decided to return to reality and to those poor idiot friends who'd been worried sick about her disappearance.

It then occurred to me the bozo who stashed his bag and kit in her apartment was at that very moment tucked away in a sleeping bag with her on some mountaintop somewhere, wallowing in the joys of that perfect skin and long legs and . . .

Fuuuuck thaaat . . .

Not *even* gonna let my head go there. To silence the thoughts I needed a sleeping pill. So I got up, reached into the freezer, and cracked open a fresh bottle of Ketel One. Flipped through the movie channels, found nothing, settled on the Golf Channel, and fell asleep in the chair watching old black-and-white lessons with Bobby Jones.

Sunday was a workout day. Two hours in the gym. Two hours at the Ranch's practice range. Then eighteen holes at Malibu Country Club playing four balls at a time, trying out different shots from similar lies in conditions, if not surroundings, that mimicked those of Pebble Beach.

For instance, the number five is comparable to Pebble's seventh and seventeenth holes, but for different reasons. Pebble's number seven is a short par-three with an elevated tee and miniscule landing zone. The par-three seventeenth at Pebble plays twice as long and requires some imagination in club and shot selection, depending on conditions.

Malibu's five is a combination of both: a long par-three with an elevated tee box looking down on a fairly tiny green. Two hundred and thirty-six yards to the center. Wind was eighteen to twenty knots, typical for Malibu, which is this gorgeous course that runs along the hills overlooking the Pacific Ocean. It's practically my home course. It's never crowded during the week and because of the narrow fairways, slick bent grass greens and those ocean breezes, always a challenge.

Like they say in Scotland, *If there's nae wind, it's nae golf.*

And Pebble *always* has wind.

So here's the math: From the back tees I was looking at 236 yards to center of the green. The cup had been cut pretty much dead in the middle so no give-and-take for that. Subtract thirty yards for the elevation and add back twenty for the wind, giving me a 226-yard shot.

There are greenside bunkers to the left and right, but the front is open. The cart path meanders along the right side, framed by a rail fence.

I still carry a four-iron in my bag. Even though a lot of the guys have switched everything longer than a five to hybrids, I still find the four a versatile blade. Last year I did switch my three-iron for a hybrid, and I have to say, it's pretty damn fabulous. But my four gives me more angles to play.

And contrary to popular belief, it is possible to shape your shots when hitting into a stiff wind, but you have to realize everything is exaggerated. Any spin you impart on the ball will have greater effect.

So first shot I tried: a low four-iron straight at the pin. I took a little wider stance than normal to keep balanced and focused on swinging level and smooth. You can't help thinking, *Hit it harder,* but you really don't want to pound down on the ball in a wind because that'll give it too much backspin and cause it to balloon. I looked at a spot just ahead of the ball to catch it clean, and my Titleist snicked nicely, although it bore a little too much through the wind and skipped off the back of the green.

Probability of birdie: low. Par: pretty good.

I teed up again with my four-iron in hand and set up for a right-to-left draw, aiming out over the cart path. It, too, was a solid hit and the ball turned nicely, taking a low trajectory back onto the right edge of the green and nestling to within seven feet of the pin.

Probability of birdie: high. Par: certain.

Next, out came the hybrid. This time I set up for a power fade, aiming out over a clump of oaks that menaced the fairway's far-left edge. It's usually hard for someone who can draw the ball also to be able to fade it, sort of like a cut-fastball pitcher also having a good changeup—the two have completely different wrist actions—but long ago I worked on developing that shot and it's come in handy many times.

I adjusted my grip and concentrated on keeping my lower body quiet through the swing. I could tell it was a good cut just by how the impact felt and sounded. Sure enough, the pill arched high in the air about twenty yards left of the green, reached its apogee then carved right, executing a graceful swan dive onto the front of the green, bouncing a few times before skittering backward four feet. It was inches from the hole.

Probability of birdie: certain. Par: not on yer life.

I got a little too cute with my fourth and tried to muscle a five-iron into the wind, but it floated up and left and found the greenside beach.

Probability of birdie: nil. Par: fair to good.

And indeed I came away from that hole with two birdies and two pars. But more important, I came away with a great deal of understanding about how my ball flight was shaping up and how well my eyes were judging the angles. My aim was spot-on target. I also learned the greens weren't sticking so I'd have to bring my shots in higher and softer, regardless of the wind.

And that's what a practice round is for, even if you're not playing on the actual tournament course.

In my case, I also managed to leave behind Joniel and the growing cast of characters surrounding Holly's murder, if only for a day. It was worth it. The hook in my drive was gone. My short game was dialed in. The putts were dropping. I wished I was teeing off at Pebble that day. I fell in love with the sport all over again.

Most people play golf for the camaraderie. They chat with their buddies while on the links and gossip like hens in the clubhouse afterward. For them, golf is mainly a social outing with the added bonuses of fresh air and exercise. And that's fine.

But that's why country-club players and professional players seem so far apart in their abilities. It's more than natural skill. To play golf at a professional level takes a commitment and maniacal drive that weekend golfers can't fathom. It's a solitary game played, as Bobby Jones famously said, on a five-inch course, the space between your ears. You can't play that course well if it's crowded.

Which is why, to be honest, I'm at my happiest playing solo. Working on shots. Trying to be creative. Focusing on the game. In my very best moments as a touring pro I've found that five-inch course inside myself and played it well and quietly and privately while in the midst of a tournament. Sadly, I can't seem to get there often enough.

So when you see Tiger or Phil or Lorena knocking shots stiff and curling putts in from ridiculous distances with this placid, peaceful expression on their face, the commentators will marvel that they're in the zone. They are. And the *zone* is, for us, the five inches.

Kenny came over that night and we played Pebble Beach hole by hole on my Xbox, plotting our real-world assault on the course as carefully as Eisenhower planned D day. But I'm betting we had more fun.

The next morning I went over to Century City to see Joniel's attorneys. They wanted me to sign some nondisclosure agreements that basically had me promise to cut off my own balls with a rusty nine-iron if I told anybody anything about anything. I wasn't too happy with what they'd drawn up and decided to use my legal acumen to hammer out something a little more advantageous. The negotiations went as follows:

Me: This is too vaguely worded.

Them: We have a check here for your expenses.

Me: Can I borrow a pen?

There was a branch of my bank on the ground floor of the same building. I deposited the check immediately. The bank would only let me take out two hundred bucks in cash against the check until it cleared, but that was enough to get me off of credit cards for a day or so. I pulled out my cell and pushed the 2. Lindsey. No answer. I left her yet another message for her to fucking please call back fucking a.s.a.p., that I had something fucking important to tell her.

Like, her friend was dead, I didn't add.

My phone buzzed as I was crossing the street.

Hello?

Huck, it's Judith.

Judith . . . ?

I just finished the preliminary autopsy.

Oh, that Judith.

I'm limited in what I can tell you until I give the full report to my boss, but if you want to meet later I can give you the headlines.

Sure, that would be great, thanks. When and where?

Eight? Do you like seafood? How about Crustacean?

Crustacean, in Beverly Hills. The specialty of the house is garlic-roasted Dungeness crab. Their prices were as high as the ocean is deep. The two bills in my pocket wouldn't even cover the liquor tab.

Perfect. I'll make the reservations.

Please, please be booked up.

Okay, see you then. And Huck, one thing I can tell you now because you're sure to hear it soon is the news is, well, the news is very bad for your client. I'm sorry. I'll explain at dinner. Bye now.

I made my way to where my truck was parked, still staring at the phone in my hand. *Very bad for your client.* Why would Tiffany's murder be very bad for Joniel?

Dad's phone rang twice before he clicked on.

Doyle.

Pete, it's Huck. What do you know?

Well, well, well. I figured you'd be callin'. Hate to say I told ya so, but . . .

What, Pete? Bring me up to speed, I haven't heard anything.

Some detective you are. It's all over the news. Your boy, Joniqua, seems he not only killed the old girlfriend, he eighty-sixed a new one. Dumped her body not far from your place, as a matter of fact. They hauled in his ass about ten minutes ago. Gonna officially charge him with both murders sometime today.

On what evidence?

Well, let's see, how about this, the lab report came back on some DNA he deposited in the dead chickie. Seems the bleach didn't get it all. Ding ding ding! We have a winner in today's genetic roulette! As usual, Huckleberry, you backed the wrong horse.

I hung up without saying good-bye. I was too stunned to make a witty retort, anyway.

The phone buzzed again, giving me a start.

Yes?

Mr. Doyle? Detective McIntyre.

So you arrested Joniel.

That we did. It would seem he's been very busy over the past few days.

You feel good about what you have on him?

Let's just say I am as confident that we have the murderer as I've ever been in any investigation. And I've been a detective for fifteen years.

Are you calling to gloat?

No, certainly not! This is a courtesy call to let you know your work on this case may be short-lived. Which may be good news for your other career, come to think of it. But also, I want to thank you for leading us in the direction of the strip club, even though Mr. Johnson was not very helpful. Some of the ladies who work there were.

Who?

Mr. Charles H. Johnson Jr. The manager of that laudatory establishment.

Charlie.

The same. Mr. Johnson refused to answer any of our questions, so we had no choice but to bring him downtown for interrogation. He was not a happy man.

I can understand that. I wouldn't be, either.

He was not very forthcoming in the end, so we let him go after a few hours. But I must tell you, he's not happy with you, either.

With me? Why would he be unhappy with me?

It seems he didn't appreciate your mentioning him to us during our initial conversation. Citizens who dutifully cooperate with law enforcement aren't popular in certain circles.

My stomach shrank to the size of a raisin.

Did he say that?

He didn't have to, Mr. Doyle. When you've done this line of work as long as I have, you can read the signs. Consider this a prudent warning. I'd advise you to find another exotic dance establishment to patronize, at least for a while. Mr. Johnson has a notable résumé, to include a few stays in prison and a dishonorable discharge from the United States Army with what I have only been able to tangentially discern were undertones of a threatened court-martial.

I knew about the time in prison part. Not about the Army part. I thanked him and clicked shut the phone, wishing like hell I'd done the same thing with my mouth yesterday.

I got in the truck and headed toward the 5 Freeway. I needed to talk to Joniel, but he was going to be a little busy for a few hours getting booked for murder. Even if the judge granted bail I probably wouldn't be able to have a private conversation with him until late afternoon at the earliest. I turned down the tunes to make a few calls.

Lindsey. No answer. Didn't leave a message. *How can she be so goddamn inconsiderate?*

Crustacean had a table available. Damn it.

I dialed my home number to check messages. I fast-forwarded through two from Louie, my business manager, who was sounding much relieved. The new deposit must've already shown up on his computer. The third message was from a satellite-dish company offering me a marvelous discount on a new system. Obviously they hadn't run a credit check yet.

I called Pete back. His voice was full of food.

So you dropping this shit-ass case?

Maybe. Looking like it.

Good. Get back to whatever it is you should be doin'.

Pete still wished I'd become a prosecutor.

I just don't understand why a guy who has everything would do this.

Happens all the time. All the fuckin' time. Guys like that think they can get away with it, 'cause they've gotten away with everything else their whole lives.

Pete went on about all the cases of spoiled rich kids thinking they were smarter than anyone else. But, see, honestly, the problem I was having with absorbing all this was Joniel never struck me as that kind. Don't get me wrong, he's no Mother Teresa; he loved his toys and his money and his women, all the trappings of fame and wealth, but he never gave off the attitude of being above everyone else. Joniel was a rare sports-prodigy success story that came from a bad part of town, as pure and gifted an athlete as you'll ever see, but one who'd known hunger and fear and who'd been surrounded by the razor wire of limited opportunities. He'd been a poor kid who'd heard the gunshots at night, seen neighbors hauled off by the cops in the morning, and attended the funerals of friends on the weekends. A childhood like that makes it impossible to believe that things are ever really as good as they seem.

Did that make him more likely to commit murder thinking the law couldn't touch him, or more likely to not do anything to wake himself up from his childhood dream?

Then again, if there's one thing you learn about people when you start scratching past the surface of their lives, it's that most folks are capable of pretty much anything.

Listen, Pete, what're you up to?

Now? Ain't doin' shit. Why?

Wanna go see Blue?

He was silent. I thought the cell had dropped out.

Pete? You hear me? I'm going to give Blue a quick visit.

Yeah, I heard.

You could meet me there . . .

The phone clicked dead.

Traffic was light. I made it to the Rancho Los Amigos National Rehabilitation Center in half an hour. Sprawled over two hundred acres, Rancho looks like a cross between a run-down farm and an aging resort. Most of its Spanish-style buildings date back to the late 1800s, when family members of the resident patients often pitched in to help run the dairy farm that kept the facility in the black. Now the cows are gone and with the county that finances the medical center looking at almost a billion-dollar budget deficit, Rancho's future is looking as bleak as the prognosis of many of its long-term residents.

I understand why Pete hates coming here. *I* hate coming here. But that's nothing compared to what it must be like to have to *be* here. Rancho is where people with serious spinal-cord injuries go to learn how to live without use of part, or most, of their bodies.

People like my big brother.

I walked through the glass doors of the only modern building on the lot, the Jacquelin Perry Neurotrauma Rehab Center, signed myself in, took a breath, and went to his room.

He was watching ESPN on a TV mounted in the corner. He smiled big when he saw me.

I knew it. I bet Gables you'd be in this week. You always come by when you miss the cut.

Gables was his nurse. Big black dude, gentle as a kitten.

If that was the case, I'd be here every week.

I sat on the corner of his bed. There wasn't much room for me, between the pulleys and bars and things that keep his head still. Beneath the covers, the lump of his body looked like it was melting away into the mattress, but Blue's face still looked as fresh and strong as it did when they brought him here, three years ago.

Aw, come on. You played beautifully. You almost made it. I think you're not keeping your head still over the ball and that's what was causing the hooks.

You and my coach. Next time why don't you just call my cell and leave a message when you see something like that? I could make some adjustments. Kenny doesn't always see the problem.

How is Kenny?

Good. Patient. Guy's a saint.

We talked about golf for a while. Then other sports. Then what was going on at Rancho; who came in new and why they were there. Most spinal-cord centers are populated by car-accident victims. Not Rancho. Gang-related gunshot wounds are the main cause of the injuries they see here.

That's what put my brother in this bed. Bullet to the neck. Only he wasn't in a gang.

He was a special agent for the FBI.

He was also the guy who taught me how to play golf. And baseball. And football. And basketball. And stand up to our dad. And figure out how to do well in school. And how to talk to girls.

The only thing we can't talk about, the only thing we never talk about, is Mom. Twenty years since she left us and we still haven't come to grips with it. A shrink could spend a career working on my family alone. If we ever let one get close enough.

Blue was the one who pushed me into law school after I washed out my rookie year on tour, and figured out how to pay for it with a creative mishmash of grants and scholarships.

He could've been a lawyer himself. Or a pro athlete. Or hell, handsome as he was . . . is . . . a movie star. Instead, he wanted to be a cop. Like Pete.

Only . . . not like Pete.

Vida Blue Doyle wanted to be a *good* cop.

He was named after the southpaw flamethrower who burst onto the baseball scene the year Blue was born, 1971, winning twenty-four games by hurling one-hundred-miles-per-hour fastballs. The young Oakland A's pitcher was Pete's favorite player. The old man obviously has a thing for unusual names. I can remember seeing Vida Blue pitch years later in the shadow days of his career, and I have to admit I wasn't that impressed. But once upon a time, he possessed some wicked stuff; throwing a no-hitter just a few weeks after getting called up from the minors, and winning both the Cy Young and the American League MVP his first full year in the majors.

Pete says if the A's bastard owner, Charlie Finley, hadn't insisted on wearing out Vida's arm in a single year he would've gone down in history as one of the greatest pitchers of all time. Finley paid his superstar $15,000 for throwing 312 innings in 1971. A pittance, Dad says, a fucking crime.

My brother never seemed to mind our parents' wacky taste in names, not nearly as much as I do. To this day he introduces himself with the full thing, Vida Blue Doyle. I think he's secretly proud of the fact that he was named for a black athlete. Which makes you wonder how it is our dad is such a racist prick. I've never been able to figure that one out. I asked Dad about it once and he looked at me in shock.

I don't hate black people! I hate bad people. Where I work, they happen to be black.

But not all of them.

Show me one who ain't around here. They're either crooks or will be crooks or are covering for crooks. Now shut the fuck up about stuff you don't know nothing about.

After the academy and a few years in D.C. and New York, Blue finagled a transfer to the Los Angeles field office. Most of the agents in that office worked the epidemic of bank robberies that plague Southern California, but Blue's specialties were crimes against children and cybercrimes, which are often related.

On weekends he volunteered to work with gang members, trying to show them what life could be like away from the violence and the crime. It was one of these stupid city-sponsored programs that are dreamed up every other day by politicians as fodder for their stump speeches to show they care about people they don't care about, and are taking action where no action is having any kind of real effect. I couldn't understand how Blue believed the bullshit. He really did. He insisted that if one kid stayed away from a gang, even for just a little while, it was worth the effort.

So Blue catches a bullet leaving a midnight softball game. Goes down like a fuse was blown in an elevator. He's lying there, face in the dirt, as shots are flying everywhere and nobody's getting hit but him, and all he can think about, all he's asking the guys around him about, is whether I'm okay. 'Cause I was across the field, gathering up the gear, about to run and catch up with him when the cars pulled up and all hell broke loose.

Of course, I was fine. My brother's life was all but over, but I was fine.

How's Pete?

Any conversation between us always gets around to that question.

Pete's Pete. He's helping me out on this thing I'm working on.

What thing?

I'm looking into something for a friend.

It's gotta be dirty for you to let Pete get involved. What's up?

So I told him. About Joniel, the murders, Dr. Filipiano. Everything. And when I finished I could see the computer inside Blue's head working. His eyes were alive.

When is Baker being processed?

About done now, I'm figuring.

He's a big fish. He'll probably get a huge bond and they'll take his passport as insurance, but they won't risk spoiling the case by locking him up this soon. He's not going anywhere. Fame is its own jail.

That's what I think. He just doesn't seem the kind.

Maybe he is and maybe he isn't, but you need to clear up a few things to make sure.

He told me a few questions I hadn't thought of. Then told me a few questions for Judith I hadn't thought of. Then raised an interesting point I *had* thought of.

If he's guilty, you need to drop this thing as of yesterday. And if he's not, it sounds to me like that's going to be a very tough thing to prove.

Right now I'd just like to prove it to myself. Then I'll figure out the rest.

Gables came in to check on Blue. He told me there's a bedsore on Blue's hip that isn't clearing up and they may have to do a skin graft on, and he needed a document signed since I had power of attorney. I did so, glanced at my watch, saw it was time to go, and said my good-byes. Blue was looking sleepy, but happy, like he had something to work on during the interminable hours of prison inside a once-glorious body that could no longer heed his wishes. I knew he'd come up with something to help me figure this one out. He always did.

I stopped on the way home to pick up some beer, booze, and chips. Waiting to pay for the stuff I remembered I'd turned off my phone in the rehab center like the sign says, and when I powered it back up the beep told me I had a message waiting.

The voice was that of a woman identifying herself as the personal assistant to one Pierce Fanagin, requesting a meeting. I wondered how they got my number. She left hers on the message. I called it.

Progressive Sports Enterprises, how may I help you?

Pierce Fanagin, please.

Whom shall I say is calling?

Huck Doyle.

She put me on hold. As I stood outside the bodega, listening to the Eagles on the phone's tiny little speaker, I ran through everything I knew about Progressive Sports Enterprises, which, frankly, wasn't much.

PSE was one of the small boutique agencies that handled negotiations and endorsement deals for professional athletes. The bigger agencies like IMG and Octagon had a lot more clout with corporate sponsors and the various sports franchises, but PSE had a reputation as a classy family-owned outfit.

A man's voice came on the phone. I couldn't quite place the accent.

Huck! Pierce Fanagin. How ya doin'?

Call me Huck. I'm fine, thanks. What can I do for you?

Ah, man, it's what I can do for you. That's what I want to talk about. Joniel Baker's a big fan of yours. You know he's one of our main guys.

I didn't but didn't say so.

You must be pretty busy putting out that PR fire these days.

A rueful chuckle.

No kidding. Phone's ringing off the hook. But the best thing for us to do right now is keep a low profile and let this work itself out.

Work itself out? A murder rap?

He was still talking.

. . . not to discuss other clients. The actual reason I'm calling you is we've been watching you for some time now and we think you're on the brink of breaking through. It might be a good idea for us to get together and talk about your future plans.

I'm sorry . . . you think I'm on the brink of breaking through? I'm barely hanging on to my tour card.

Minor detail. You'll straighten it out. Thing is, you have star quality and looks, and those things are almost more golden when it comes to product endorsement than pure athletic talent. Look at Anna Kournikova. What tennis tournament did she win? But she's worth millions to advertisers. But you, you have all that plus you can really play the game. So what we're thinking is to partner with you before you start winning majors, which we're sure you will, and that way we can help guide you through all the minefields.

I was, honestly, in a rare state of speechlessness.

Huck? You there?

Yes, I'm here. Just absorbing.

I can understand that. Look, why don't you come on over and we can meet about this in person. You know where our building is?

Uh . . . no.

My girl will give you directions. Let me get her on the line. How's this afternoon looking for you?

Not bad. That should work fine.

Great! Say, four?

Great.

Great! I'll pass you back to my assistant. See you later. And Huck, you're going to look back on this phone call as one of those life-changing events. I promise.

You're quite the salesman, if you don't mind me saying.

Not at all. That's what we do. And I want to make you our newest product.

Sounds . . .

. . . *amazing? Interesting? Please, God, give me any adjective but* . . .

. . . great. See you at four.

His girl—did he even know her name?—came on and gave me directions. I jotted them down on the damp paper bag my cold beer was condensating into and mumbled a thanks, still not quite believing what had just transpired. Then it occurred to me Joniel must have set this up, tit for tat, a favor for helping him out. What Fanagin was saying couldn't really be true. Me? PSE's *newest product*? Not possible.

Right?

A bum shuffled up to me and asked for some money to get something to eat. He looked more thirsty than hungry, and not for water. I handed him my pen and climbed into the Bronco.

Hang on to that. Pierce Fanagin thinks it'll be worth something someday.

He snorted, cursed, and tossed it to the curb.

Some people are just no good with long-term investments.

CHAPTER ELEVEN

Progressive Sports Enterprises has offices on the top floor of one of the many soulless glass towers that dot downtown Los Angeles. This city is segregated by industries, and like gangs and their respect for turf, most corporations hew to the rules. Moviemakers have their headquarters in Hollywood, Century City, or Culver City; television is for the most part based in the Valley; and downtown Los Angeles is reserved for, well, the money. Banks, investment houses, and the plecostomi of the entertainment aquarium, agents. It's a power thing. A separation of church and state. Art is art and money is money, and in the corporate side of the entertainment industry, art is appreciated only so long as it makes money.

After clearing some no-nonsense security on the ground floor, I rode the elevator up to the twentieth-fourth floor. The doors opened onto a marble-floored lobby with a reception desk at the opposite end flanked by two black-leather-and-chrome couches. The walls displayed half a dozen energetic LeRoy Neiman prints, suspended in individual beams of halogen light, their primary colors practically jumping off the canvas.

An extremely attractive young woman was smiling at me from the reception desk. Above her head hung the three giant gold-toned initials of the company for which she worked. It struck me that the gilded letters didn't really match the chrome arms of the couches, but what do I know about interior decorating?

The young lady spoke. Have I mentioned she was extremely attractive?

Mr. Doyle?

Somebody told you.

Excuse me?

Nothing. Yes. Huck Doyle to see Pierce Fanagin.

She pretended to check her computer.

Yes, of course. You're early but I'll see if he can fit you in now.

She pushed a button and spoke into a tiny flesh-colored microphone that extended on a thin wire from her ear to the corner of her mouth. I hadn't noticed it before. But now I couldn't take my eyes off it. It looked like a mole. Or drool. It almost ruined the effect of her perfect jawline and Angelina Jolie only-not-real lips.

He's finishing up a call now. It will only be a moment. You may have a seat if you like.

She glanced toward the nearest couch. I walked around and looked at the Neimans instead, the original of any of which one was worth more than I'd made in my lifetime. Even the limited-edition prints were worth thousands, if not tens of thousands.

Which made me wonder, for the umpteenth time, if I'd really chosen the right career path. Didn't Mom once say I showed tons of talent with crayons?

I looked closer at the print before me, *18th at Harbourtown.* There was a slight wrinkle in the canvas near the signature, which I realized meant it wasn't printed on canvas, it was printed on paper, which meant it wasn't really an authentic print, it was a copy of a print. A poster. In an expensive frame.

The halogen lightbulb above it probably cost more than the picture itself.

The extremely attractive young woman appeared at my elbow. I caught a whiff of a slightly sweet yet tangy fragrance.

Mr. Doyle? Mr. Fanagin is ready. This way please.

Is that J. Lo you're wearing?

She blushed and smiled.

No, Britney's Curious.

That her perfume or state of mind?

I'm sorry?

Nothing. Trying to be funny.

Uh-huh.

She knocked on a door and opened it, stepping aside for me to enter.

Mr. Fanagin? Mr. Doyle.

This town is replete with nothing if not clichés. So I admit, I was expecting a small guy, maybe with a soul patch or ponytail or some other vain Hollywood attempt at sad passé hipness, in too-tight jeans with the collar up on his Polo shirt. I was wrong on every count.

Fanagin was a big dude. He looked like a former athlete, maybe even a current athlete, although the gray at his temples hinted he was at least in his forties. He had on a well-tailored gray suit with a fashionable pink tie. His feet were up on his huge desk. He didn't rise when I entered. He simply smiled and waved and pointed to the mole-mike attached to his face.

It's twelve points backend or take a hike.

He was looking at me but obviously not talking to me.

I'm not going to say it again. You know he's worth it.

I took the opportunity to glance around his office. Lots of framed pictures of Fanagin with some noteworthy athletes, including Joniel. A shot of him shirtless on a fishing boat revealed an impressive pair of guns with those razor-wire tattoos bodybuilders get around their biceps to accentuate the positive.

On the credenza behind him was a collection of trophies and photos of Fanagin in front of a Ferrari, dressed in one of those Nomex driver suits the NASCAR guys wear, holding a helmet under one arm.

He was wrapping up his call.

Send over the papers. John's out sick this week so I'll handle the legal review myself. Hey, you still showing for the race Wednesday night? Don't chicken out on me. Yeah, right. Well, fuck you. Riceburners are for pussies. *Ciao.*

Or did he say "chow"? I can never tell. Maybe that word is code for "we'll do lunch" among the entertainment elite and the rest of us only think it sounds pretentiously European. He brought his feet down from the massive desk and extended an equally massive hand.

Pierce Fanagin. Thanks for coming in.

No problem. So you race?

Yes, foolish hobby. But man, I love fast cars. You know, I got tired of getting expensive tickets and even more expensive insurance bills so I've started entering legal races. They have them all over the place now to cut down on street racing, and at great tracks, too. The one this week's at Irwindale Speedway. See that picture? That's my baby. Yellow Maranello, five hundred fifteen horses. Race it in Super Street. What do you drive?

I motioned toward the photos.

Not one of those.

Ah, you will someday, I'm sure. Because we're going to make you a very wealthy man.

I started to say, I've heard that before. From a very slick investment adviser. But I swallowed my cynicism. Almost.

That would be terrific.

You have a curious look in your eye, Huck, suspicious even. Is it that you can't believe we'd be interested in representing you?

This is my normal expression. I'm a curious guy.

It seemed like he started to say something else, then put on the brakes and showed his teeth.

Yes. So I've heard. Word is you're a smart guy, too.

Well, I guess if all it takes is intellect to win golf tournaments, Einstein would've been a scratch golfer.

True, true. But it does take intellect to make the right decisions at the right moment, and you showed yours by coming here today. Truth is we really see enormous potential in you. You may not be playing up to your abilities right now but we believe it's just a matter of time before you do.

Okay . . .

Still not convinced. Look, our approach is like surfing. You surf?

Do politicians lie? I nodded helpfully.

You know, then, you have to catch the wave before it crests, or you'll miss it. It's not rocket science. You're a good-looking guy. You look in shape, no golfer's belly. Young. Single. Got all your hair. You have all the signs of a marketing gold mine. Endorsements. Commercials. Maybe even some commentary work on one of the networks when you have the time.

He was good. I felt like the drunk girl at closing time hearing all the right things. Part of me was ready to lie down and spread 'em, figuratively speaking, of course, except for one itsy-bitsy little problem. My bullshit alarm was ringing off the wall.

I'm flattered. Really. How do you know I don't already have an agent?

He smiled again, but his eyes narrowed and said, *Give me a fucking break. How stupid do you think I am?*

Actually, once upon a time, I did have an agent, Rickie Sandazor. They were all over me after I won the Amateur and came out of college the number-one-ranked rookie, promising all kinds of fame and riches. I picked Rickie because he repped some other notable Tour pros, and he seemed sincere about growing a long career together. After a dozen missed cuts, Rickie stopped answering his phone. So did the others. So I'm a little wary of agents, I guess. Most of the guys on tour sign with IMG, the largest and most powerful management company for golfers. But I could never swallow the idea of handing over a 20 to 25 percent commission. Which, in reality, means I've saved about 25 percent of nothing.

So, that's great to hear, really, very nice, thanks, but what I don't get is, what exactly are you proposing?

To the point, huh? Me, too. So, this is it. We want to represent you. Start marketing you around as the next great thing, the next Adam Scott, the next Camilo Villegas. See what we can scare up. Thing is, Tiger's getting overexposed and Phil's, well, Phil's, you know, a brilliant player but he's up and down and besides, he's locked into some seriously exclusive deals. So they're looking for someone new in golf to be the it guy.

And it doesn't matter that I haven't won shit?

No. Think that's hurt Michelle Wie at all? Our angle will be you're just about to. So to sponsors it will be like signing up Sharapova before she won Wimbledon, a bargain at the price.

Maria Sharapova was seventeen when she wowed 'em at the All England Club winning Wimbledon; I'm more than a decade older. Fanagin reached into his top drawer and pulled out a manila folder.

This is just a boilerplate agent agreement. Sole representation, blah blah blah, we take 15 percent, you get millions, you know the drill.

He handed it over with a big smile. I took a few moments to scan the pages. There were two basic documents. One, as he said, was a standard representation agreement, no surprises. But the other was a nondisclosure contract, and a pretty hard-assed one at that. Fanagin noticed me zeroing in on it.

Let me assure you, Huck, that's standard, too, the nondisclosure thing. This is a competitive business, kind of like war, you know? We simply can't have clients revealing our strategies and negotiation tactics. Gotta keep an upper hand.

That's understandable. But I'll need to have my lawyer take a look at this.

Fine. Of course. Who's your lawyer?

Me.

He paused. He smiled. He blinked.

You? A lawyer? No shit . . .

No shit . . .

No shit. After my disastrous rookie year on tour, I tried to find a backup career path. And, after said disastrous rookie year on tour, law school was a relief. But the main thing graduate school taught me was I didn't want to be a lawyer. The Monday I was scheduled to take the bar I finished on the number, tied for the fortieth-best finish, at the grueling 108-hole Qualifying School Tournament. A PGA card was once again mine. And a horrific career in law was abated.

In fact, the only thing about law that was better than professional golf was that once you passed the bar, you never had to take it again no matter how bad a lawyer you actually were. On the Tour, you could become a pro by passing Q School, but if you didn't play well enough you'd have to go through it all over again. And again. And, in many cases, again. Some guys have visited that particular level of Dante's hell half a dozen times. I lived every day hoping I wouldn't be one of them. Some years, I feel the flames licking at my ass. Like every other professional golfer bouncing along the bottom of the money list, thoughts of the Q visit my dreams and inform every moment of every tournament I play.

Fanagin blinked a few more times, then stood, signaling it was time for me to leave.

Janet here will give you my personal mobile number. Call me later.

Janet here beamed at the chance to do something for her lord and master, and handed me Fanagin's business card with his cell number scrawled on the back. She leaned close as we walked back through the valley of the shadow of Neiman.

Not many people get his private number. You should feel very important.

I did. At least, my head did.

My gut wasn't quite so sure.

CHAPTER TWELVE

I had just enough time to crawl my way home through rush-hour traffic, put on some nighttime duds, and hightail it to Beverly Hills. On the way my phone buzzed. It was Detective McIntyre. I faked bad cell reception and hung up.

I stopped in front of Crustacean at ten past eight. The guy at valet parking looked down his nose at my Ford until he gave it a bit too much gas pulling away from the curb and practically did a wheelie. His buddies had a good laugh at that one.

Incidentally, valet parking is to Beverly Hills what the subway is to Manhattan. The city would be nothing but gridlock without those eager dudes in the penguin suits who squeeze every spare millimeter out of a parking lot. But that doesn't mean I have to like it. Nobody puts Baby in a corner.

Dr. Judith Filipiano was seated at the end of the bar with about fifteen hungry-looking suits clustered around, vying for her attention. She was smiling politely, sipping some bright red drink from a martini glass, but actively scanning the room. Her dark eyes zeroed in on me and I saw what looked like a mixture of relief and agitation cross her face. This was a woman who didn't like being kept waiting, and I couldn't blame her one bit. Damn L.A. traffic. I wedged myself between two Armanis and gave her a peck on the cheek to tell the wolves the alpha male had arrived.

Damn L.A. traffic. I'm sorry.

You're not late. I'm just early. My place isn't far from here.

She's an enabler. I like that. Her perfume was subtle but absolutely delicious. The kind you smell all the way down to your belly.

Nice try, Doc, thanks, but I'm ten minutes late and it's unacceptable to keep a woman like you waiting. I had a meeting go long and you know what the ten is like this time of day. I could've walked faster.

It's really no problem. Should we see if our table is ready? I'm starving.

We squeezed out of the bar area and made our way to the maître d', who promptly escorted us to our microscopically small table. As we sat I got a better look at my dinner guest. Or, more to the point, a better look at the rest of my dinner guest. The little silk spaghetti-strap dress she wore was a dark purple, almost black, and moved when she moved, nicely and loosely. And she moved nicely and loosely under it. This was definitely not business attire. Nor was her understated but perfect makeup.

Realization dawned: I was on a date. Suddenly, I was very glad I took the time to change clothes.

A waiter appeared and asked about drinks. I ordered a Goose straight up for me and a . . . I raised an eyebrow at the good doctor . . .

Manhattan.

Manhattan for the lady. I'll take a look at the wine list, too, if you don't mind.

He nodded and sniffed. I'm not kidding, he sniffed. Like some French poof. All the waiters in Los Angeles are struggling actors. The ones who've been struggling longest can be a little bitter.

I'll send the sommelier right over.

You do that. And while you're at it, I'd like to talk to the guy in charge of the wines.

I crack myself up. Judith ignored my hilarity and was already studying the menu with a look of rapt anticipation.

The last time I was here I had these wonderful little salmon wraps. Here they are, with the chili dipping sauce. They're marvelous.

Count me in.

And the crab. I have to have the garlic crab.

That whooshing sound was the remainder of my brass in pocket headed out the door. I didn't care. I was overdue for a classy night out with a beautiful woman. It had been, well, let's see, a very, very long time.

And besides, that's what plastic's for. I just hoped mine wouldn't be declined. Again.

I always switch my phone to vibrate when I'm with other people and it buzzed just as I was about to launch into a funny story I'd heard from a studio exec friend about the making of the movie *Titanic*. It wasn't a number I recognized, but considering everything that had happened that day, I answered it anyway.

Hello?

Huck. Pierce Fanagin. I know you're at dinner so I won't bother you for long.

Call me Huck. You're not bothering me, except for the fact that you knew I was at dinner. That's a nice little trick. What can I do for you?

Hey, we always keep a close eye on our newest clients. Can't let you get into any trouble, can we? I'm kidding. It's dinnertime and it sounds like a restaurant in the background so I just assumed.

I covered the phone and whispered to Judith.

It's my agent. Or rather, my agent-want-to-be. PSE's trying to sign me.

Hold out for IMG. They've done well for Sergio.

I just stared at her.

You're scary.

She laughed. I liked her teeth. White, and just a tiny bit crooked.

Fanagin was still talking.

. . . get to know each other. So how 'bout it?

Sorry . . . my cell dropped out for a minute, Pierce. What were you saying?

I said let's play a little golf tomorrow. Got a tee time at Bel-Air. You up for it?

Let me check my schedule.

I put my palm against the phone again and smiled at Judith. She smiled back, a quizzical look in her eye. After a ten-count I put the phone back up to my face.

Looks pretty clear tomorrow.

Great! That's great! And let's make it interesting. Say, a grand a hole?

I blinked a few times. I must've looked ready to pass out because Judith started to rise to give me CPR or something before I waved her down.

A thousand dollars a hole . . .

Judith's turn to blanch.

Fanagin chuckled.

Yeah, that's right. I figure you must be extremely rich to not jump at working with us right away, so you can afford a little side bet, right?

I began to zero in on New Jersey as being the underlying accent in Pierce Fanagin's voice, that or Long Island, but I wasn't sure yet. He definitely had an East Coast bravado.

Right. Sure. You are aware, of course, that I'm a professional golfer.

He guffawed like a drunken sailor.

So I'm hoping! Don't worry, I'm no fool. I know you're way better than I am, so we'll work out the details of how to even things up tomorrow. It'll be fun. Bring cash!

He hung up.

The sommelier arrived with a thick book listing all the wines in their cellar. I'm sure half of them don't exist down there anymore, but size matters when it comes to restaurant wine collections so most places never bother to update their book. Truth be told, what I know about wine could fill half a Post-it note. So I let him recommend a few and picked one that wasn't the cheapest. Looking at all those numbers made me begin to think taking a few grand from Fanagin might be a fortuitous turn of events, fiscally speaking. Maybe not beat him too badly, but take just enough holes to tide me over for a while.

Then I replayed the end of the conversation back in my head.

How to even things up . . .

It'll be fun . . .

Fanagin had something up his sleeve. It occurred to me that guys like Fanagin *always* have something up their sleeves. That's how they get to be guys like Fanagin.

When the wine steward left, Judith made some further comments about the food here but I wasn't really listening that well. My brain was chewing on Fanagin's call. Which then made me think of Joniel. Which then made me wonder how his highly paid agent could manage to play a round of golf when his most important client was looking at life in prison for murder.

Those mind games led me to a mental image of Holly Ann Cramer, which took me over to Tiffany's crime scene, which parked me in front of the autopsy Judith had just conducted.

She was going on about some recent trip to Napa. It took every bit of my self-control not to interrupt her to ask her what she'd found out. I gallantly waited until she paused for a sip of wine.

You mentioned earlier you had some bad news for Joniel.

She laughed that delightful, kind of husky laugh.

Easy there, big boy. It's a long night. What else will we have to talk about if we rush through the meaty stuff first?

Answerus interruptus . . .

True enough. We have nothing else in common, do we? This is doomed.

Her eyes twinkled.

What do you mean by *this*?

Nothing. Dinner. Conversation. *This.*

Mmm-hmm. Well, I think we do have quite a lot in common. We're both curious people. We're both relatively smart and educated. And we both love golf.

What the hell makes you think I love golf? I despise the damn game.

I don't believe that.

It's true. I only play it because otherwise people would think it's strange that I walk around hitting a little white ball everywhere I go.

Ah, I get it. You have OCD.

Oh seedy? Is that another dig at my strip-club habit?

O ... C ... D, silly. Obsessive-compulsive disorder.

There you go. Five years of therapy, wasted. You're a helluva doc, Doc!

And that's all of our inane yet endearing dinnertime conversation I'm going to subject you to. Mainly we talked about the world's hardest game and our wonderfully dysfunctional city.

Judith kept me entertained through the appetizer, which was every bit as great as she said, through the entrée, which was even better than she said, and on into dessert, which was something called the Music Box and so utterly fabulous I swear I could hear the crackling sound of my arteries hardening. The topic of Joniel Baker didn't come up again until we were served espresso with a brandy chaser. She patted her mouth, folded her napkin, and set it before her.

At that moment, somewhere inside Judith, my delightful dinner date, a switch was flipped, and she became Dr. Filipiano, forensics investigator, sometime college lecturer, expert in death. Her voice lowered. We both leaned forward over the small table until our heads were practically touching. Her breath was a pleasant mix of chocolate and wine.

So, to more serious matters . . . my initial observation at the crime scene was correct. Elisabeth Sarah Hadrich, the woman you knew as Tiffany, had dozens of old bruises that indicate a history of violence or self-abusive behavior, further evidence of such was the presence of anal fissures and rectal scarring. I found numerous puncture marks that reveal intravenous drug use. And, in fact, toxicology showed a considerable amount of heroin in her blood, in addition to smaller amounts of cocaine and MDMA.

MDMA?

Methylenedioxymethamphetamine. Also known as Ecstasy. Presumably because she was an exotic dancer it appears she was careful with her heroin habit. It's obvious she didn't want people to see track marks, so she injected herself mainly under her toenails, under her tongue, even in her genitalia. There were only a few puncture marks on her arms and behind her knees.

So she wasn't just a casual user.

No. She was a hard-core addict.

Was heroin the cause of death?

No, it wasn't, but she was pretty high at the time. Judging from bruises on the face and, well, technical bits of information like relative lung weight and pulmonary vessel contents, it's my opinion cause of death was palmar strangulation. To be exact, she was asphyxiated by someone forcing her nose and mouth closed with their hand. It's a horrible way to die if you're conscious, and I think she was. Ligature marks on her wrists indicate she was tied up during the murder but had struggled against the bindings.

Do you get fingerprints from this sort of thing?

Not on the face, if that's what you mean, where the fingers are pressing against skin. In fact, we found no discernable latent prints anywhere on her or her clothes. Her shoes are missing. We think the killer was wearing gloves. The body has traces of cornstarch powder such as the kind used with older-style latex gloves, the type usually still available in consumer drugstores. Hospitals use a different kind now, powderless, because of allergies.

The gloves mean it was intentional.

Yes.

Not a crime of passion.

Unless his passion was killing beautiful young women. But yes, in my opinion it indicates premeditation.

Any reason to believe there was more than one person involved?

We couldn't rule that out, but as you know she was a very slight woman. One relatively strong man could have handled her, especially if she was incapacitated by the drugs. And as I said, there's strong evidence she was tied up.

I found myself hoping Tiffany was so blitzed on H she didn't know what was happening to her. It was still hard to reconcile the image of the corpse lying next to La Cienega Boulevard with the beautiful girl I saw dance a few weeks ago.

I didn't really know her at all. But she seemed . . . well . . . nice. You'd never know she was strung out.

Many addicts are very, very good at fooling everyone around them. Except their suppliers and fellow junkies.

So, but, forgive me if I'm being dense here, but what I don't understand is, you mentioned there was bad news for Joniel.

Judith flashed a surprised look, like I must have been kidding.

Other than the fact that he was seen by at least thirteen witnesses leaving the strip club with Hadrich . . . *Tiffany* . . . the night she disappeared?

Uh. Yeah. Other than that tiny insignificant detail.

Well, forensically there's the hair evidence found on the body. Specifically pubic hairs from an African-American. We can't tell the sex until the mitochondrial DNA tests are completed. But odds are good they're from a male.

Just for kicks, why do you say that? Some of those exotic dancers play for the same team, you know.

I didn't. Thank you for that fascinating bit of inside knowledge. I know because there also was a small amount of dried seminal fluid on the victim's stomach.

On her stomach? Not in her, ah . . .

Vagina?

That would be the place.

No. None in her vagina, although there are definite indications she had had intercourse shortly before her death. We won't get the DNA results back for another day or two, but that's almost a foregone conclusion because of what else we *did* find in her vagina.

A confession note?

She didn't laugh. Thank God. I'd hate to be around someone with my sense of humor.

Almost. We found traces of the spermicidal compound nonoxynol-9.

And?

The good doctor gave me a moment to connect the dots. I wasn't seeing any dots, though.

You do know Joniel Baker's semen was found at the Cramer murder scene.

Yeah. Someone apparently tried to erase it with bleach.

Another pause. Her eyes were urging me to get it, like a patient parent helping their kid with a math assignment.

That's true. But we didn't have to bother with testing the damaged specimen.

I looked at her blankly.

Huck, you do know where the rest of the DNA evidence was found?

I was beginning to feel really stupid. On a lot of levels.

I assume the usual places. The front door was pretty much washed clean with bleach, so I'm guessing back door? Upstairs window?

She shook her head.

It was in the condom.

The condom.

The condom. The used condom found lying under Holly Cramer's body. That hasn't made it into the media yet, so I shouldn't be surprised you haven't heard.

I was staring at the little flower arrangement on our table now, having that out-of-body feeling that was like falling into a deep abyss. Judith let me absorb it for a moment, then pushed me the rest of the way.

The condom was the same brand Detective McIntyre found in Joniel Baker's glove compartment. An open box of Durex Extra Sensitive, which contains the spermicide nonoxynol-9. Two packets were missing. Baker's prints were all over the box.

I could find nothing at all to say. Judith changed the subject but it was too late. I couldn't possibly feel any worse.

Until the check came.

CHAPTER THIRTEEN

The valet guys brought Judith's car around first, a little red Japanese convertible with the top already down. The mood had dimmed considerably and our good-bye was on the awkward side. She opened the tiny trunk, rummaged through a box of files, and handed me a copy of Holly Ann Cramer's preliminary autopsy report. When she slid behind the wheel I leaned over and gave her a peck on the cheek. That's like shaking hands in L.A.

I had a lot of fun. Except for that last bit of information, if you couldn't tell.

I know. I'm sorry. I know you were hoping he was innocent.

Yeah. Kind of knocked me off balance. It's still hard to believe he's actually capable of such violence and, shit . . . I don't know . . . deliberation.

That's the way most friends of murderers feel. I'm sorry. Thank you for dinner.

Well, I still have some questions about Holly's autopsy we never got around to. Can I give you a call?

Tying up the loose ends?

A little. Not really. I would like to understand a few things better, just for my own piece of mind. Maybe it's just an excuse for me to see you again.

She patted my hand.

Silly man. You don't need an excuse.

All heads turned when she goosed the engine and drove away. Some women are just made for convertibles.

The Bronco arrived just as my phone started vibrating. It was my client. The one who had apparently been killing beautiful young women all over town. I let it buzz a few times so I could think of what to say.

Hello, Joniel. I'm off the case. I'll drop off the advance money tomorrow.

Wha . . . fuck you say?

I'm done.

He made that sucking-on-his-teeth sound but didn't respond. I waited.

Joniel.

Yeah.

Good luck.

I didn't mean it.

Wait a goddamn minute, Huck. Listen. Shit, just listen for a minute. Why you think I did it, huh?

What?

I didn't kill them, man. I didn't. I know it looks like it. I know about all the evidence they say they got.

You should shut up. You're on a phone.

Like that's going to make things worse for me? Somebody's set me up, Huck. Set me up real good. Somebody with money and fucking cops in their pocket.

The row of penguins were enjoying our conversation, as were the people waiting patiently for their Jaguars and Porsches.

Just a minute. I can't talk here.

I pulled away from the curb but parked half a block down where there were no people standing around.

It couldn't look worse if you'd left autographed baseballs behind, Joniel. Jesus Christ, Johnnie Cochran himself couldn't have gotten you off this one! They have witnesses and DNA evidence, all of which say you're guilty as hell.

Just like Pete had said. It was going to be really painful to admit to the old man he was right. The nice glow from all the good wine and brandy had evaporated. I was ready to hit a bar.

You gotta come talk to me, Huck. You owe me that much. You can keep the advance money if you just let me have my say in person. I'm asking you, man.

I have to be somewhere . . .

No I didn't.

. . . and your place is out of the way.

No it wasn't.

I'm not at home. Too many fucking cameras and reporters and fucking satellite trucks around there. You wouldn't believe it. What a circus. They love this shit, what do you call it, like leeches or vampires or something. I'm at the Marmont. Ask for Leroy Paige. That's the name I signed in with.

The Chateau Marmont was only a few blocks away. I looked at my watch again. A couple walked past me on the sidewalk, talking and laughing as if murder and death were nothing more than words in a dictionary.

Huck? Man, if . . .

I'll be there in five.

All right. Really? All right. Thanks, man. See you.

I had no idea why I'd agreed to see him. He was most likely a murderer. Not just that, a cold-blooded serial killer. For some reason, just a few days ago, he'd looked me in the eye and told me a lie. And instead of working on getting in shape for Pebble Beach, I'd been chasing that lie thinking maybe, just maybe, it was really a truth.

I sat there beating myself up for being so stupid, until I remembered why I really wanted to look into this in the first place. It wasn't about Joniel. It was about Holly Ann Cramer.

The girl who'll never again get to dream. To make love. To swim in the ocean. To have a kid. To breathe.

To walk down a street arm in arm with the person she loves and laugh about nothing at all.

At that same party where she told me about trying to save that rabbit's life all those years ago, some guy and his girlfriend got into a nasty fight. A real throw-the-glass-against-the-wall, get-the-fuck-out-of-my-life screamer. Holly moved between them as gently as a lace curtain being drawn, put her hand on both of their wrists, and said something very quietly. They both looked down at the floor. Holly said something else. They each mumbled something, and the three of them walked together out onto the deck.

Thirty minutes later, Holly sat down on the couch next to me again, with a little smile on her face as she watched the guy and his girlfriend slow dancing outside.

I started the Ford and turned up the street toward Sunset Boulevard.

I was going to tell Joniel exactly what I thought of him. For Holly.

There was a metered parking space on Sunset a block away from the hotel. I zipped my credit card in and out of the box and entered the space number. It gave me a list of time options and I chose the minimum one hour.

Walking down to the Marmont I promised myself I'd never stick my nose into someone else's business again. I'm a professional golfer. I'm not a detective. Not a real one, anyway. If I don't get serious about playing golf real soon, I'll be back trying to win Qualifying School again, or worse, eking out a living as a club pro somewhere. Why can't I just live the dream while I'm still in it? Is there something defective in my family DNA that makes us want to solve other people's problems?

I have enough of my own to mess with.

There was a dark sedan parked illegally right in front of the hotel. In it sat two men. One was Detective McIntyre. He was looking the other direction and I quickly slipped past the car and into the lobby.

The guy at the front desk nodded when I mentioned Joniel's *nom de hide* and dialed the phone. He told whoever was on the other end that I was there, nodded again, and hung up.

Bungalow three. Do you know the way?

I did. I walked through the lobby and out back past the lush pool area. Joniel stood in the doorway of a little house, wearing a cap pulled low and dark sunglasses, talking to a really large fellow in a black suit with a really large bulge under one arm.

Hey, Huck. Thanks for coming. This is Nate. He's my pit bull. Anti-media patrol, you know?

Nate barely nodded. Joniel turned and I followed him inside. No one else was there. It wasn't the nicest room the Marmont offers; their penthouse and suites were much more sumptuous, but the bungalows are favored by celebrities who stay at the hotel for the one thing they do have in abundance: Privacy. I walked over to the little fridge, found a couple of tiny blue bottles of SKYY, and poured myself a very dry martini.

This is the one where Belushi OD'd.

He looked around.

No shit? Who?

Belushi. John Belushi. Comedian?

He shrugged.

Blues Brothers. Animal House. Saturday Night Live?

Oh, yeah. Yeah.

He OD'd on speedballs in this bungalow I think, number three. Top of his game at the time, hottest guy around back in the eighties. My dad used to watch tapes of his movies all the time. Said he was the funniest fat guy ever.

Mmm.

Pete had actually been in on the investigation into Belushi's death, back when it looked like it might've been murder. He was in a mean mood for a week.

You don't give a shit, do you?

Not really, man. Got some other concerns right now.

Yeah. So I'm not sure anything you tell me now is protected by privilege since I just quit. You might want to just keep quiet.

He have any friends try to help him?

Who?

Fat dude.

Belushi. Yeah. I think he did.

Or they just disappear like fucking smoke the minute things turned bad for him?

You're accused of murder, Joniel. Two murders. People tend to stay away from murderers. Nothing personal.

Man, everything's personal. I hate it when people say *nothing personal.* And I know what I'm accused of, motherfucker. I'm telling you I didn't do it. Neither of them. And my question to you is, Are you the kind of friend who believes? Who helps? Or are you like those other fucks who don't answer their phones no more unless they're on my payroll?

I'm the kind of friend who has an autopsy report probably linking you to both murders. I'm the kind of friend who has just been informed there are at least thirteen people who saw you with one of the girls the night she was killed. I'm the kind of friend who remembers how sweet a girl Holly was and how if she hadn't been dating *my friend,* I might've tried to get to know her better, and she might still be alive.

Man, I knew you had a thing for her. You couldn't hide it.

I didn't know her enough to have a thing for her. I just thought she was a cool girl. Pretty and nice. I hoped you didn't just use her and dump her like most guys in your position would.

Joniel was looking at his hands, probably imagining what a couple of World Series rings would've looked like if he hadn't screwed everything up so royally. Leroy "Satchel" Paige pitched three shutout major league innings at the age of fifty-nine. The guy hiding in this thousand-dollar-a-night bungalow under Paige's name had probably thrown his last ball ever. Outside a prison yard, anyway.

Yeah, well, truth is I was about to. Things was winding down. She was thinking we was getting more serious and I was just having fun, you know? I'm too young for that. Shit, does every bitch think about marriage as soon as you can remember their fucking name?

Call her a bitch one more time and I'll break your nose.

He stared at me in surprise. I was kind of surprised myself.

I mean it. Show some respect.

He sucked at his teeth, but nodded.

Not *she* was a bitch, man. Just women in general. You know what I mean.

Respect, Joniel.

All right. Respect. But I didn't kill her. And I didn't kill the other chick, Tiffany.

In light of what I know, you're going to have a hard time proving that.

I walked over and pulled aside the curtain. It was like living in the middle of a garden there. The little brick paths that meander between the bungalows were landscaped with every kind of tropical plant you could imagine. I saw no dead leaves. No litter. It was truly a sanctuary for the very rich, or the very secretive. The guy in the room with me happened to be both. I heard him open the fridge and get something out. A soda can hissed. I turned back around. Joniel was sitting on the arm of the couch, just watching me.

Huck, man, think about it for a second. Just think about it. It's too perfect, right? Right? I mean, who the fuck is stupid enough to do that? Leave shit like that lying around? I'm a lot of things, man, I know it, but I ain't stupid and I sure as shit ain't a murderer! Somebody set me up.

Look, you've got the best lawyer in town. If what you say is true, Bert will find it out.

Bullshit. He don't walk in that world, man. You do. Your old man's history and all. This is some dirty shit. Ask me anything. I'll answer everything you want to know, man. I got nothing to hide from you.

That's a foolish thing to offer. I told you, I'm not on your team anymore.

Whatever. Ask your questions.

Okay. Fine. Did you leave the club with Tiffany that night?

Yeah, I did. So what? I didn't kill her.

Did you have sex with her?

Why the fuck you think I left with her? Yeah, I fucked her.

Where?

He snorted.

Man, you perverted or just nosy? I'm not into no anal stuff.

I meant, at what location did you have sex with her?

We drove about a block to a crappy hotel she said she knew. I gave her some cash and she went in and got the key so I wasn't seen. Went into a room around the back and did our thing.

You remember the name of the hotel?

He thought for a second, then shrugged.

Airport Manor, I think. Something like that.

I know the place. On Sepulveda near Westchester.

Yeah.

Your Ferrari must've stood out like a circus elephant.

I was in the Lambo. And it looked just fine parked between a Jag and a big ol' Benz.

The Manor has rooms by the hour. Popular place for cheap little love trysts when you don't want to be recognized by people you know. Like your wife, for instance.

My phone vibrated but I ignored it.

So you were there about how long?

I don't know. Two hours, maybe. A hour.

Then what? Did you take her back to the club?

Naw. She said she wanted to take a shower and have a nap. Said she'd get a ride back to her car.

You use a rubber?

'Course, man. Always. Nasty shit out there.

How about with Holly?

He fell quiet. The index finger of his right hand was scratching idly the back of his left.

Naw. Not with Holly. She was the only one I could keep it pure with. I trusted her. She was clean, you know?

You didn't use condoms with Holly? Ever?

First few times, yeah. Then what we had became, you know, special. So we just stopped when she moved into the place at the beach. She said she had this thing in her kept her from getting pregnant.

IUD.

Yeah, that's it. IUD. Said she couldn't never remember to take the pill so she had one of those put in. Said I didn't have to worry about wearing a condom if I didn't want to.

When was the last time you had sex with Holly?

Like I said, things was winding down. I hadn't seen her for maybe a week before she was killed. She kept callin' and all but I kept making excuses for why I couldn't come over. I was just kinda hoping she'd get mad and make the move on her own.

She was living in your apartment. Pretty tough to move out of that sort of arrangement.

Tell me. I thought maybe I'd let her stay out the lease. Rest of the year. Season starts soon anyway and I'll be on the road a lot.

But you never had that conversation.

No.

You guys ever fight?

Naw. That's the thing about Holly. She's so damn calm about everything. I think she knew I was a player but she didn't sweat it none. Like maybe she thought I would always come back to her. She knew I'd be careful and not do nothing that put her at risk, too.

Or maybe she thought this was a fun thing while it lasted but when it was over, it was over.

Yeah, except she said she loved me. That's when I started to get nervous and all.

Maybe she did. Maybe she loved you but she knew you so well she knew it wouldn't last. Maybe she was fine with the arrangement as it was. She ever talk about marriage to you?

No.

Was she pressuring you to let her move in with you?

No, she liked her place.

So what makes you think she was wanting to take things to the next step, marriage?

Man, I told you. She said she loved me. People say they love you, they want something.

Yeah, Joniel, they probably do. They want love back.

He looked at me like I was the thickest brick in the wall. I started to leave. We both jumped when Joniel's cell phone blared out a hip-hop ring tone. He looked at the display and flipped it open.

Yeah.

He listened for a beat.

Don't worry, I'm not leaving the damn hotel. Tell the prosecutor he's got my motherfucking passport and a couple million bucks of mine so what else does he want? My feet in chains?

As he said this, he pulled out a little blue book from his front pocket and waved it at me with a wink. It had gold lettering and an embossed eagle on the front. He was looking closely at my reaction. I gave him none. He put the passport back in his pocket.

Cops are out front. I'm not going nowhere. Yeah, I know, they're nervous their big black ticket to fame is going to disappear. Tell them I'm fucking innocent, motherfuckers, and I'll prove it and then sue their asses silly for wrongful persecution. Whatever, prosecution, same fucking thing. Yeah. The hearing, I know. See you then. Naw, I'm fine with that. See you, man.

He flipped shut the phone. I stood.

Two passports. Nice trick. Not easy to get.

The extra passport's just a backup, man. Just in case. Don't mean nothin'.

None of my business. But it does mean something. It means you knew you might need it someday.

I got it to travel incognito sometimes, you know? I'm famous, man. It's hard to get around sometimes. It's just insurance, that's all. I'm innocent. I'm going to beat this, Huck. But I need your help. You gotta believe me. Nobody else does. I don't even think Bert does, really. I'll pay whatever you need. This is like some nightmare I can't fucking wake up from. Like I woke up in some movie about someone else's life gone real bad. You can't imagine how much money this is costing me, not just the lawyer fees, man, but all this goddamn bad publicity. It's killing me, man. It's ruining my name! Nike just dropped me!

I'd worry about spending the rest of my life in San Quentin if I were you. Good luck.

Again, I didn't mean it. Nate glanced my way when I closed the door and walked past him.

I'd find another client if I were you. No bodyguards in prison.

His voice was low, like a shift in the tectonic plates.

You'd be surprised.

CHAPTER FOURTEEN

It wasn't just where I learned how to really play golf; it was where I learned to love golf.

Bel-Air Country Club, with its spidery bridges and steep canyons and beautiful hills and luscious fairways and treacherous greens, taught me that the sport of golf is like being married to a breathtakingly beautiful, fickle woman; she makes you work for it. All the time.

But when she loves you back, my God . . . does it all become worth it.

Bel-Air is the kind of rarefied place the vast majority of golfers will never have the joy of setting foot on, and that's a real shame, but that's the thing about golf that makes places like Bel-Air and its cousin down the street, Riviera, so special. There's not just one heaven in golf; there're a couple dozen. And everyone who ever picked up a club is dying to get on one.

Growing up the son of a cop, I wasn't a member here, of course. And although a tour card can get you on pretty much any golf course in the world no matter how exclusive, I hadn't played Bel-Air in years. But as an undergraduate at UCLA, I'd walked these fairways and crossed these bridges hundreds of times, as both a caddie and a player.

Bel-Air was the Bruins' golf team's home course. I knew it as well as I knew the mug that looked back at me in the mirror every morning.

Only, Bel-Air is a helluva lot prettier.

Fanagin was standing next to the bright yellow Italian sports car I recognized from his office photos, chatting with a twosome, when I drove into the parking lot. They all three turned to look at my Ford as I parked it, with something akin to disgust on their faces. Mine was by far the lowliest cow on the feedlot.

Fanagin's face brightened when he saw me get out, and he said something to his buddies to make them laugh before stepping over to where I was pulling my bag out of the back. He slapped me on the shoulder.

Thought one of the Pedros had gotten lost and was trying to park in the wrong lot!

One of the Pedros had just appeared at my elbow to take my clubs from me. I'm pretty sure I saw his face flush. I offered a thanks and hoped he caught the apology in my tone. Fanagin paid him no attention whatsoever.

Got time for a drink. Let's hit the clubhouse.

I checked my watch.

It's not even eight A.M. yet.

Happy hour starts early out here!

Maybe Pierce Fanagin was my kind of guy, after all. He strode up the stairs into the massive main building.

We sat down in the big leather chairs and ordered. Fanagin was in full country-club mode, being the hail-fellow-well-met to everyone who passed by, many of whom seemed not to recognize the man who greeted them like old friends.

Arnie's a member here. Not a real member, you know, just honorary. Saw him the other day. Still booms 'em high and long.

Really? I'm pretty sure Arnie always struggled with trajectory. Thought his drives went too low.

Oh. Didn't know that.

Fanagin then changed the subject.

Lots of the greats were honorary members at Bel-Air: Palmer, Norman, Venturi. And because the club was in the vicinity of the entertainment capital of the world, membership also included a fair share of names that appear on your movie screen even before the title of the film. But the way Fanagin was pointing out features of the building and giving me a history lesson on the club, I figured he didn't know I had my own history here. Which gave me a tremendous advantage.

And at a grand a hole, that was an advantage I wasn't going to reveal.

My opponent leaned forward conspiratorially. I caught a whiff of his breath, a mixture of gin and halitosis.

They sort of frown on the betting thing here even though everyone does it, so we have to keep that to ourselves. But this is what I'm thinking. You know that golf movie, the one with what's-his-name, Kevin Costner?

Tin Cup.

Yeah, *Tin Cup.* Costner should have stuck with sports movies. That was a great one. Except the ending, you know? What the hell was that? He's gonna blow the Open just to prove he can hit that shot? No way.

Fanagin's voice had risen above the level of country-club acceptability, causing some of the others in the room to glance over. He caught their looks and toned it back down. I gave a shrug.

Even the best screw up. It's happened before.

I thought about Angel Cabrera's meltdown at the PGA Championships a few years ago, posting a ten on the par-three sixth. But, to be honest, I hated that part of the movie, too. Why couldn't Roy McAvoy just learn his lesson about sometimes par is good enough to win and taken the drop? Writers, what do they know? People who aren't professional golfers should never be allowed to write about it. They'll just get it wrong.

Fanagin was waving his drink in the air.

> Anyway, so I saw that movie again on cable a few days ago and it got me to thinking, that part about him breaking all his clubs and having to finish the round with just a seven-iron? Do you think that's really possible, I mean, with a really good player?

I didn't like where this was going.

> I guess. Sure, you could maybe shoot par with just a seven. Wouldn't be easy.

> Wow. You think? How about you? You think you could do that?

I really didn't like where this was going.

> I don't know. Never tried. And anyway, it wouldn't be legal.

> Not legal? You don't have to play with all your clubs! Nobody can tell you that!

> That's true. But they can tell you how you can use your clubs, and not use them. In the movie, Costner turns his seven around to putt with the flat edge of the back. Can't do that. Rules say the putter's the only club you can hit on any side.

> No shit!

> Yes shit.

> Damn. Wow. Well, damn.

He slumped back and thought for a moment.

So don't turn it around, how about that? Just putt the regular way.

With a seven-iron? No way. The face is too lofted.

I didn't say this to him, but theoretically, I guess someone could learn to use just the leading edge of the club face, sort of blade every putt, but it would give you absolutely no feel for distance. And putting is all and only about *feel*.

Fanagin wasn't happy.

Rules. Damn it. Who thinks these things up? I mean, who actually sits in a room and decides they won't let players use a club any way they want? What, like they have security cameras on the golf course or something?

You can tell a lot about a person by how they play the game of golf. That's why you should think twice about playing a round with someone you admire.

Gotta follow the rules, Pierce. Even when you don't like them.

He rolled his eyes.

No, you're right. You're right. Okay, then, how about this . . . you play with a seven and your putter, that's all. Match play, a thousand a hole.

Half a dozen heads around us turned in unison. Somebody behind me spoke up.

I'll take some of that action!

Another guy at the bar asked in, too. Then another. Pretty soon we were surrounded by four guys wanting in on the wager. Which meant there was absolutely no fucking way I could back out of it now. So much for keeping the whole gambling thing on the lowdown. Fanagin was loving the attention. I was picturing how much cash I had in pocket and in the bank, not that I should've bothered; I didn't have nearly enough money to cover this bet.

But like Lee Trevino once said, a hungry dog hunts best.

I wanted to figure out my potential agent. A few hours on a golf course together would tell me pretty much everything I needed to know.

I shook Fanagin's extended hand. The battle was joined. We made our way to the driving range to warm up, then it was off to the first tee.

Fanagin had the full complement of weapons, Nike by the look of his head covers; I had naught but my TaylorMade seven-iron and Odyssey two-ball putter. But there were two other big things in my favor: one, I knew this course as well as anyone alive, with the possible exception of Eddie Merrins, who was the pro here for forty years and the former UCLA golf coach, and with whom, years after he retired, I spent many happy hours walking the course and talking about the game . . .

. . . and two, I absolutely, positively, had to win.

CHAPTER FIFTEEN

Golf is a game of math; simple addition, subtraction, and geometry. You learn through practice and experience, some of it quite humbling, how far you tend to hit each club, and then as you stand on the course with a certain distance to the green before you, you figure out how far you want the ball to fly and what club—and for pros, what kind of shot; a trap draw, a power fade, a three-quarter—would best get you there.

A seven-iron, for most golfers, is a highly reliable middle-distance club. Even high-handicappers can hit it solidly more than half the time for distances of between 130 and 160 yards. Because it has more loft than, say, a five-iron, it's also useful for chipping and even bunker shots. That versatility has caused some people to call the seven-iron the perfect club. I was hoping it would be for me, anyway.

I knew there were a few holes that would be tricky for me to manage, but chances were very good with the accuracy my seven would give me, I'd be approaching most if not all of the greens from the short grass. There was no way I was going to pull a hook into the woods today.

The only question was, could I match the math and the shot selection well enough to get me to the greens—and near enough to the hole—to go low. Or at least par.

The tumbled green valley of the number one fairway lay before us, a par-five, 482 yards from the back tees. So, doing the math, I didn't have to crush a 200-yard drive to make it to the green in regulation on this one. All I needed was to hit two of my regular easy sevens in a row, which go about 175, and then depending on the lie, hit either a half-pitch or a chip to the green for the remaining 130 yards.

We tossed the tees and Fanagin won the honors.

Out came the big-headed driver. I watched closely as he set up over the ball, adjusted his stance, eased the Sasquatch back, and pulled the trigger, launching the ball a mile down the right side of the fairway with the cacophonous ping of a Coke can shot by a .22.

Fanagin, it was immediately apparent, had game.

But he was still just an amateur. I played with gods.

I put my Titleist down the middle right at almost exactly 300 yards from the center of the green. Fanagin's drive had gone almost 280 so we rode up in the cart to my ball first and I hit my second shot. And again, it landed just about where I wanted.

Fanagin had just over two hundred to the green. But just as I suspected he would, he got greedy. He pulled out a hybrid iron, intending to go for the par-five in two shots, and proceeded to chunk it fat. The ball scuttled into the sand short of the green. Fanagin whomped his club into the ground.

Shit!

I see this all the time, because I play with amateurs all the time. All the pros do. Except for the Majors, there's a Pro-Am on the Wednesday of every tournament week, and if you're asked to play, you have to. Period. And because those amateurs pony up a few thousand bucks for the honor, they want to get the most of your time and knowledge. They also want to impress the pro, which is almost always a big mistake. Word to the wise: Play the first few holes conservatively until you get a clear picture of how your swing is working that day. There's always a par-five in the future to go for the glory on.

Not that I said that to Fanagin. I wanted him to show off. The more he tried to play beyond his abilities, the more cash I was taking home.

The yardage marker on the sprinkler head five yards behind my ball said 140, so I had 135 to the middle of the green. A four-knot wind caressed my face. The rule of thumb with wind is for each knot add or subtract a yard, depending on which way it's blowing. Add three yards or so for the pin placement, which that day looked to be slightly back and right of center, and I had a 142-yard shot to make.

But, and here's where things get dicey, I didn't want to fly it on the green, not with a seven-iron. There was no way I could land it softly from that distance. So I put the ball back in my stance, hooded the face slightly, took a half-swing, and hit a punch shot.

It skipped on the fairway in front of the green like an eight-year-old headed to Sunday school, skidded to a halt about ten feet from the pin, then spun backward another four.

My opponent made a decent sand shot and two-putted for par.

I rolled mine in for birdie and smiled inwardly as Fanagin cursed under his breath.

This was going to be fun.

By the time we made the turn I was ahead by four. We'd split one hole and Fanagin had recovered from an errant drive nicely to make par and take the number six, on which I'd overshot the green with my second and had a difficult flop shot to get back on the plate for bogey five. He managed a birdie on the short par-four ninth, which I parred.

With fresh beers in hand, we stood before one of the most awe-inspiring and terrifying sights in all of golf: number ten at Bel-Air. The Swinging

Bridge. Par-three, 200 yards from the back tees over a canyon so steep the designers of the course, George Thomas and Jack Neville, had to build a suspension bridge to get golfers from the tee box to the green.

The story goes that in 1925, when Neville and Thomas were just beginning to lay out Bel-Air's back nine, California bought a huge parcel of relatively flat land in Westwood for what would become the University of California, Los Angeles, leaving Bel-Air nothing but canyon land to complete its nascent golf course. Like putting together a gigantic puzzle without knowing what the picture on it will ultimately be, Neville and Thomas hiked through the rocks and scrub, trying to imagine how their finishing half could possibly take form.

As they stood at the edge of the canyon we were gazing out on, the design partners made a wager. If Neville could hit a golf ball across the canyon, a carry of about 150 yards with treacherous winds, they would make that the first hole of their back nine. They returned with clubs and balls, and Mr. Neville put one on the other side. Then Mr. Thomas did the same. And the world of golf received one of the greatest gifts a sport could ever have: a defining, enduring image.

Fanagin had the honors. He pulled a five-wood from the bag, put it back, pulled a hybrid, put it back. Looked at me. Smiled.

Can you believe it, Huck? Here I am, trying to decide which long club will cut through the wind and knock it close, and all you have is that puny little seven. My, oh my, boys, my shot suddenly seems a lot less difficult!

He settled on the hybrid. Took a nice, even swing. Faded the ball onto the green ten feet from the pin. Pumped a fist in the air.

Yes!

I patted him on the back as he came off the box.

Nice shot, Pierce.

Why, thank you, sir. Honestly, that's how I normally hit it. Now let's see what you can do.

I had to laugh. Mr. Pierce Fanagin, amateur golfer, sports agent, Ferrari driver, was pushing me: Huckleberry Doyle, professional golfer, amateur detective, Bronco driver.

In my senior year at UCLA, I aced the number ten. But that was with a five-iron. This day, as my gaze shifted from the graceful white suspension bridge, to the canyon walls below, and up again to the seemingly postage stamp–size green on the far side, I held in my hand a shorter club with a more tilted face, and wondered what the hell the winds were doing and could they please, God, blow eighteen to twenty knots from behind me?

Because I'd need all the help I could get on this one.

I tossed some grass into the air. It slanted out toward the gap.

I tossed another tuft. It landed on my head and shoulders.

The flag was lazily pointing toward us, then directly away, then falling limp.

The treetops were swaying in cadence to some Cole Porter ditty.

The wind, I deduced, was swirling. No help. No guidance.

Golf, in that way, at that moment, is like life. Sometimes we stand at the abyss, alone, and all we can do is all we can do.

I set my ball on the tee and tapped it lower into the sod. A seven-iron sends the ball much higher than a hybrid or a five-iron, which means mine would be hanging in the air a lot longer than Fanagin's had, and thus a lot more susceptible to being held up or even pushed back by the breeze.

I took the club in my hands and went through my mental checklist. But as I started my backswing, I stopped, and stepped away from the ball, realizing I was gripping the club so tightly my knuckles were white.

And then, I remembered.

When I was a caddie here, I marveled at how those capricious winds would damn one player to purgatory and lift another to heaven, all within moments of each other. You couldn't possibly be sure what it would do between the second you hit your ball and the second it approached the target.

Or could you?

Out of sheer curiosity, or perhaps it was nothing more than a caddie's boredom, I began keeping notes about how players did on the tenth on breezy days, and the timing of their swings relative to what the winds were apparently doing. And, as with so many things in nature, a pattern emerged. One moment the wind would die, then sweep in from the west, then switch to the east, then die again. Wash, rinse, repeat. It wouldn't happen every day, but when the winds were pumping in, there seemed to be a fairly consistent rhythm to them.

Standing there, as Fanagin nattered to our small gallery sotto voce about how he didn't think even J. B. Holmes could carry 200 in those swirling winds with a seven-iron, I realized I might be able to time my ball flight to coincide with that rhythm. If I chose the exact right moment, it could work.

I counted the seconds between changes in the flag position.

I already knew I didn't have to carry 200. That number was to the center of the green. I'd have to hit 190 to clear the canyon rim. Still, Fanagin was right. It was a hell of a long way to hit a seven-iron.

The thing about hitting farther than you normally do is, you don't want to swing faster, you don't want to take a longer backswing, you simply want to make absolutely solid, firm, *perfect* contact with the ball. But smoothly, and with tempo. Tempo. Always the tempo. Without tempo, a golf swing is nothing but ugly violence. With tempo, it's a controlled nuclear reaction; incredible power released from those tiny atoms on the face of the club and the innards of the ball.

I readdressed the ball, breathing out evenly and calmly. I relaxed my grip. I pictured the flight, the landing, the roll.

I turned my eyes to the flag and watched it rise from a dead hang to pointing toward us. I waiting four beats and started my backswing.

My last thought as I swung down on the ball was to keep my head still enough to see the club make clean contact with the back of that poor little about-to-be-terribly-abused ProV1.

The canyon echoed with that sound, that beautiful rim shot, the snick and whirr of a well-struck iron. The ball arched high into the air like an arrow loosed, straight and true and headed toward the heart of the green. It flew, and flew, reached the top of the parabola, and then began its gentle fall toward earth.

And not for one moment did I doubt it was going to make it. The flag was pointing straight away.

One of the guys with us urged it on.

Get some legs! Go! *Go!*

Fanagin was, I'm sure, offering the opposite prayer.

The ball, now tiny in the distance, approached the canyon's edge at increasing speed as it fell. It looked for a second from our vantage point like it would just keep going all the way down to the bottom. If so, I would have to take a drop, make an impossible chip onto that tiny green, and hope for, at best, a double bogey.

But. Then.

Just as it appeared ready to plunge past the edge of the green and into the gaping maw of hell, my little white pill hit the front of the green. And bounced. And rolled.

Coming to rest a foot from the pin.

Our witnesses erupted in cheers and laughter. Fanagin stood with hands on hips, aghast.

Jesus, are you lucky. The wind turned at just the right time.

Yeah. Funny how that happened.

He just grunted. Two-putted for par against my tap-in bird.

Securely in the five-inch zone, I then posted pars to his consecutive bogeys on the next two holes. But the thirteenth was a problem; a long par-three, 213 yards. I managed to lay up clear of the hazards, but my chip found a steep greenside bunker near enough to the pin to make a normal sand shot, especially with my seven-iron, way too tricky. I simply couldn't lay the face open enough to pop it out anywhere close to the hole.

I was pondering my options, wishing like hell Kenny was with me to bounce some ideas around, when I remembered a Fred Couples shot Coach Merrins once described, an out-of-the-blue stroke of creative genius.

Sometimes golf takes more than skill. Sometimes you have to headbone a way out of a situation where no swing in your repertoire will get you where you have to go.

Instead of splashing the ball out of the sand only to have it run all the way across the green, I choked up on the shaft and used the edge of the iron to give the ball a firm plink in its middle, like the kind of tap-in you do with your wedge when the ball is near enough to the hole not to have to bother with your putter, only with considerably more English. My sweet little Titleist rolled up the face, popped over the lip, and trickled to within eight feet of the pin. I still two-putted for a five, but I filed away that shot for my next practice session. It'll come in handy someday, when it really counts.

By now, Fanagin was done. His mechanics were in the trash: hands too quick, lower body too loose, and he was beating himself up after every shot. Nobody is better at self-loathing than a golfer. The things we say to ourselves about ourselves out loud on a golf course would be rewarded with a punch in the nose coming from anyone else. Fanagin was cussing like Curtis Strange, and the madder he got at himself the worse he played.

He finally caught a break on the fourteenth, when his tee shot pinballed around in the woods before being spat back onto the fairway, not too far back from where my drive ended up.

The worst thing a struggling golfer can do is start overthinking everything. You could see the wheels inside his head churning every time he stood over the ball. As we carted over, I decided to try to help the poor guy by changing the subject.

Pierce, listen, what you said in your office. I'll be straight with you. I'm still trying to figure it out. I'm not a name. I haven't won shit since the Amateur. What makes you think I'll ever be more than a scrambler?

He blinked a few times. I could see the lines on his forehead relax. A smile crept back onto the corners of his mouth. The salesman returneth.

Look. Huck. Your skepticism is completely understandable. But honestly, it's what I told you. You have the looks and the skills. And fact is, to tell you the truth, in my world it's not about how many tournaments you win. It's about how likeable you are. We choose who the stars are, who the next big guy is. Joniel's the perfect example. Before this mess he's in, he was maybe the most marketable athlete in the world, because he's young and fresh, and he's got that hip-hop thing going on. Well, if it wasn't for us, he'd just be another great baseball player with a few commercials here and there and his face on a bubblegum card. That ghetto act would eventually work against him, but we turned it into a positive. We made him who he is, whether he thinks so or not.

Joniel is one of the best in the game. His marketing success can't just be the packaging.

No? Do you know how many ballplayers are popular outside their own fan base? Maybe five. They're a particularly hard sell because people are so loyal to their own ball clubs. I mean the Yankees and the Red Sox are the only franchises to have global marketing appeal. But in golf, outside the Ryder Cup anyway, there are no home teams and there certainly aren't enough Tigers out there to fill the demand. In the aggregate, people who play golf spend more money on their chosen game than any other sport, with the exception maybe being motor sports but hey, you gotta be rich and or stupid to do that, right? Another thing about golfers, they're devoted rabidly to their favorite stars and, here's the important part, to the companies those stars represent. So we're the ones who look around and say, hey, what about him? Guy's got what it takes. Will people take to him?

Kingmakers.

Not quite. Starmakers. Tennis is the same. Hey, that chick looks good, nice smile, nice legs, so what if she never won a goddamn tournament? Not about that. Not anymore.

Fanagin settled over his ball with a five-iron in hand. I replayed in my head the thing he'd said in his office about me being on the cusp of winning, of starting to take Majors.

So you're saying it doesn't matter if I win, all that matters is how you market me?

Well, not exactly. It'll get easier for all of us when you start winning. But for now, just make sure you keep your card. I'll do the rest.

He gave me a Jack Nicholson smile and smacked his second shot one-eighty down the middle. Turned to me like it's as easy as that, leaning on his iron like a walking cane.

There are two winners in professional sports, Huck. Those who win the game and those who win the bucks. In most sports it's the same guy. But why do you think great players like Els and Singh never had the huge sponsorships? Nobody *sold* them the right way. Plus, reality check, they aren't as good-looking as you.

Since you mentioned him, let me ask you. How's Joniel holding up?

Shit. What a mess this is. It's tearing him up. I feel so bad for him.

And the girls.

The girls?

The murdered girls.

Oh, yeah! Of course, them too. I hear they're both real lookers.

Once upon a time.

Yeah, right.

So what I don't get is, why aren't you neck-deep in the middle of this? Seems to me the media should be all over you for comment.

They have been. But that's what we pay our PR people the big bucks for. They've been fielding all the press requests. I like to keep a very low profile. The more invisible I am, the more our clients realize it's really all about them. They're the stars. *You're* the star.

Not yet.

Give it time. Give us a chance to work. If Joniel had listened to me, you know, maybe he wouldn't be in this mess.

What are you talking about?

Fanagin leaned in close. He had a pained expression on his face.

I shouldn't be saying this, but you're his friend. I warned him to be careful. I'm sure you did, too.

Careful?

You know, that temper of his. His partying ways. It was bound to get him into trouble.

I took a moment to recall what I knew of Joniel's life.

Okay, sure, he likes to have a good time, but I never saw him out of control or whacked out on drugs or booze. He seems too careful about his conditioning for that kind of behavior. And I certainly never saw a temper.

No, don't get me wrong. Joniel's a great guy. Love him. But there's another side of him most people don't see. I know I'm breaking my own rules about client confidentiality here, but maybe I'm feeling a little guilty myself.

Why?

Like, you know, I could've done something. Gotten him some help to curb those inner demons or something.

Joniel? Inner demons?

Wow. That's not the Joniel I know.

Huck, look, I know I shouldn't be saying this, but what *I* know about Joniel makes me wonder if maybe he really did it. Really killed those girls, you know? I'd never say that in public, but just between friends. I gotta wonder. I know you've been looking into things for him. What have you found?

I could hear Joniel's voice in my head, *Are you the kind of friend who believes? Who helps?*

Nothing, really. I'm hitting a lot of dead ends.

Dead ends.

I nodded. Debated how much to say. Chose the better part of valor.

I'm not even sure why Joniel asked for my help. There's very little I can do that his attorneys haven't already covered.

Oh? But I heard from somewhere you've definitely been nosing around. Find anything at all that might help get him off? He's convinced he's being framed.

I know he does. Not really. Not yet. Still hoping, though.

Yeah. Well, if I can help clear things up in any way. You know, you got any questions about stuff, need any kind of help to open doors, that sort of thing, feel free to call.

Thanks. I will. Thanks.

And I know he wouldn't mind if you kept me posted on stuff, seeing as how he's one of our most important guys and all.

Sure.

Although if Joniel wanted Pierce to be kept in the loop, he'd be more than capable of doing that himself. I wasn't naïve enough to think agents are friends. Agents are agents, a subspecies. A genetic mutation formed to branch the gap between the haves and the wants. And I could see how Joniel was becoming a problem for PSE, not only the bad PR of a high-profile client being mentioned as a murder suspect on cable news every five minutes, but he was probably becoming a financial liability. They're expending resources behind and in front of the scene putting out this raging publicity wildfire, while he's bringing in fewer and fewer endorsement deals. You don't see many serial killers on cereal boxes. And, like it or not, Fanagin's little confessional made me wonder anew if the guy I *thought* I knew was, indeed, capable of murder.

Even though we managed to redirect the conversation to more mundane topics and get back to the business of golf, I wasn't completely successful at exorcising the dark thoughts from my mind.

The fourteenth at Bel-Air is a long par-five; long enough, at 577 yards, to land a small plane on. Which, by the way, Howard Hughes actually once did. Legend has it he wanted to meet Katharine Hepburn, who had a house just off the fairway and played a fine game of golf herself. The club executives were not amused. Hughes lost his membership.

But he got the girl.

When Tiger Woods was fifteen, he reached the green here with a driver and a three-iron. I came up short even with three perfect seven-irons. Despite his lousy drive, Fanagin recovered and was on in regulation. He two-putted for par.

I chipped it close and holed out with one putt, splitting the hole. And that's pretty much how we brought it in on the back nine, matching pars and bogeys. We finished the round with me nine in the pink.

Or rather, in the green. I had a warm glow all the way down to my wallet.

Three clubhouse Vodka Transfusions later and I was saying my good-byes to our jovial, slightly drunk group of witnesses. Fanagin pulled out a folded wad of hundreds and began peeling them off.

. . . thousand nine-hundred, two grand. There you go. Nice round.

I just stared at the money in my hand. One of the guys who'd walked the course with us spoke up.

Uh, Mr. Doyle took nine holes. You owe him seven more.

Fanagin looked at him, winked, then turned back to me and slipped the scorecard out of his pocket.

You took nine, but with my handicap you had to give me strokes on seven of them.

The man spoke up again. The others had gathered closer.

Pierce, playing with the seven-iron was the equalizer. You never said anything about giving strokes.

That's true, we didn't. But I just assumed anything not stipulated beforehand would be according to established rules. I'm sorry if there was any misunderstanding, Huck, but, what was it you said? Gotta play by the rules? Whether we like them or not?

The men around us murmured in disbelief. Fanagin slapped me on the shoulder.

Right? Next time we'll spell things out a little more clearly. No hard feelings?

Like I said, golf reveals character. And sometimes, the lack thereof.

No hard feelings, Pierce. He's right, fellas. We should have been clearer on that. Hey, it was a great day of golf. Thanks, guys.

We said our good-byes and shook hands. The group dispersed.

I handed back the two thou.

Pierce, you must need this a lot more than I.

He actually looked surprised.

No, don't do that, it's yours. You won it. That was a great round. Go ahead and take it.

No thanks.

Well, all right then, suit yourself. Hope you're not upset about this. Rules are rules. You really did play a nice round. I was a little off today or else I'd have given you more of a fight. Hey, I'll give you a call tomorrow and we can talk business.

I turned to leave. I was pissed off, I mean really, really pissed off, but I was going to let it pass. Until, that is, Fanagin gave the slightest little satisfied chuckle as he settled back into the leather chair. That sound did it. Broke my resolve. I stopped and turned and let out a long sigh, and tried not to raise my voice.

I'm not upset, Pierce, just a little disappointed. In you. Here's some advice, take it or leave it. Don't short a guy you're wanting to go into business with. It certainly doesn't assure me you're someone I can trust.

His mouth was open, the hand holding the drink paused halfway between table and teeth. I wasn't finished.

And, by the way, it's never a good idea to make bets you're not willing to pay on, because sooner or later guys will just find a reason not to take the action. You and I know strokes were never part of the deal. The seven was my handicap. That was a bullshit play and you know it.

So much for not raising my voice. The entire club heard me deliver those last few lines.

Fanagin's neck turned the slightest shade of purple at the collar. His eyes narrowed. The muscles in his cheeks tightened almost imperceptibly. He set the drink back down. I thought for a moment he was going to stand up and deck me. I thought for a moment that was probably going to hurt.

Instead, he folded the money he was still holding and put it back in his pocket. He showed his teeth in some semblance of a smile, but his eyes stayed out of it.

Hey, so sue me, I hate to lose. In business and in play I find every angle and exploit it to the maximum. You should appreciate that. It's why I'm great at what I do. I always win my negotiations.

Always winning isn't the same as being a winner.

He laughed out loud.

Huck, *Jesus*, what are you? A Boy Scout? Winning is winning! Christ almighty . . .

He pulled out his cell phone and pushed a single button.

Excuse me . . . some unfinished business with one of my guys. I just realized I should have made this call earlier . . .

Into the phone he said,

Got it? Okay. Just a sec . . .

And back to me he said,

So I'm no saint. You don't have to like me personally, you just have to like what I can do for you. So, what's it going to be? Give me an answer. Do you want a tough, take-no-prisoners agent who can make you a millionaire? Or do you want to be a nobody forever? This is the moment. Time to reach for what you can be. Let's do this. Let's get on the same side and make some fucking money.

In a lifetime of difficult choices, this was probably the easiest I'd ever have to make.

Fuck off, Pierce.

His expression didn't change one iota. He snorted, made a dismissive gesture with the phone, put it back up to his ear.

You there?

His eyes met mine.

Make the deal. Yeah. That's right. Do it.

And he slapped the phone shut and held it up admiringly.

It's as easy as that. It really is. Another happy client getting what he so richly deserves.

He arched his brows and feigned sympathy with a shake of the head.

What a shame. I thought you were smarter than that. Someday you'll realize business is business. Can't take it personally. And hey, since we're giving advice, Mr. Huckleberry Doyle, *esquire,* I have some for you, too. You really should stay away from Joniel Baker. You're not doing any good for him, and you're really not doing any good for you. Stick to golf . . . for however long you'll get to play it, anyway, which my money's on not for long.

Pierce . . .

I turned to leave.

. . . what the fuck do you know about playing golf?

CHAPTER SIXTEEN

It was the last place on earth I wanted to go. And he was the last person on earth I wanted to see.

But Charlie was the last guy on earth I wanted to be sideways with.

I found him where he apparently lived twenty-four seven. At the club, keeping an eye on his girls and counting his money. I sat down at the table next to him.

When do you ever sleep?

He didn't even look up.

Someone once told me you were pretty smart. Guess not.

You mean me coming here? After mentioning your name to the cops?

Meaning that.

Yeah, that wasn't so smart. I apologize for that. Really. I've been trying to figure out who killed someone, and then Tiffany turns up dead, and I just, I was trying to help the cops find out who killed her, too. But your name shouldn't have come from me. And I'm sorry.

Silence.

I fucked up, Charlie. Trust me. It'll never happen again.

He didn't hug me, or shake my hand and tell me everything's okay, or even so much as nod, but I got the sense somehow that my apology had been accepted. Maybe because I was still breathing. And had all my teeth.

He motioned with one finger to the bartender, who'd obviously been keeping that finger in sight for just this moment, like a Labrador retriever anticipating a tossed ball, because a fresh glass of club soda appeared in front of Charlie a split second later. He turned his head and raised an eyebrow at me, which I guessed meant, Did I want anything to drink.

Absolut, neat, please.

I guessed wrong. His voice was subterranean. I felt it from my gut up.

Fuck you doin' still sitting here? You said your say.

The bartender snorted and retreated to his rows of sparkly glasses. I stood to leave. Charlie returned to counting his money, then spoke up in a growl.

And tell Lindsey to turn on her fuckin' phone. She misses another shift I'll fire her ass.

You haven't heard from Lindsey? For how long?

Three days.

That would've been Saturday, the day I woke up in her apartment. I sat back down.

Tiffany's been murdered and you haven't heard from Lindsey for three days?

He met my eyes, the curtain of inscrutability pulled back just for the briefest of moments.

You?

No.

Fuck.

Yeah, fuck.

We both tilted our gaze to the stage as the music changed and another girl began her dance. I was rifling through all the notes and files and calendar pages in my head, trying to put it all together.

Did Lindsey work on Saturday?

He nodded.

Early shift.

She leave with anyone?

Not that I saw.

Hey, did you know Tiffany used? Autopsy says she was hard-core into H.

Charlie took a sip of his club soda and held the glass up to the light, inspecting it for cracks or whatever the dishwasher didn't get off.

I knew.

Does Lindsey?

You a narc now?

I'm a friend.

You such a friend you'd know there's no fuckin' way.

That's what I thought. But I found a kit in her apartment.

Don't give a shit what you found, it wasn't hers.

Yeah, right. You're right.

The girl on the stage was pretty good. Skin like caffe latte. Little birthmark on her left thigh. Or maybe it was a bruise.

Let me ask you something, Charlie. Lindsey told me Joniel Baker was in here the night Tiffany went missing. There's some pretty good evidence he may have killed her and another girl.

Heard that.

Did you ever meet him?

A nod.

What did you think of him?

The music ended and the girl left the stage, replaced by a redhead twirling to an old Queen song.

... Mama, just killed a man. Put a gun against his head, pulled the trigger now he's dead ...

She had stripped down to a G-string and stilettos and was about to prove whether the carpet matched the drapes before Charlie spoke up again.

You learn, in my world, there are some folks who can do that sort of thing, some who can't. Joniel can't. But the evidence ...

Fuck evidence. Evidence lies.

The redhead's performance ended with a crescendo of Brian May's electric guitar and swirling spotlights, one of which came to rest on our table, splashing some reflected light onto our faces. That's when I noticed the tears at the corner of Charlie's left eye.

Not real tears.

These were tattoos, two of them, and they were black. The kind you are awarded in prison for doing something very specific. Something very few people, as he just said, are actually capable of doing. I stood, again, to leave.

What about you, Mr. Charles H. Johnson Jr.? Which kind of folk are you?

The spotlights slammed off, plunging the stage in momentary darkness. Charlie was silhouetted against the dim lights of the bar, his face, and the black tears, no longer visible to me. His voice came to me so quietly and low, had the music still been playing I would never had heard him say,

The other kind.

CHAPTER SEVENTEEN

I'm not sure how long I stood outside the club, leaning against the Bronco, trying to get my thoughts straight, but I didn't notice the two big guys approach until the one on the right spoke.

You Huckleberry Doyle?

I hoped they didn't see me jump.

Yeah?

I wasn't flattered to be recognized because they didn't look like golf fans. Unless San Quentin was pushing it as therapy.

Got some advice for you. From people who care.

He began poking me in the chest with each syllable.

Take your fuckin' nose and stick it some fuckin' place else other than where you been.

His equally large buddy moved in closer. I could smell his breath. In terms of health risks to me, it was much worse than the chest thumping. Vampires were dropping dead all over Los Angeles from that toxic garlic cloud. They had me pretty much pinned against the Bronco. Cars passed on the way to the airport with the people inside pointedly looking the other way: Don't get involved, this is Los Angeles. Someone will invariably have a gun.

The friendly advice–column guy was still dishing out pearls of wisdom.

> . . . and don't say nothin' about nothin'. It ain't your business and you ain't helpin' no one. Now, you should just get back to playin' that little game . . .

The human brain really is an amazing thing. Even with all this going on, a part of my mind wondered why someone would bother to send two comic-book thugs to warn me off of the investigation when Joniel looked guilty as hell and was probably going to stand trial for not one, but two murders. I mean, what was the purpose? To make sure I was going to drop it? It occurred to me maybe these guys could clarify. I tried to pace my words between impacts.

> Can. You. Stop. That. For. A. Second? I. Have. A. Question.

> No, I ain't gonna fuckin' stop! YOU'RE gonna fuckin' st—

And that's when I chopped him in the throat. Not hard enough to crush his larynx, just enough to make his eyes go wide, bring his hands to his neck, and rock him back on his heels. He was also having a hard time keeping his balance as he fought for breath.

I turned to his buddy, who was staring at Thumper.

> Boy, that was a surprise, wasn't it? He's one big dude to be in so much pain.

The guy raised his arms like he was going to rip my head off. He had a crazy mad look on his face. It changed. When his left knee snapped backward. After I kicked it.

He screamed—forgive me, ladies—like a woman.

I had to step out of the way as he folded in on himself and went down, still screaming. I was embarrassed for him. Somebody yelled something from a passing car but nobody stopped.

Thumper was now sitting down on the asphalt, his hands still on his neck, fighting hard for every tablespoon of air he was hauling in through his rapidly swelling windpipe. His face was very white. He looked up at me as I approached but there was no fight left in his eyes.

I reached into his jacket pocket and pulled out his wallet. Credit cards and money fluttered to the ground between his legs. Driver's license and business cards went into my pocket. Billfold became a nifty little tent on top of his head. I knelt down and got right in his face.

You're going to want to get even for this. You may even already be thinking about how many colorful ways I'm going to die. But for your own sake, please reconsider and leave the area. I have friends in the LAPD who will have your name within the next half hour. Get it? I'd think about relocating.

He tried to say something but all that came out was a glob of bloody spittle, which landed, unfortunately, on the front of my shirt.

I'll take that as a yes. Have a nice day.

The other guy had passed out. As I fished for his DL in his pants pocket—he evidently doesn't like the unsightly bulge a wallet makes—I noticed a wadded-up cocktail napkin.

The logo it bore was very familiar. An identical one blinked above the entrance next to where I stood.

And under the silhouette of a dancing woman was scribbled a phone number.

On a hunch, I pulled out my phone and dialed it. A cheerful voice said she couldn't answer the phone right now and to please leave a message. I was pretty sure I recognized the voice.

Tiffany's.

I suddenly felt very, very cold.

I started up the Bronco and rolled out of the parking lot. I was buzzing from the adrenaline.

No fucking answer on Lindsey's phone. No messages from her, either. Kenny had called but that could wait.

McIntyre picked up on the first ring.

Mr. Doyle! I was wondering if we'd ever talk again.

Have you located Lindsey Feller?

Who?

Lindsey Feller. Friend of Tiffany's. The other dancer from the club.

Oh, yes. The young woman you know. No. I've left messages but she hasn't called back. I take it you haven't, either?

No.

You sound concerned.

Getting there. If you do end up hearing from her, could you please ask her to call me?

Certainly. And vice versa, if you don't mind. She's a material witness.

No problem.

As I flipped shut the phone, I noticed some blood on the back of my hand and wiped it off on my already stained shirt.

The thing about big guys is they never expect someone smaller than they are to fight back. Because, frankly, we hardly ever do. Bullies, kind of like terrorists I guess, depend on intimidation and the threat of bodily harm. If they're going up against someone their size, they're ready for a fight. But the last thing on those two yahoos' minds was the possibility of a punch coming their way. They each had three inches and at least eighty pounds on me. That's what gave me the advantage.

That and the fact that I was raised by a cop with a mean temper and an encyclopedic knowledge of every weak spot in the human body.

Pete taught me how to fight. By personal example. My last few years at home as things grew worse between us, I'm pretty sure he came to regret sharing his secrets with me.

I had another thing in my favor: These guys knew I was a golfer. Golfers are wimps. Golf is a game played by pussies in funny clothes. That's the stereotype, at least among people who don't play golf. But the reality is most of the guys on tour are real athletes. Most of us played other sports in school in addition to golf. There are training trailers and sports physiologists at every tournament. Most of us try to stay in good shape, although there are still some doughy bodies walking around, and what people don't realize is professional golfers are probably the most aggressively competitive athletes around, because it's us against the world. With the exception of the Ryder Cup, we have no teammates. Our caddies are advisers, but we do battle against ourselves and terrain and wind and physics and the other golfers, ultimately and inescapably alone.

I realized I was really hungry. I grabbed a burger at a drive-through and headed home.

This little side job was beginning to take up way too much of my time, not to mention becoming riskier than I'd expected. I had a golf tournament coming up. I had my real career to salvage. I needed to focus on deadening my hands on my chips, and not overrotating with my backswing on my drives. I needed to study the course layouts for Pebble and get together with Kenny and work up a plan.

But now this thing had become something else. It wasn't just looking into a murder investigation. It wasn't just seeing if Joniel Baker had been framed.

Now Lindsey was somehow involved. And that, as they say, was a game-changer.

I'd just finished toweling off from draining the hot-water heater dry with a blissfully long shower when I heard the beeping sound my cell makes when I've missed a call. The message was from Lindsey. I almost passed out from relief when I heard her voice.

Until I heard what she was saying.

> Huck, Huck, listen, I'm sorry I haven't called back, I've been so scared. I lost my phone somewhere and, I'm, I'm hiding right now. If you can believe it, I, I, you know, I, I'm in real trouble. I know it sounds so dramatic but please. Meet me at the place we went after prom, you know the place. I don't want to say it over the phone, you know, just in case, you know. Just, meet me there tonight. Later. I'll be there after midnight. Please come, Huck. Please.

CHAPTER EIGHTEEN

I called Pete, told him about the two thugs, and read him their driver's license numbers.

I think they're looking for Lindsey.

Shit! Why'd you get Sweetie mixed up in this?

Pete always liked Lindsey.

I didn't. I don't know how she fits into things yet but my guess is these guys want to hurt her.

That would be the last thing these assholes ever do. I'll tell the boys to keep an eye out for her.

We hung up. I stretched out on the bed and closed my eyes for just a second to try to organize all the scribbled notes and random bits of information and mixed-up index cards in my head.

When I awoke an hour and a half later, I shuffled out of the bedroom and toward the kitchen to make some coffee. Pete was sitting on my couch, feet on my coffee table and a beer resting on his sizeable gut. I wore nothing but a few pillow creases on my face.

Did I give you a key?

Fuck needs a key? Mind putting something on? Been a long time since I changed your diapers.

You never changed my diapers.

He rolled his eyes.

And am I ever thankful for that.

When I reemerged in some jeans and a T-shirt a few moments later, Pete was flipping through a notepad.

You got some interesting friends there.

That so? How interesting?

Interesting enough to upgrade my equipment when I came here.

That's when I noticed the chrome .357 lying on a *Golf World* magazine at his feet. He normally carries just a little .25 in his boot.

You really did it this time, boy. These goombas are bad-asses. We're talkin' fuckin' *Sopranos* shit here.

Whaaaat? No way.

He found the page he was looking for and read from it.

Peter Francisco DiCarmelo and Jason Patricio Dano Jr. Multiple arrests on illegal possession of a firearm. Multiple arrests on aggravated assault. Assault with a deadly weapon. Attempted murder. Possession of stolen goods. Driving while under the influence . . .

Jesus Christ!

He listed about six more impressive offenses, including aggravated sexual assault.

I realized I was still standing, mouth agape, so I plopped down into my recliner.

What the hell are they doing still out on the street?

That's the interesting part. They got no convictions. Not one. They get hauled in and the cases get summarily dropped every time. And there's something else. All these arrests happened back east in Jersey. And they just come to a stop a little over a year ago. *Presto magico!* No more busts with either of them. Like they disappeared or cleaned up their act or joined the monastery or something. Nothing, until you meet up and have a little dance with them today.

So they're *mafia*?

Of fuckin' course they're mafia! I said Jersey, didn't I?

Holy shit.

You kicked the asses of two guys whose friends really won't appreciate that very much. If I was you, I'd think about moving to another state. And changing my name to Cindy.

I sat mulling that over.

Pete downed his beer and stood with a belch. The notepad went into one rear pocket, the .357 into his belt, somehow, and was almost completely concealed by his belly.

No sign of Sweetie yet, but I've got the guys lookin'. There's also an official APB on her. Looks like McIntyre's a man of his word, at least. You said she was hiding out. That's good. Smart girl. You talk to her again, tell her she'll be okay. We'll protect her.

I opened the door, only halfway paying attention.

I will. Thanks.

You got a piece?

I blinked a few times, thinking he was still talking about Lindsey.

What?

A piece! A fuckin' piece! You know, a gatt, a nine, a fuckin' gun for chrissakes!

I pictured my Sig Sauer .45, sitting in its mahogany gift box under a pile of sweaters on the top shelf of my closet, a birthday present from Blue. I hadn't pulled it out, or fired it, in years.

Yes. I've got one.

Well, you better start carrying it. If you were smart you'd have a concealed license to go with that private dick piece of paper you got. And listen, cowboy . . .

He moved past me out the door, took a careful look around the street, then turned.

. . . if you carry it, you better fuckin' be prepared to use it. These guys you're fuckin' with, they sure as shit are. Better to do time for illegal possession than to do time in a cemetery.

Then he was on his Harley, and gone.

I checked my watch. A quarter to eight. I changed into a pair of dark jeans and a pullover sweater, and stuck a pair of thin leather gloves in my back pocket.

I thought about getting the Sig, even started toward the closet, but ultimately talked myself out of it. Pete was being melodramatic. The idea of me getting into a shootout with mobsters was absurd.

Right?

Of such decisions is Darwinism based.

The first address was in West Hollywood, a crappy apartment complex on South Flores Street. His driver's license said one Jason Patricio Dano Jr. lived in unit number 5B. I was relieved to see it was on the ground floor.

I parked the Bronco across the street, half a block down, and watched. No lights in the windows. No one coming or going.

When I was fairly confident there was no one home, I pulled on my gloves and made my way around the back of the building. Like most cheaply constructed apartment buildings, this one had thin walls and loud residents. The heavy-metal music blaring from an upstairs open window competed with the explosions and machine-gun fire coming from the surround-sound system of the apartment directly next to Dano's.

I eased up to his back window and peered in. Total darkness. But when I turned away I caught the slightest movement out of the corner of my eye and froze. The movement stopped. I waited a full five seconds then dared a glance back. Again, a vague sense of something stirring inside the room.

If Dano was in there and had seen me chances were I'd already a bullet in the face. I looked closer and realized someone was, in fact, staring back at me.

I was.

From a bathroom mirror.

I let out a breath. A cat moved past, scurrying between the bushes. Somewhere close by a siren wailed, or was that from the TV next door?

Dano's back door looked solid and had a dead-bolt lock on it. But the wood around the window frame looked creased and water damaged. I took out my pocketknife and tested it. Sure enough, the blade pushed all the way in to the hilt.

Between the old caulking and the dry-rotted wood, I was able to cut almost entirely around the frame. The only part that offered any resistance was the very top, which had been protected from the elements by the overhead casing. That's actually what I'd been counting on.

I put both hands against the sides of the window and pushed. The wood at the top held firm. I pushed harder. There was some popping and cracking and it finally began to move. After some effort the entire window, frame and all, eased inward as if on a hinge.

I had it almost far enough that there was room for me to climb in when the whole damn thing gave way and came crashing down onto the bathroom floor.

I dove behind a spiky patch of maguey plants, ready to dash down the street if anyone showed.

But I was pretty sure they wouldn't.

Even if the neighbors had heard the breaking glass, even if they'd wondered what that was about, they most likely wouldn't do anything. Because people usually don't. It's a sad sociological fact. Most neighbors if they hear breaking glass they think some drunk dropped his forty or the kids next door are acting up again.

What they do not do is stick their nose out. Especially not for neighbors like Dano. I was betting he wasn't exactly Mr. Lend a Cup of Sugar.

Nobody turned the music down. Nobody peeked out a window.

And best of all, nobody appeared at Jason Patricio Dano Jr.'s door with a mighty big gun.

Still, there was an off chance someone called the cops so I had to move fast. I muscled myself over the windowsill and stepped right into the open toilet bowl. I didn't want to think about what might be floating around in there. Glass crunched underfoot as I made my way out of the bathroom and into the tiny apartment.

Out came my Mini Maglite and I put it on narrow beam. I made a quick once-over. The apartment was a mess. A couch, two chairs, folding table with dirty dishes on it. Clothes everywhere. A gigantic flat-screen TV mounted on one wall. The smell of stale cigarettes and spoiled food.

Beer, old pizza, and leftover mold in the fridge.

I didn't see a phone anywhere but there was a cell charger plugged into the wall next to the coffeemaker.

The bed was an unmade tangle of sheets and blankets. Porn magazines stacked on the floor, an impressive collection. *Barely Legal* was by far his reading material of choice.

I found a pile of bills on the dresser: power, rent, cable, nothing interesting. Nothing in the drawers worth noting. Four bundles of hundreds in the nightstand, still in the wrappers, next to a .32 and a half-empty box of condoms.

The closet held two shotguns, an AR-15 assault rifle, and a little automatic I'd never seen before, something that resembled an Uzi, only nastier with a big long clip. There were cases of ammunition stacked next to cases of liquor, cigarettes, and beer.

This wasn't answering any questions, other than one I already knew the answer to, namely, I was in a world of shit.

And so was Lindsey.

I eschewed my point of entry for the more traditional egress, and walked out the front door.

Twenty minutes later I was at DiCarmelo's address on Laurel Canyon. I parked a few blocks up the street.

His house appeared to be a rental, but much nicer digs than that of his compatriot. It was a dark brown Craftsman set back in the woods. There were a few lights on inside but no car in the carport.

I waited ten minutes before kicking in his back door.

No alarm. No yelling. Not even a barking dog.

And you wonder why burglary is such a popular occupation?

I had no idea, of course, when the current occupant would return home, but I was betting he was either still in the hospital or out trying to find the guy, me, who put him there. Mr. DiCarmelo was the opposite of Mr. Dano when it came to cleanliness. The house was moderately sized, nicely furnished, and very, very neat.

The kitchen had very little food in it, mostly bags of pretzels and chips, with salsa and cheese in the fridge. Beer, of course, and lots of what seemed to be expensive wines stacked in the cupboards. Bottles of top-shelf liquor in the cabinets. The sink was empty of dirty dishes and appeared to have been wiped down—not even a water spot to be found.

I really must get the name of his cleaning lady.

A short hallway led from the kitchen, with two rooms branching off, right and left. The door to the left was closed and, I discovered, locked. The room to the right was a bedroom DiCarmelo had converted to a game room, with big-screen TV, various video-game consoles, and one of those combination miniature billiards, foosball, air-hockey tables in the middle. Game boxes, stacks of gossip magazines, and a DVD collection of first-run movies in the closet.

I returned to the locked door. I knocked once. With my foot.

Inside was a queen-sized bed. A professional-looking video camera on a tripod. And half a dozen movie lights on stands.

I turned on the camera and hit eject. It was empty.

On top of the nightstand was a bottle of Astroglide lubricant and a box of Kleenex. I opened the drawer and gazed upon a gazillion condoms of various makes and sizes and colors, and a half-roll of breath mints.

Lots of men's and women's clothing hanging in the closet. Regular clothes as well as a police uniform, a prison guard uniform, what I think was a Catholic schoolgirl's skirt and blouse, and, yes, a French maid's outfit.

I started to close the closet door when I spotted something shoved to the back. A black cargo bag, identical to the one I'd seen in Lindsey's apartment. In fact, I immediately realized it had to be the same one, because it had a tear identical to the one I'd noticed earlier at the base of one of its looped cloth handles.

Inside it I found a few articles of clothing, size zero, a small cosmetics bag, and five whitish brown rectangular bricks of something powdery, tightly wrapped in cellophane.

Holy fuck.

The sound of my own voice made me jump.

Then the sound of the phone ringing in the next room practically put me through the ceiling.

It was in the office. On top of a big desk that took up most of the room. Next to a digital answering machine. Which picked up after the fourth ring.

Silence. Then the click and buzz of a dead line.

DiCarmelo's was one of those fancy answering machines that resets when it hears a dial tone. The blinking red counter on the top changed from 1 to 0. I pushed play anyway, and was greeted by an electronic voice.

You have no messages.

But the little window above the play button showed a ten-digit number. Caller ID. It was vaguely familiar but I couldn't quite place it.

I jotted the number down on a sheet of paper from DiCarmelo's desk, then pushed the arrow button on the unit to show all the prior callers.

The list had a memory of twenty calls. Fully a third were the same number as the last. I copied them all down, and the time and dates of the calls.

The drawers on the massive desk were all locked—*who the hell locks his desk drawers at home?*—and from the solid look of them it would take a chainsaw to get them open. The top of the desk held some blank legal pads, Post-it notes, and a Notre Dame beer stein full of pens. No family photos. No bills. No incomplete letters being composed to Mom. This guy kept his cards very close to the vest.

Next to the desk sat a computer table with a large flat-screen monitor, keyboard, mouse, and a monstrously large Apple computer underneath. There were four dictionary-sized external hard drives stacked on the floor next to the Mac, their icy-blue lights blinking expectantly.

I powered up the computer. It hummed and bleeped for a few seconds, then a log-in screen appeared on the monitor, requesting a user name and password. I turned the computer back off.

A bookshelf against the back wall held dozens of computer software boxes and manuals. *Final Cut Pro. Toaster. DVD LabelMaker.* There were also stacks of blank DVDs, two additional one-terabyte external hard drives still in their boxes, and twenty unopened digital videotapes.

I couldn't find a single used DVD. Nothing that showed what Di-Carmelo was shooting and editing in his little home porn studio.

His own bedroom and bathroom revealed about as much about him as his desktop. He liked dark sheets and towels, prescription pain medications of dizzying sorts, teeth-whitening toothpaste, and *Sports Illustrated.* There were side-by-side closets in the bedroom. One held everything from expensive suits to Hawaiian shirts; the other opened up to another closet. A gun closet. Metal, and locked tight.

I checked my watch. It was almost time to go meet Lindsey.

I did another quick scan of the house. No basement. Couldn't find the access point for the attic.

I was closing the door when I remembered the external hard drives.

The first thing DiCarmelo'd check when he got home, once he saw the number I did on his back door, is his computer. Judging from all the locks everywhere, I figured he probably had a pretty damn sophisticated encryption on it so he likely wouldn't worry about it being hacked. But he'd damn well make sure the computer itself was still there, as well as those hard drives.

The lawyer in me . . . the one who tends to look the other way with a shudder when I, you know, kick in doors and climb through windows . . . knew he'd destroy every bit of evidence on those drives if he thought they'd been compromised. So I couldn't just take them with me. Not only would the drives I took be useless as evidence because they were obtained illegally, but the drives I left behind would be wiped clean long before police showed up with a warrant. If I could even convince them there was anything illicit going on here, which I wasn't even sure there was. Unless you have an objection to pornography, that is. Which I really don't. Not because of any personal predilection, of course, just because it's a big employer in our fair city and not technically illegal unless it involves children. Yeah, that's it.

I knew I was rambling, but this was a fair representation of my train of thought at that moment.

I wanted those hard drives. I just didn't want him to know they were gone.

So I went back into the office and unplugged two of the hard drives from the computer. I then took two of the new ones from their boxes and plugged them in, careful to put the empty boxes back on the shelf just as they were.

Out the door, up the street, back into the Bronco, and off into the night.

I made it all the way to the Palisades before a cop car pulled me over.

Someone must have 911'ed the break-ins, I thought.

Nope. My right brake light was out. After radioing in for any outstanding warrants, of which there were as yet none—emphasis on *yet*—the nice officer let me off with a warning.

As I pulled away from the curb, I noticed my shirt was soaking wet.

CHAPTER NINETEEN

When Lindsey was my girlfriend in high school I could barely afford movie tickets and a bag of popcorn for both of us to share. So we spent a lot of time hanging out at the beach, surfing, or just driving around. One of our favorite things to do was to hike the Backbone Trail, which meanders along the Santa Monica Mountains all the way up to Malibu. There are lots of places to be alone along that trail, which for me was the main point.

The night of my senior prom, after I blew everything I had on a dinner out, rental tux, and corsage, we decided it would be nice to watch the sun come up from those mountains. We changed our clothes, packed a blanket and a bottle of Boones Farm Strawberry Hill wine, and drove up to a little-known entrance to the trail at the Will Rogers State Park near the Palisades.

That's where Lindsey was waiting for me now.

Hardly anyone but the folks who live nearby knows about that particular trailhead, and more important, that there are actually legal places to park along the street. I found a spot just before midnight half a block down from where the street ends and the trail begins. It was on the other side of the road so I turned the Bronco around and parked facing downhill. I didn't have to wait long. Lindsey appeared from behind some trees and hurried over to the passenger side. She climbed in and gave me a kiss on the cheek. She was shivering.

You're cold.

I know. I didn't bring anything else to wear. When Nancy dropped me off here it was still warm.

Nancy is her older sister.

You've been at your parents'?

Yeah. I didn't know where else to go, but then I thought, how hard could it be for them to find out where my parents live, you know?

Who to find out? Hold it, first let me get you a blanket.

The fact that Lindsey had gone home was in itself a major shocker. Her self-righteous parents had long ago passed judgment on their daughter, and never let a moment go by without some kind of condemnation. Each rare trip to Ojai gave her a little taste of the ultimate hell they were so certain she deserved. I mean, I know Lindsey is far from perfect, but isn't Christianity based on the concept of forgiveness? And if you can't forgive your own daughter, what chance does the crook, the cheat, the casual liar have in that heaven?

I turned the heater up high but with the Bronco's top off it didn't make much difference, so I reached under the backseat for a gym bag I keep there with various sundries in it, including a fleece throw. The Bronco doesn't have an actual trunk. I pushed DiCarmelo's hard drives aside but instead of the faux leather of the Nike bag, the knuckles of my right hand bumped into something hard and square.

I glanced back but couldn't see what it was in the dim light from the streetlight. I leaned across Lindsey and fished a flashlight out of the glove compartment. She must've seen a look on my face.

What is it? What's wrong?

Just a minute.

It was whitish, rectangular, neatly wrapped in clear plastic, about the size of a brick . . .

Fuck . . . me.

. . . and identical to the five others I'd just seen in that cargo bag in the bottom of DiCarmelo's closet.

Lindsey turned to look.

Oh my God! What is that? A bomb?

No, it's okay, calm down. It's not a bomb.

Not the kind that explodes, anyway. *What the hell did this mean?*

Then what is it!?

In her fear and exhaustion, Lindsey was about to lose it.

I'm not sure, but it's not a bomb. I think it's . . . I'm pretty sure it's drugs.

Oh my God!

I reached past the package, being careful not to touch it, pulled out the gym bag, and handed Lindsey the fleece.

When the hell did they have a chance to plant this?

Answer: any number of times, and places. Bel-Air. The strip club. Joniel's hotel. At my house. I didn't realize I was thinking aloud until Lindsey, with her eyes barely visible above the edge of the blanket, spoke up in a terrified whisper.

Who? Who planted it?

She whirled around in her seat, panicked, looking more closely at the white brick.

Oh my god! I've seen that before! Those were in her bag! It must be them! The guys who killed Tiffany!

Her words were like a punch in the gut.

What did you say? Lindsey! What do you mean? You know who killed Tiffany?

Yes! And they want to kill me!

I noticed the bright light on her face before I turned and saw the car, just as Lindsey screamed.

Oh my god! It's them! There they are! There they are!

The car's high beams were on and a third spotlight extended out from the driver's side window, waving around the darkened street like a water hose before settling on us.

Instinctively, I turned the ignition key to start the Ford, before the grinding noise told me I had never shut it off.

Is that the trouble you were talking about?

Yes! Yes!

That black bag was Tiffany's?

Yes! And they killed her for it! And they want to kill me! Go! Go! Get away, please, Huck!

That's when the siren blipped and the blue lights started throwing those weird moving shadows against the houses and parked cars.

They were cops.

Which ordinarily would be a good thing under these circumstances. Except for that package of something almost certainly illegal sitting on the floor behind me, a very large package that any halfway decent prosecutor could convince any halfway decent jury was not intended for personal use, but for distribution. Class A felony. A long time in the joint.

Oh yeah, and the two hard drives that linked me to a recent burglary. Breaking and entering. Another felony. Throw away the key, please, this cell will do just fine.

As I contemplated how ridiculous any explanation would sound, Lindsey slumped back into her seat with a sigh.

Oh, thank God!

And then the paranoia really set in. This was probably the most crime-free area in all of Los Angeles. Cops almost never come up here. And when they do, since this is the Lover's Lane of the Palisades, seeing two people sitting in a car, talking, is about as unusual as Botox at a menopause party. The timing of these guys showing up right at that moment was just too damn coincidental. I handed the flashlight to Lindsey.

Put on your seat belt.

What?

Put on your seat belt.

No! What? It's the police! They'll protect us. They'll know your dad.

Do it slowly.

Huck, why, you, what's the matter?

But she did what I asked. I heard her seat belt click.

The police car blocked the road down the hill. The only way out was up. But the moment I put the Bronco in reverse, the back-up lights would go on and the cops would know something was wrong.

Hang on.

She just whimpered and brought her knees up to her chin. I waited until the police car's doors opened and slammed the gearshift into reverse, spinning the steering wheel counterclockwise and popping the clutch at the same time. The Ford practically jumped off the ground. In forward, the Bronco will turn on a dime. In reverse it's even tighter. We were away from the curb and flying backward up the street in a split second.

We careened between parked cars and trees, brushing up against a few. The occasional screech of metal against metal competed with the noise of the Ford's tortured 350, which, at red-line rpm's, was roaring like a jet engine on takeoff.

It was all I could do to keep us headed in a relatively straight line. I couldn't look to see what the cops were doing but I had a pretty good idea. Then I heard the siren above the din we were making, and the houses and trees and cars around us got much brighter.

Just as we reached the end of the road.

The trailhead was directly behind us. Someone was shouting something over a loudspeaker but the words were incomprehensible, if not the meaning. I kept up the speed as we hit the two posts and wimpy little chain that barred the park entrance after dark. They folded under us like an empty beer can against the head of a drunken frat boy.

The path at this point is wide enough for a group of six weekend hikers to stroll leisurely abreast. It had only about a twenty-degree incline and went straight up the gentle slope for about thirty yards. I risked a quick glance around. The cop car was right up against the front grill. I could see two very angry faces through the dust-covered windshield, not six feet away. One was shouting into a radio mic, and his mouth movements corresponded with the indecipherable *wa wa wa* of the loudspeaker.

I turned back around and concentrated on my driving. Such as it was. Four-wheeling uphill on a dirt road at speed is hard enough. Try it going backward, in the dark, with about fifty cc's of adrenaline firebombing your heart.

The first turn in the trail was approaching. I knew the grade steepened considerably just after the bend and I was counting on the cop car not being able to make the turn, or, in the event it did, not being able to get up the rest of the hill with its rear-wheel drive and smooth tires made for asphalt.

I waited until the Bronco's rear bumper cleared the bushes at the near end of the turn, then cut the wheel sharply. The knobby front tires hopped a few times then bit, and we spun around the corner and continued up what was now almost a forty-degree incline.

But there was one problem I hadn't counted on. The lights went out.

The police car had sloughed into the brush, unable, as I'd guessed, to make such a sharp turn. But when it did so, its headlights immediately stopped illuminating the path behind, or, rather, in the direction to which we were headed. Not even the spotlight could find us from their angle. We were plunged into darkness with only the revolving blue emergency lights dancing on the treetops around us, and the feeble back-up lights of the Ford spilling into the dirt a few feet in front.

I eased off a bit and tried to picture the trail ahead. How many times had we walked it? A hundred? More?

Then the path suddenly grew visible again. I glanced over at Lindsey. She was turned completely around in her seat and had the flashlight out, holding it up over her head to show as much of the trail as possible.

We wove around the next bend without much trouble, but then things got more interesting. The trail narrowed to four feet and became much, much steeper. We slowed to a crawl.

A coyote appeared in the spill of Lindsey's flashlight, its eyes an unearthly red. She screamed. He looked stunned. I guess that's understandable. I didn't want to hit the dumb thing but couldn't chance stopping our progress. Had we hesitated at that grade we could very well have just slid all the way back down the hill and into our friendly neighborhood law-enforcement officers.

The coyote jumped out of the way at the last second.

We crept upward. The Ford's engine growled and snarled and popped in protest. I tried not to think of what might be happening to the rocker-arms or the clutch plate or the differential under the strain. I smelled all kinds of things burning.

The incline exceeded all manufacturer recommendations. Warranty null and void. Kiss your ass good-bye.

At a certain point, as the path grew steeper and steeper, the fact that we were backing up the hill rather than driving up it normally became the only thing keeping us rooted to the earth. The weight of the engine was on the rear of the vehicle. Had it been in the front we probably would've flipped ass over eyebrows by now.

The Ford's motor really began to labor. The tires were hopping and buck-ing, trying to keep purchase in the loose dirt. I was forced to work the steering wheel back and forth to help them grab. I caught sight of Lind-sey, dodging the thorn bushes that lined the path while holding the light as high up as she could.

I don't think we're going to make it! If we start to slide back downhill, you need to jump out to the side! Undo your seat belt!

I couldn't see if she did, because just at that moment we crested the hill and practically flew off the other side into the darkness, and certain death, below. I slammed on the brakes and let the engine stall. Silence washed over us. All I could hear was two very scared people breathing heavily and the sizzling and popping of a red-hot motor.

Lindsey clicked off the flashlight. I took a moment to get my bearings. We sat on the first in a series of mountain ridges on a widening of the trail where it splits into three different directions. There was an orange glow in the sky to the east. Los Angeles. There was a smaller orange glow to the south. Santa Monica.

Then I noticed them. Or rather, the lack of them.

No revolving blue lights below.

No sirens.

And most interesting, no police choppers hovering overhead.

Which is not to say we were safe.

We still had a damn mountain to get down from.

CHAPTER TWENTY

In physics, in life, in golf, what goes up must come down, and eventually we did, too. Although it took almost two hours of carefully easing the Ford down a series of hiking trails until we ended up on an old fire road. That led us to Sunset. Which led me to a dilemma. If those cops were legit, there was a be-on-the-lookout for the Bronco right now. If they weren't legit, they were probably still cruising the area, hoping to finish the business.

I thought about tossing the brick of *what-the-hell* into the woods, but the image of some kids finding it changed my mind. Lindsey had grown silent, probably from the sheer terror of car-skiing pretty much out of control down the hill. She was wrapped up in the blanket, eyes closed.

One thing was for sure: I had to get us off the street. Hide the Bronco. For a while anyway, until I could find out what was going on.

The closest friend to where we were happened to also be my closest friend. I knocked on his door a little after two thirty in the morning. A light came on upstairs. I knocked again to make sure he didn't go back to sleep. Three minutes passed and he opened the door.

Huckleberry.

Hi, Kenny. Sorry about the hour.

Come in.

Can I ask a favor first? Can we put the Bronco in your garage?

He blinked a few times, peered out at the Ford and Lindsey sitting in it, and nodded.

I'll move Bernie's car. Let me get the keys.

Kenny disappeared inside for second. When he came back he looked a little more awake. He nodded toward the huddled figure in my car.

That somebody's wife?

It's not like that.

We walked to his two-car garage and he entered a code into the automatic opener.

What's Bernie's car doing here?

She and the new guy took K.J. to Hawaii. They're having the house completely repainted. Garage included.

The door hummed and squealed open. The car was a big shiny black Chrysler 300.

Nice wheels. New guy must be doing okay.

Kenny gave half a shrug.

I suddenly had an idea. Not a *pretty* idea, but hey, any port in a storm.

Kenny, do you think this car is registered in his name or Bernie's?

His.

His look asked, *Why?*

I need a car that can't immediately be traced to me or you.

He raised an eyebrow but said nothing.

I was going to get a rental but time is short.

Planning on taking me along to prison?

I'm trying my best not to go there myself. But no . . . you won't be in any trouble. If I'm asked I'll say I took the car without you knowing.

No hesitation. He dropped the keys in my hand and turned to go back inside.

'Night, Huckleberry. You might think about golf once in a while. Rumor has it you're pretty good.

Thanks, Kenny. Really. Thanks . . .

Practice week at Pebble starts Saturday.

I'll be done with this one way or another by then.

I sincerely hoped that wasn't a lie. The front door shut and I heard the lock turn. I wondered again, for the millionth time, why Kenny stuck with me.

I switched the cars out and loaded a half-asleep Lindsey, the computer drives, and the mysterious package into the Chrysler. I sure as hell wasn't going to leave it anywhere near Kenny, and now that I had a clean car the chances of those cops, or any cops for that matter, stopping me were infinitesimal.

The Chrysler started with a deep rumble. I put it in drive.

And then just sat there.

I couldn't risk taking Lindsey to her home. Or mine for that matter. If she really knew who killed Tiffany, and if they really were after her, I'd have to find a safe place to stow her until I could figure things out. I felt her eyes on me.

How're you feeling?

Hungry.

Good enough reason to kill a few hours and give me some time to think. We headed to an all-night diner I knew in the Valley.

Lindsey ordered waffles, two eggs over well, hash browns, coffee, and an extralarge OJ. How is it skinny girls can eat so much? I had a Spanish omelet and coffee. Lots and lots of coffee.

By the fourth refill I could tell Lindsey was sated enough to talk, so I started her off gently, like the sensitive guy I am.

Who killed Tiffany?

Well, gently considering the time of night. She blanched, understandably.

What?

You said you knew who killed Tiffany. A certain homicide detective I know thinks Joniel did. Did he?

She stared at her plate.

Lindsey.

Yes.

Who killed Tiffany?

I don't think I should tell you now.

What the fuck?

What the fuck?

My inner censor was obviously sleeping. She looked up with fresh tears in her eyes.

I don't think I should tell you. They'll want to kill you, too. I can't have that on my conscious.

Conscience.

What?

Nothing. Listen, I appreciate your concern, but two things. One, they probably already do want to kill me. And two, a man is accused of murder who you say didn't do that. I have to know who did to help him.

She looked confused. And scared. Mostly scared.

Maybe he did do it, though. I don't know. Maybe he just hired those guys.

Which guys? No, wait. You know what . . . back up. Just tell me exactly what you saw and we'll work up from there, okay?

She nodded. Took a swig of orange juice. Which was probably at most 2 percent real juice and 98 percent, just orange-flavored crap because these places never give you the real fresh-squeezed stuff, just the concentrate that's usually water and lots of sugar with a little artificial flavor and color.

I had time to think of all that because she was still not talking.

Lindsey . . .

Okay, okay, okay.

Big breath. Pause. Wringing of the hands. Swig of OJ. I was just about to reach across the table to slap her (okay, not really, but I rather liked the mental image) when she finally thank the precious Lord baby Jesus started telling the story.

Here's the gist: The day I woke up in Lindsey's bed she had gone off to work the early shift at the club to cover for Tiffany. It seems there are always men wanting to ogle naked girls, even on weekend mornings. Go figure. I'm a late-night ogler myself. Anyway, after dancing for a few hours she returned home only to discover two very large fellows ransacking her apartment. The black cargo bag lay on its side, with a couple of those bricks of whatever tumbled onto the floor.

The two large fellows were extremely unhappy to see her. She thought at first they were cops but she didn't think to ask to see a badge. When she walked in on them they grabbed her, slammed her up against the wall, and said in no uncertain terms she'd better talk or she'd end up like her friend.

That's when she knew Tiffany wasn't off playing hooky with some rich client. Tiffany was dead. Lindsey was pretty sure she was next. She also figured out at that moment these guys probably weren't cops. But she wasn't completely sure about that. This, after all, being L.A.

So she talked. They asked her what she knew about Joniel Baker. She said a friend of hers was looking into the case. A certain golf pro who imagined himself a part-time P.I.

You told them about me?

I was scared!

You told them about *me*?!

Sorry! Give me a break! They'd already killed Tiffany! I'm sorry!

It took a few seconds of hyperventilation on my part, but I eventually realized I really couldn't blame her. Contrary to movie myth, when most people are faced with the option of violent death or ratting out a friend, life suddenly appears more precious than anything else on earth. Their own life, that is. The concept of the friend's life becomes more abstract, like that of a stray dog on the highway you talk yourself out of stopping to help, because maybe it won't really be flattened.

Maybe the friend you just ratted out won't really be hunted down and shot or beaten or stabbed or otherwise transformed into a hundred-and-something-pound pile of meat.

Actually, it doesn't even have to be violent death that's the alternative to talking; sometimes it's just minimal jail time. Cops count on this. It's how 90 percent of their cases are solved. The friend who turns out not to be.

So, when Lindsey mentioned me they grew very interested. They pushed harder and she tried to remember everything we talked about. They wanted to know if we had sex. Never, she said. Not even when we were dating.

I bet they thought that was funny.

Yeah. They kinda did. They looked at each other and kinda laughed. One of them said "Pinocchio" or something like that and they laughed again.

Finocchio.

Yeah. What's that?

Nothing.

Finocchio is an Italian slang term for gay. These guys were calling me gay because I hadn't slept with Lindsey. I didn't give a crap what they thought. But the fact that they used an Italian word confirmed what I already knew.

Describe them to me.

What do you mean? They were big and scary.

How tall in relation to me? What color hair?

She proceeded to paint a detailed picture of Thumper and friend, aka Peter Francisco DiCarmelo and Jason Patricio Dano Jr. They of the bruised larynx and busted knee.

Is that it?

What do you mean?

What else did you tell them?

She said she told them I was sarcastic about her acting in an adult feature and that had made her angry.

And that's when I recognized them.

I'm sorry? What? You recognized them? From where?

From the night I met the producer. The one who wants to put me in adult films. These two guys were hanging out by the door, but I remembered seeing them.

Unfortunately, as soon as she mentioned acting in an adult feature, they recognized her, too. Which meant they knew she'd be able to connect them and the now-deceased dancer with their boss, the adult-movie producer whose name she couldn't quite remember.

They just looked at each other and I could tell I was in serious trouble.

No kidding.

They took me out to their car and said we were going to meet the big guy.

They actually said that, *the big guy*?

Yeah.

So where did they take you?

Nowhere. When they opened the car door I scooted across the seat, opened the other door, and ran for it. They weren't very fast.

I could only stare.

It was really that easy?

Yeah. I don't think they're very smart. But they sure are scary.

My head began to hurt. I needed a drink. Or five.

Lindsey had a look on her face like a puppy that had just peed on your best Oriental rug.

Huck? Why are they doing this? What's it mean?

I didn't say, it means you're already a corpse. It means I'm already a corpse. It means there's a really pissed-off bad guy with lots of other pissed-off bad guys under his employ who are even now scouring the city for two very tired, very stupid, very formerly alive coffee drinkers in order to tie up some nasty loose ends on a few murders they've already committed. What I did say was,

Nothing. It doesn't mean anything. I'm just trying to make sense of all this. Don't worry. I think I've got it figured out.

Yeah. Like we move to Antarctica and get enough plastic surgery to make us resemble penguins. Lindsey didn't believe my assurances; I could see it in her eyes. But she was smart enough to shut up about it.

I made a decision, paid the check, put Lindsey back in the car, and took her to the one place they'd never think to look for her.

Along the way I couldn't help but wonder if I'd live long enough ever to hit another golf ball.

CHAPTER TWENTY-ONE

It took some explaining, a few lies, and a couple bucks, but the security guy at the door agreed to let her in. Halfway down the hall she turned and gave me an entreating look. I managed an easy smile and a thumbs-up. She was not fooled.

After dropping Lindsey off, I drove to a beachside parking lot in Venice, turned on a classic rock station, and reclined the Chrysler's seat as far as it would go. I watched the waves until the windows fogged up from my breathing.

I think there are snapshots from your life that become sort of touchstones, icons of self-identity that are forever powerful but calming, definitive but philosophical, even when you're far away from them, or even if you can never go back there again. They're the moments you think of when you're troubled or struggling or confused and want to start at the point of who you are absolutely certain you are and what you are absolutely certain you know and work outward from there.

In times like that, I find myself in the ocean.

Before he got shot, before he joined the Bureau, back when I was still in high school, Blue and Lindsey and I used to spend a lot of time sitting on boards out beyond the break at Zuma. Like every other sport he ever tried, Blue was a natural at surfing. He had this yogalike balance thing, where he never seemed to struggle against the wave. I would pop up and try to get the most out of the ride; Blue flowed along with it like he was part of the sea. He was just beautiful to watch, making easy turns with graceful footwork, hardly ever wiping out. And even when he did eat it, it almost seemed like it was deliberate. He'd come up laughing, white teeth flashing in the sun, muscled brown arms pumping his longboard back to where we bobbed in the swells.

Every Betty on the beach was crazy for him. I'd even catch Lindsey, who was used to the never-ending stares of man and boy and woman alike, watching him with admiration. Funny thing, I was never jealous of Blue, because I felt so damned lucky he was my brother. He dated a bunch of girls, but never any one for very long. I remember wondering, as I watched the parade of gorgeous creatures come and go out of his life, what could it possibly be he was looking for?

I awoke a little after nine, found a public phone, of which, by the way, there are very few in these days of cell phones, and started making the calls.

The first was to Blue.

How's she doing?

She's fine. She's sleeping. Good idea, bringing her here. No one would guess it. How're you? *Where* are you? Wait . . . don't say anything over the phone.

It's okay, I'm on a pay phone. And I'm safe for now.

I doubt that very much. Lindsey told me a little. Fill in the blanks.

So I gave Blue everything I knew.

Funny thing about my brother, he can't lift his arms so he can't take notes, but he would ask me about something I'd told him five minutes earlier and cross-reference it with something I'd just said. He has this uncanny ability to keep it all straight in his head, even just in hearing something once.

I, of course, have no such ability. I still didn't have it straight in my head.

He groaned when I got to the part about the burglaries.

Huck . . . *no* . . . B and E! What were you thinking?

I know, I know.

You're better than that, Huck!

No, I'm not.

I know. I was desperate. Someone's trying to kill Lindsey, and probably me now, and I had to find out who. It was the only way.

It's never the only way!

It's done, Blue. I have to find out what's on those hard drives.

He knew my tone, knew it was useless to admonish me anymore.

Well, look, Huck, let me make some calls. See who DiCarmelo and Dano are working for out here.

You got it, thanks, Blue.

The second call was to Detective McIntyre. He didn't answer his phone so I left a message asking him to call back.

The third was to Joniel.

Hey.

Hey.

How're you holding up?

How you think? Waiting for the noose, man. Waiting for the noose.

Listen, I don't want to get your hopes up, but I think I'm onto something. And I think the hangman might just have to look for someone else.

He was silent.

Joniel?

I could hear him breathing. I think it was breathing. His voice was a little strained when he finally answered.

Yeah, man . . . yeah . . . please tell me you're not shittin' me.

I'm not shitting you. I don't have enough to get you off the hook, there's still a ton of evidence linking you to the murders that I can't explain, but something really fucked up is going on, with some really bad dudes. I have to ask you, do you know two guys named Peter DiCarmelo and Jason Dano?

Let me think a sec. Naw, don't think I do. Why? Who're they?

They're the bad dudes. I'm pretty sure they killed Tiffany, but I don't know if they had anything to do with Holly's murder. And I still don't understand yet why your DNA is all over both crime scenes.

I told you man, I'm being set up!

I know. But I have to know the why and the how before we can prove that.

I hear you. You'll do it, man. I know you will.

I wasn't so sure. But Joniel was suddenly in a chatty mood.

Hey, man, I heard about your match with Pierce. God-*damn*! You played the whole round with just a seven-iron?

And a putter. Yeah. How'd you hear?

It was on *SportsTalk,* the radio show. Somebody from Bel-Air called it in. Man, I wish I'd seen that. See the big man get humbled.

Well, not sure who was humbled. I hate to tell you this but he pulled a fast one on me. Took strokes and cheated me out of some large cash.

No shit? Motherfucker. Well, ya know, I have to say that doesn't surprise me.

What do you mean, that doesn't surprise you?

Him cheating you. I think he's been cooking the books with my shit, too. I ain't no math genius but I started thinking the numbers don't add up on what I should be putting in the bank and what I am. Ya know? Like, they send a monthly statement of what's coming in and all, it's confusing as shit, but I'm seeing a lot of fees and taxes and shit that are costing me a hell of a lot of Franklins. PSE used to be good people, straight talkers and all, that's why I signed with them right outta college. Had a good rep. Now, that group that bought them out, I don't know . . .

Did you ask Fanagin about it?

Yeah. Told him I was going to have an accountant take a look and he said he'd have Anderson go over it all with me to explain . . .

Anderson?

Dude at PSE who does my taxes and shit. But I told him fuck that, I was going to get someone outside to make sure there wasn't anything funky going on.

And did you?

Got a name from someone but I haven't called him yet.

Why not?

Man, 'cause a certain girl turns up dead in a certain ballplayer's condo and the world turns all kinds of crazy.

He fell silent. I did, too. But only long enough for it to sink in.

Sonofabitch . . .

Naw . . . man . . . Huck . . . you don't think . . . ?

I don't know.

Naw, come on, I mean, he's a motherfucking thief and all, but . . .

Yeah.

And . . .

Yeah.

Shit . . .

Yeah.

Before hanging up with Joniel, I asked him to e-mail me the financial records in question. Because I, unfortunately, had a lot of practice tracking down misappropriated monies.

Then I called Blue again.

Hey, what's up? I don't have any info on those guys yet.

I know. I have another name for you to check.

CHAPTER TWENTY-TWO

There's an Internet café on Pacific Ave. I was relieved to find, in addition to a row of PCs, a newer model Mac sitting unattended on a table in the back. It wasn't loaded with *Final Cut Pro* so I couldn't look at the edited movies, but since (thank you, Steve Jobs) every Mac has an iMovie program on it, I could plug in the hard drives and view their raw video files.

Which ordinarily would've been somewhat enjoyable, since they consisted of mpeg movie clips of sex being had by very attractive people in every imaginable position.

But the twelfth clip featured a certain young woman who was at that very moment residing on a cold, stainless-steel examination table at the Los Angeles County Morgue.

Tiffany, aka Elisabeth Sarah Hadrich.

I couldn't watch. Seeing her alive, in those circumstances, knowing how she died, was just too gruesome.

I clicked through the remaining files. Tiffany was in a total of thirteen clips. I didn't recognize any of the other women or men on the video but I could distinctly hear the director's voice from behind the camera giving occasional instructions. And in one scene he actually moved around in front of the camera to adjust the actors on the bed.

It was unmistakably Peter DiCarmelo.

So, here's the thing. I had proof of a connection between DiCarmelo and Tiffany. But it was illegally obtained and absolutely inadmissible. And since I was staring at the drive that contained those clips, chances were good there'd be no such proof on the drives that remained at DiCarmelo's house.

I had a witness, Lindsey, who could swear that DiCarmelo and Dano verbally implicated themselves in Tiffany's murder. Slim testimony, to be sure, and from an easily impeachable source. Plus the fact that were Lindsey ever to take the stand, she'd be marked for death from that point on.

Not that she wasn't already.

In a nutshell, I had jack shit. Legally speaking.

An hour later, as I sat at the front of the café, sipping a coffee, going over a printout of Joniel's financials he had e-mailed me and that the girl at the counter had printed out, my cell buzzed and the Rancho number came up. I didn't answer it.

Joniel had been right. He'd been screwed to the tune of more than five million dollars, and that was just the obvious skims. And if this was ever brought up in court, Progressive Sports Enterprises would have a dozen polished lawyers explain patiently to an uncomprehending jury what each and every charge was for, and how it was all so very legal and aboveboard.

That's how the truly great crimes are committed. With lawyers. Not guns.

I made my way to the pay phone and called my brother back.

Hey, it's Huck.

Hi. I've got bad news.

Worse news than murder, drugs, rape, and assault?

Yes, I'm afraid, worse than that. DiCarmelo and Dano were, in fact, mafia. Both appear to have been what they call *sgarristas,* made men, foot soldiers in the Giordano family, which is one of the seven mafia organizations operating in New Jersey. They disappeared from the radar screen out there about two years ago. Showed up here. Clean slate. No arrests, no convictions.

Just like Pete said.

Yes. No help there. But that's not the bad news.

Oh?

The other guy you asked me to run, Pierce Fanagin. He doesn't exist.

He doesn't exist.

Not on paper anyway. No records of any kind before last year. I had a guy I know check the NCIC. Ran his DL for anything, anywhere. Every public database. He even Googled him. Nothing. No birth cer-tificate. No tax records. No divorce records. No criminal records. No utility bill. No political affiliation. Not one thing before he shows up at PSE. It had been sold by the founding family to an investment group that then installed Pierce Fanagin as president.

That's weird. How can Fanagin have no past?

It's more than weird. I'd say it's impossible.

Can someone live such a clean life off the grid that they leave no clue as to who they are or where they're from?

No. Not in this day of computer databases and credit files. Not unless you're going to live in a cabin in the woods or something and only pay for things with cash. That's obviously not the case here. Fanagin has a past, it's just been wiped clean.

Wiped clean? What do you mean? How does someone do that?

Someone doesn't. Some*thing* does.

Holy shit. Then it dawned on me.

Something, meaning the government. The U.S. government.

That's my guess, but I have no way of being certain. And neither do you.

Jesus Christ.

You're in way over your head on this, Huck. It's time to let the professionals take over.

Who's stopping them?

You are. Give that detective everything you've got. Come clean. Let him handle it.

Mmm-hmm . . .

Right, I thought, and what can the good detective do? Fanagin's a ghost. There's no hard evidence against those two thugs. The only thing McIntyre will be able to prove is that Joniel Baker committed those murders and I committed some serious felonies, to include but not limited to: two counts of burglary, tampering with evidence, possession of narcotics, fleeing from police, and, shit, speeding on a jogging trail.

Thanks, Blue.

Huck.

I'll call you back when I figure this out.

Huck.

I hung up and walked back to the Mac, fired up its Internet browser, and typed in the word *Giordano*. There were literally thousands of Web sites and articles about the mob family and its rich, crooked history. They ran trucking companies, sanitation facilities, construction, even retirement communities, half a dozen such legitimate, or what appeared on the surface to be legitimate, businesses, and were linked to every kind of illegal activity you could imagine: running tax-free cigarettes from Canada. Prostitution. Fake phone cards. Extortion. Gambling. All the good vices, and plenty of the bad ones. It was obvious the heat was being turned up on their activities by the state's new attorney general.

Then I found a *New York Post* article from a few years ago, with the headline: MAFIA UNDERBOSS FLIPS.

The family's number two guy, the *Capo Bastone* named Frankie "the Ear" Licante, testified before a grand jury in exchange for immunity from prosecution. His testimony led to the arrests of six mob members from the Giordano and two other mafia families. I clicked through more articles. Near as I could tell, whatever Frankie the Ear said on the stand was still under court-ordered seal.

After his testimony, Licante disappeared. Of course. He and his family had been granted the ultimate mulligan of the Federal Witness Protection Program.

I could find no more mention of him, other than references to his single appearance in court, in any follow-up articles. So I went backward, to stories written about Licante and the Giordano family prior to that calamitous day. And that's when I found the picture of dear Frankie the Ear.

It was from 1952. Black and white. A little blurred, probably scanned in from an old newspaper clipping. A group of young, tough-looking guys, leaning against a big Cadillac. The caption said, "The Next Generation," and listed the names of the guys in the photo. Frances Licante was second from left. He looked to be in his mid to late twenties. Muscular. Black hair slicked back.

It was the eyes that gave him away.

The girl at the counter handed me the stack of pages I'd asked her to print off. I was reaching into my pocket to pay for the computer time when I felt the folded-up piece of paper I'd swiped from DiCarmelo's house, the one I wrote all the phone numbers from his answering machine down on.

Outside I unfolded it and looked at the first number. I suddenly knew where I'd seen it before—scribbled on the back of a business card. I opened my phone and dialed.

Yeah?

Hi, Pierce.

CHAPTER TWENTY-THREE

A couple of local girls wandered by in bikinis, one of them casting me a shy smile. I smiled back. The voice on the phone sounded impatient.

Yeah, hi. Who is this?

It's Huck.

Not a sound.

Huck. Huck Doyle. The guy you're trying to find.

Pause. Measured response.

Hello, Huck. What can I do for you?

Not sure yet. Just wanted to make certain of something.

Yes? Is that so? What's that?

I'll tell you later. Hey, did I ever tell you about my brother?

Your brother. Yes, you did. I believe, in fact, we were on number fourteen. Terrible tragedy.

It was. It really was. And you know what? They never did find the guys who put him in that bed, you know? The guys who unloaded on us that day.

Oh?

Nope.

That's a real shame, but this *is* Los Angeles. Unfortunately happens all the time.

Yeah. I guess some bad guys just get away with it, you know?

He didn't bite. So I stuck the needle in a little further.

Some people, well, they can do just about anything and still be untouchable. Get it? *Untouchable?* That was another great Kevin Costner movie. Anyway, I mean some guys can kill, rape, steal, God knows what else, and if they've got the right connections, they never get caught. Do you think that's right? I mean, is that the way the world should really be?

He remained silent for another moment, then spoke very quietly.

Huck. I told you. Winning . . . is winning. And you lose.

The line went dead.

Judith was in the middle of an autopsy but she had left instructions to be interrupted if I called. I was really beginning to like that girl. Even if she did have a creepy job.

Hi, Doc. What are the chances you could take another look at the Holly Cramer case today? What kind of permissions do you need?

None. We have access until the chief coroner closes the case, and he hasn't yet. Why?

I have a theory.

Good enough.

When can I come by?

How's three?

Perfect.

My office can be pretty gruesome. Are you squeamish?

Only around newborns. And infants. Children in general.

Are you trying to tell me something?

You asked.

I think you're just joking.

They always do.

One more thing, Doc?

Yes?

How long would it take to get details on the DNA evidence?

The trace amount of semen found in her vagina, you mean?

Sheesh. The V word again.

That would be it, yes.

Well, you know, even with the new federal funding, our forensics case-load is way backlogged. Still, this is a high-profile investigation, so it shouldn't be impossible. I'll check and see if Esteban can rush it. But I told you, there was plenty found in the condom that we've already typed.

I know.

As belonging to Baker.

I *know.*

Another theory?

Same one.

Okay. I'll know if there's a match with your client by the time you get here. If it is, which I have no reason to believe it won't be, by the way, it's just another nail in his coffin. And you realize if it's not a match, that's not nearly enough time to check it with CODIS.

She was referring to the government's Combined DNA Index System, which is a massive database containing the genetic profiles of a couple million convicted bad guys.

That's fine. At this point I just need to know if it's Joniel's or not.

Shouldn't be a problem. See you here. You sound tired.

Stayed up late watching *Letterman.*

Oh? Was he at a strip club?

Ouch.

I locked the Chrysler and walked to the Marriott at Marina Del Rey, which was about a mile from where I had parked. There are always cabs hanging out there and I got one to take me back to my neighborhood.

He dropped me two blocks away from my house. I gave the cabbie an extra twenty for his UCLA woolly and pulled it low over my eyes, hoping that the guy didn't have lice.

The alley was narrow and full of garbage bins and illegally parked junk heaps. A few dogs spotted me and took up the alarm, but other than that it looked empty of life. I was betting that whoever had the job of watching my place was parked out front.

I eased my key into the lock and opened the back door, half expecting a bullet to the brain as I stepped inside. I listened intently for two full minutes. No breathing. No scrape of magazine pages being turned. No conversations. No *shink-SHUNK* of a shotgun shell being chambered. I slipped off my shoes and tiptoed into the bedroom.

It was as I had left it.

I slipped around the corner and looked into the living room.

No one. Nothing disturbed that I could see.

Same with the kitchen and the guest bedroom.

Nobody home.

I peeked out a corner of the front window, being careful not to move the curtain. The street looked normal but with the glare from the sun on all the parked cars' windshields, I couldn't tell if any of them had occupants. With guns. And orders to use them.

Speaking of which. First order of business, get the Sig Sauer from the closet. Check the ammo.

Then, take a hasty shower. I stank.

Change of clothes, and on second thought, a bag with a few others just in case.

Then I rummaged around the bottom of my closet and found the main thing I'd come back for, the only thing really worth the risk. If my hunch was right, this would go a long way to proving Joniel was innocent.

But what I'd realized earlier was even if I could show those other men committed the murders, that still wouldn't be enough to save all our lives. Not with people like these. I had the genesis of a plan forming in the back of my mind, but I had to be sure. And once I was sure, I had to have the tools I'd need to end this thing.

I made two bologna sandwiches in the kitchen, ate one, and put the other in a quart-size Baggie, careful to hold only one corner of it. That went into my blazer pocket. The .45 and ammo went into a side compartment of the overnight bag. I went out the back and started the long walk back to the car.

It was mid-morning by the time I made it to the club. The parking lot was nearly empty. Inside, I found Charlie interviewing a prospective dancer, a blond Midwest cheerleader-looking girl who disconcertingly resembled Reese Witherspoon. I had to look twice to make sure it wasn't really the actress. You never know with these Hollywood types, always up for new adventures.

I had a double Ketel One while he and I watched the girl audition. She had a tattoo on the small of her back I couldn't quite make out. I turned to Charlie, who seemed a little bored. But then, that was always his demeanor, like a Mack truck idling. You just knew the power was there when he wanted to turn it up.

What's the tat?

He squinted.

Some kinda bird.

I squinted.

Oh. Yeah.

She worked it hard, lots of hands rubbing over her breasts and hips, and come-hither looks like she'd been studying bad porn tapes or something.

Poor girl had it all wrong, though. What the customers want isn't teasing in a place like this. They want the girls to make them think they're giving it all to them. No secrets. No shyness. No shame. Here, mister, here's want you dream about. Right in front of you. Close enough to reach out and touch.

But you better not. Touch, that is. Not with Charlie just a few feet away, with arms strong enough to snap you in half if you tried.

She finished without much finesse, but she was toned enough and pretty enough, and the bird was a nice flair. I thought she'd probably get the job.

I was wrong.

Charlie shook his head when she asked how she did. She looked even less like Ms. Witherspoon when all those lovely curse words started flowing out of her mouth. He just gave her the baleful ghetto-gaze until she grabbed up her clothes and stormed out.

Another cut of music started and the next candidate took the stage. Charlie glanced at his clipboard and made some notations.

Just curious, what didn't you like about her?

Would you fuck her?

One millisecond, two millisecond . . .

Uh . . . yeah. You keep her number?

That's what.

I took a long sip of vodka to cover up my utter lack of comprehension.

You mean, the kind of girl I'd like to fuck isn't the kind you'd hire?

I mean, the kind of girl you assume you *could* fuck.

He waited until the smoke started to waft out of my ears from thinking too hard.

Psychological, man. My girls are fantasies. Unattainable. Guys don't jack to girls they know they can have. But they'll pay good money to watch girls they'll never have.

Girls . . . like Lindsey.

He shrugged. I sat up and turned to face him.

And Tiffany.

He cut his eyes to mine. I saw the muscles in his jaw tighten.

Yeah. And Tiffany.

Police not having much luck with that one.

Nope.

Shame if those dudes get away with it.

Cut the shit. You got something?

My turn to shrug. I handed him the two driver's licenses. And told him a story.

When I finished he studied the pictures of the two men real close, then slipped the licenses into his jacket pocket. He settled back in his chair and returned his gaze to the stage, his face calm and blank.

Don't come back here for a while.

Okay.

I got up to leave.

By the way, Lindsey's okay. I've got her someplace safe. For now. Unless those guys get to her.

Ain't gonna happen.

Good.

Doyle . . .

Yeah.

You got one in the bank.

I thought of Tiffany lying in the dirt. I thought of Holly spread out on her kitchen floor. I thought of Lindsey, running for her life, and of Joniel, trying to wrestle his back from a nightmare not of his own making.

I have a feeling we'll soon be even.

He looked up at me. The nod was barely discernable.

CHAPTER TWENTY-FOUR

One of the first things you learn in law school is that law has nothing to do with justice.

And everything to do with lawyers.

For this reason: What almost every aspect of law boils down to is simple negotiation, most especially criminal law. The charges, the plea bargain, the jury voir dire, the admissible evidence, the presentation of cases, the closing arguments, the jury deliberation, the sentencing, pretty much everything having to do with a criminal case contains some or a lot of pure bargaining.

And that's what you go to law school to learn how to do well. Whatever actual case knowledge you retain from those torturous years is nothing more than ammunition to help better negotiate for your clients, be they the state or the crook, the divorcée-to-be, the seller, the buyer, the outraged, the outrageous.

And that's why I hate law. Because no matter how innocent or guilty someone is, it simply doesn't matter. The legal system doesn't really care. The lawyers really don't care. What they care about is winning, what is the best deal they can negotiate with the exigencies at hand; an appealing client, a preponderance of evidence, the slandering of a hardworking but loudmouthed cop. Innocence is relative. And negotiable.

Golf, on the other hand, is all about justice.

It is a pure system of punishment and reward, with an immutable set of rules that include in no small way those of physics.

Make a bad swing and you suffer the consequences. Choose the wrong club, or read the wrong line, or get greedy, or get timid, or think you just might win this one, and you have reaped that which you sowed.

Oh, you can cheat, to be sure. But if you do cheat at golf, by the way, you're a pretty sorry piece of shit. Just because you can doesn't mean you should. Count every stroke. Don't fluff up the lie. Call yourself on penalties. Replace the divot and rake the sand. And be the person your daddy would be proud of. Well, not *my* daddy, but you get the drift.

In golf there is always forgiveness and always luck. The next hole is nothing but God's green acre of possibilities, and the luck that one day lips out a one-foot par tap-in gives you an eagle three from a blind lie when money's on the line the next.

There are guys who've gone through the exquisite torture of Qualifying School three, four, seven, eight times. What keeps a man coming back when every other sensible person in the world would conclude a life as a pro isn't in the cards?

Belief in oneself.

Nobody beats you in golf. If you lose it's only because you didn't play well enough to win, and some other guy did. There are no negotiations between club and ball. There are no compromises between wind and fairway. The course is the same for you as the group playing behind you. It picks no favorites and accepts no bribes.

You hit down on the ball to launch it into the air. You swing within yourself to hit far. You consult a mental checklist of a thousand things that can go wrong, then clear your mind of everything and let the body do its mysterious dance. Golf is the algebra of opposites.

And what I love most about golf is that it isn't law.

Pierce Fanigan was perverting the law to settle a score. He is far from the first, and farther still from the last, to do that. And as I drove to his office building I kept telling myself that as law isn't about justice, justice isn't always about the law.

The Niemens still cavorted garishly on the walls. The vision of female perfection sat below the giant gilded initials, with the same technological affliction curving around in front of her puffy lips.

Mr. Fanagin is not expecting you.

That really hurts. He said to drop by anytime.

Be that as may, he is otherwise engaged at the present.

Be that as *it* may.

Excuse me?

You dropped the subject. Common grammatical error. They have pills for that.

Her eyebrows fluttered slightly, I thought for a second because I out-five-dollar-worded her, until I realized someone was speaking in her ear.

Mr. Fanagin will see you now.

She motioned with a handful of really lovely French tips.

What, I don't get you as an escort this time?

Her voice said, *I believe you know the way,* but her eyes said, *Get out of my sight you smart-ass creep.*

Pierce Fanagin sat behind the huge desk, inscrutable look on his face, feet propped up, hands behind his neck, flexing those big guns underneath the expensive wool of his bespoke suit.

Well, hello, Mr. Doyle. You either have bigger balls or a smaller brain than I thought, after your rude remarks at my club the other day.

My game is the one with the small balls. You really should take it up someday.

He chuckled, sort of a cross between a growl and a cough.

So I should. Someday. Now care to tell me why you're here?

Sure, Gino, I wanted to show you something. Your name is Gino, right? Gino Licante? Son of Frankie *the Ear* Licante?

He didn't answer, but his eyes narrowed to dark slits. His tan faded by two shades.

Where is Papa, by the way? He around? I'd love to say hi. See how the plastic surgery scars are coming along.

I'll give him this: He was smooth. Fanagin calmly put his feet down and stood. Slipped off his suit jacket. Rolled up the sleeves of his custom-made shirt and sat back down. He really did have impressive arms. Noticing them reminded me I had slacked off on my workout regimen, mainly because of all the detective work and avoiding-death stuff I was doing. I had the time to think of all that because he was just staring at me. I coolly met his gaze. For about a second.

Speaking of plastic surgery, Gino, you can change pretty much everything but the eyes, you know? You and Papa Licante, yours are exactly the same. They're the windows to the soul, you know, if you have one.

Those dark, empty sockets I'd spotted in the photo of his old man resembled sewer drains more than windows. I didn't say that to him, though, because . . . well . . . because of those fucking big arms.

He stood quickly and moved around the desk, grabbing me by the shoulders and lifting me out of the chair. His voice was a low growl.

Don't say another goddamn word.

As I expected, the pat-down was rough and thorough. He emptied my pant pockets of coins, cell phone, pocketknife, credit cards, and car keys, tossing them on the desk. He then rummaged through my jacket pockets, pulling out the sandwich bag, peering at it disdainfully before dropping it on the carpet. In my side blazer pocket he found the stack of research I'd printed off at the Internet café, with lots of articles about his father and his former life. He flipped through those pages, a look of incredulity on his face.

Finally satisfied, I guess, that I wasn't packing a weapon or wearing a wire, he motioned for me to sit and returned to his own chair. He put his elbows back on the desktop and steepled his fingers, just like all good agents are taught.

All right, Mr. Dead Man Talking. So, educate me. Why are you here?

Well, frankly, I wanted to see your reaction in person when I told you that I know who you are. And what's more, I know what you've done, or at least, *had* done by DiCarmelo and Dano to Holly and Tiffany, and what you're trying to do to Joniel.

Uh-huh. What *I've* done . . .

Yes. I mean, I don't have all the angles figured out yet, but I'm sure you had a hand in the murders of those girls and in framing Joniel for them. I know about the heroin. I know about the little porn studio in DiCarmelo's house. My guess is you don't get your hands dirty in most of these operations, can't blow your cover by any messy arrests, but you're probably taking a good cut of the profits. This is a good front, a legitimate agency. I can't help wonder why you couldn't just stay clean?

His face was that of a bronze statue. I mean, nothing moved. Not a muscle. Not an eyebrow. He just looked at me over his here's-the-church finger pyramid and let the thoughts in his head grind through the processing. Finally I heard a sound come out of him that was either a faint chuckle, a derisive minisnort, or a brain aneurysm, and he spoke.

So, here's what I'm thinking. You may know some things, but it stands to reason you haven't told the police anything yet, because if you had, they'd be here instead of you.

Fuck. Me. Didn't think about that. Time to tap-dance.

Actually, my good friend Detective McIntyre of Homicide should be outside right about now. I left him a message I'd be here.

Uh-huh. You're not wearing a recorder or wire. You're not packing. And you expect me to believe a cop let you walk in here, with what you say you know, and piss me off like this? He must really dislike you.

He does. Oh, he does. Not as much as you do right now, I'll admit.

I don't believe you, in fact—

And then, I swear to God, it happened. My cell phone buzzed. Fanagin quickly reached over and held it up, peering at the little window. He then looked at me.

And called my bluff.

It's for you.

He tossed the phone to me. The caller ID window said *McIntyre,* the name I'd saved his number under. I flipped open the phone as Fanagin settled back in his chair, eyeing me like a cat watches a mouse he has pinned beneath his paws.

Hello?

Mr. Doyle, it's Detective McIntyre returning your call.

Yes, hi. You still parked outside?

What? I'm sorry? I'm in my office. Where—

Great. I'm almost wrapped up in here so don't worry about a thing. Let's grab a coffee down the street and we'll have a good chat. No, he's being a perfect gentleman . . .

I gave Fanagin a big grin and a thumbs-up.

. . . great! I'll tell him. You look forward to meeting him. Yeah, see ya soon.

I flipped shut the phone and surreptitiously held down the off button as I placed it back in my pocket. I didn't want a perplexed detective calling back, asking what I'd been smoking.

Without taking his eyes off me, Fanagin took his own cell phone out of his shirt pocket and pushed a button.

It's me. Where's McIntyre right now?

He listened for a beat.

You sure? Okay. No, nothing. Let me know if he leaves.

The phone went back in his pocket.

Huck, Huck, Huck. Good thing we never played poker.

Guess so. That your buddy in the LAPD?

He didn't have to answer.

Say, Gino, speaking of gambling, what's the line on Joniel now? You must have some play in that?

As a matter of fact, I do. Quite a lot. And despite your presence here and what you say you know but obviously can't prove, it's looking good, which is to say it's not looking good for your friend.

On Wall Street they call that shorting a stock. Only instead of Procter and Gamble or Sears, Fanagin was betting Joniel's value would fall with a conviction, and since he had all kinds of inside information about the evidence stacked against the former All-Star, considering he orchestrated the whole thing, he stood to make millions. Maybe even enough to cover what he was no longer getting from Joniel himself.

Fanagin reached over to open his desk drawer, from which he pulled a real nasty automatic, I guessed a Glock 9mm from its black matte finish. But I could have been wrong, since I was trying hard not to stare at it. He slid the gun across the desk and let it lie there, right in front of him, pointed right at me.

I have to admit, I'm impressed with what you've done. Not many guys could've found us out, not with the U.S. government giving us a hand in starting over fresh.

Then again, why not just stay clean? I don't get it.

He laughed a nasty little laugh.

Clean? Clean is fuckin' boring, that's why. That was never the plan. Heat was on back east, so we had to come in here under the radar. Find something new to do. And boy, did we find it. This place is like a candy store run by retards. Opportunities every place we look.

If I found you, someone else can, too.

Ya know, I don't think so. Got a new face. Got a new name. New past. New profession. I just keep my head down and let my boys do the nitty-gritty, bing bang boom, no problemo.

Would it be cliché of me to say you can't get away with it?

Another laugh. Then he reached over and flipped off the Glock's safety.

> I'm starting to get tired of this conversation, Huck. I really don't know how you've stayed alive this long, but that will change soon. For you. For Lindsey Feller. For that embarrassment of a father you have. For your sad, pathetic, crippled brother. We'll find them all. And they will all stop breathing. In very painful ways.

> So, we're not negotiating I take it.

Slow shake of the head.

> What if I said I'd manage to lose everything I've got on you if you throw those two assholes who actually murdered those girls into the fire instead of Joniel, and let the rest of us be?

Slow shake of the head.

> You know, Huck, I would, but I don't have to. It's not the way we do things. And I'm certain you don't have anything on me other than a theory, with no proof connecting me to these crimes except, perhaps, *perhaps,* a loose affiliation with the two men you think did them. I know this because I know what I'm doing. I'm the professional in this game, Huck, and this time, you're the amateur.

He picked up the gun and stood, using it to motion toward the door.

> Time for you to go, Mr. Huckleberry Doyle. I'd love to blow your head off right here, right now, but that would be too much trouble to clean up. No telling who saw you come in here. It'll be much easier outside at a time and place of our choosing.

I scooped up my things from the desk and the sandwich from the floor.

> Can't let a good lunch go to waste. Might be my last meal. Hey, Pierce . . . or Gino . . . or whatever it is. One last question, you mind?

He tilted his head, sighed, raised an eyebrow.

Ever the smart-ass, aren't you? Laugh while you can.

One last question. I promise.

Why not?

Do you know what the very hardest shot in golf is? I mean the absolute, very hardest?

I could tell he was intrigued for a moment. He thought about it, then shrugged.

Two-thirty, over water, into the wind.

Wrong.

And I closed the door behind me.

CHAPTER TWENTY-FIVE

I can't believe this! It's not possible!

I was standing in a ridiculously tiny and cluttered office where every shelf and desktop and floor space was covered with stacks of colored papers, manila folders, or jars of cryptically labeled liquids. Even the numerous computer monitors had things piled on them. In fact, the only two objects not being used as file space were myself and an apparently very angry, very frustrated Dr. Judith Filipiano, who was waving a computer printout at me like all of this was my fault.

I can't believe you were right! They don't match! The semen in the condom and the semen inside Holly Ann Cramer do not match!

And you're not happy about that because . . . ?

She glared at me.

It's not that I'm not happy about it. As a professional I have to be objective. It's just that this makes the case that much more difficult to solve. It's now so much more complicated.

Really? How?

How? It's obvious! We're literally back to square one. We now have two suspects, with DNA evidence present, and absolutely no idea as to who the second suspect can be.

Maybe not.

She was, and I truly love this word, flummoxed.

Maybe not what?

Maybe not no idea who the second suspect is.

I pulled my bloody shirt from the shopping bag I'd carried it in and handed it to her.

There's a fifty-fifty chance the blood on this shirt will match the semen you recovered from Holly.

What? What do you mean fifty-fifty? Whose blood is it?

Let's call him Suspect Zero. For now.

She didn't take the shirt from my outstretched hand.

Suspect Zero? How 'bout chance of me touching that zero.

Judith. Trust me.

Yeah, right, said the spider to the fly. No way, birdie-brain. Go find another assistant medical examiner's career to ruin.

I turned on the charm and slipped an arm around her shoulder. She turned on more charm, found some sort of pressure point between my thumb and index finger, and squeezed. The pain brought tears to my eyes. I returned my arm to its proper place.

That hurt like hell!

No, that hurt like second-grade gym class. But I can show you hell if you keep pushing.

Jeez, Judith. I'm trying to save a guy's life here.

Actually, a couple of lives here, including mine . . .

How noble of you. I hope the check clears first.

It's not about the money.

Uh-huh. Then exactly what is it about?

Two girls who were murdered by someone other than Joniel Baker. It's about two lives, and soon to be three lives if Joniel is convicted, wiped away by people who think they can do anything they want.

That stopped her for a second.

Oh, throw that at me, why don't you? The whole justice thing.

Yep.

Look, I just can't do this, Huck. I have no idea where that shirt came from, or whose it is, or whose blood is on it. There's no chain of evidence, which makes it virtually useless. Worse than that, you're not a cop, you are working on behalf of the accused, so there's a motive for you to mislead the investigation. This is tainted and inadmissible. Any halfway decent defense attorney would tear me to shreds on the stand over this.

It's my shirt. The blood on it is from one of two very bad men who tried to dissuade me from looking into this case. Those men were involved in both murders. I now know for a fact, Doc . . . for a fact . . . that Joniel is innocent and is being framed. By some very dangerous, very powerful people. If I'm right, if this blood matches the other evidence, then we have the proof we need to at least get Joniel a fair trial if not a complete dismissal of the case. I'm a lawyer and private investigator. I'll sign an affidavit attesting to this evidence that will cover your concerns. You can put me on the stand. Plus, you'll then be able to get a DNA sample from the killer himself to confirm it.

There was still a great deal of doubt in her eyes, but I could tell she was weakening.

You really think he's innocent?

I have absolutely no doubt. Really.

Does Detective McIntyre know about this?

Not yet, but he will. I'm going to give him the names of the two men later today.

I held out the shirt to her again. This time she took it.

Doc, please, test the blood. This is the key to having the men who really committed these murders face a jury.

She sighed heavily, and very, very reluctantly nodded. The shirt went into a different plastic bag.

Thank you, Judith. Really. I owe you a fabulous dinner for this.

Oh? Your treat?

Of course.

Then does that mean I can't get the fries with my Big Mac?

Ha ha ha.

She marked it and began filling out the required lab request form. I watched her, feeling shitty and guilty on all kinds of levels, but mostly because I had just told this amazing woman who trusted me one whopper of a lie.

Those men would never stand trial.

CHAPTER TWENTY-SIX

On the third ring, I raised my head from the pillow and rummaged around for the cell phone. The display said *McIntyre.* I answered anyway.

Yeah?

Mr. Doyle? Detective McIntyre. You've been busy.

I sat up and looked at the clock next to the bed. I'd been in the Best Western for three hours, asleep for two hours, fifty-nine minutes and fifty-nine seconds. It was almost seven o'clock in the evening.

Mr. Doyle? Are you there?

Yes. Sorry. I was taking a nap.

Interesting. Is that part of your training routine?

No. Yes. Not really. I've been, uh, practicing hard lately.

So I'm told. So much so you've neglected to keep me in the loop of your inquiries as you assured me you would.

I was going to call you today.

I'm sure you were. I saved you the trouble, as you can see. Do you have anything for me?

Yes. I'm sorry, can you hold on a moment?

Certainly.

I put down the phone and tried to clear my head. I knew McIntyre wasn't going to give me anything, despite our little agreement, and frankly I was sure I knew a lot more than he did. But I still needed him and so I had to make him believe I was a good source of information. My dilemma was keeping him friendly without making him bring me in as a material witness. Because I was certain the moment I was in police custody, I was a dead man. I rubbed my face and picked back up the phone.

I have two names for you, two men who were seen at the same club where Tiffany worked and who also knew Holly Ann Cramer.

Mr. Doyle, there are many, many people, men in particular, who knew these women. What makes you think these two men are special or should be of interest to me?

Because they tried to beat me up in order to discourage me from investigating this case.

Oh, they did? And did they succeed? Are you injured?

No, they did not. I got in a lucky punch or two.

I see. Yes. Of course. A golfer who knows how to handle himself in a fight.

Are you being sarcastic, Detective?

Not in the least. I have seen many amazing things in the course of my long career.

Just then, my phone beeped, indicating another call coming in. It was Lindsey. I told McIntyre I had to take that and that I'd call him right back, and clicked over.

How're you doing?

Good. Great really. Gables said you called earlier while we were sleeping.

The moment I'd left Fanagin's office, I'd called to warn Blue and Pete to be extra careful. I told Gables that I'd heard some murderous psycho had escaped from a mental ward and was making threats to our family and he said he'd tell security to be on the lookout, and that he hoped the guy would show up there because he hadn't torn the head off anyone in quite some time. Not that he wasn't big enough, but the mental image of Gables getting violent just couldn't come into focus.

I left a message for Pete saying I'd call later that day as soon as I figured a few things out. But to keep his head down and his big gun handy.

Lindsey was still chatting away.

They're really nice here. It's amazing what they do here, Huck, you know? Like, I'm thinking maybe this is something I want to get involved with. Do something, you know? I want to hang around for a while, okay?

That's great. Don't tell anyone anything about what's going on, though.

I know, I know. But I feel like I can trust him, you know? Blue . . . he's like, he's *always* been family, you know?

Him, you can trust. He knows about most of this. No one else, okay? The more people who know, the more danger you . . . and they . . . are in.

Okay.

He there?

Yeah. Hold on a second, let me get the phone closer.

I heard a shuffling sound and then a familiar voice came on.

What can I do to help?

What you're doing.

Good enough.

Good enough. Just listen for a second, I don't want you to respond with anything that would scare Lindsey.

Okay.

Pierce Fanagin is in the witness protection program. His real name's Gino Licante. His father, Frankie Licante, probably got his entire family into it as part of the federal deal. But the more I think about it, the more I think there's something odd about it all. The guys the Feds took down, the guys Licante ratted out, they were kinda nobodies, you know? Some were captains and all were fairly high up in the organizations, but near as I could tell from the research, they were all sort of on the outs. I mean these guys never talk about their business, but reading between the lines, I don't think these arrests crippled the families in any real way, and it may have in some ways taken the attention off.

He was careful in choosing his words.

I see. Not the high-level individuals such a high-profile deal would ordinarily net.

Exactly. This was really just part of a strategy to get out of town. They were under a lot of attention from a new A.G., and this would allow them to move into friendlier surroundings with a clean record.

Nobody knows them. Family vacation to Mexico, everyone gets a new face, maybe some lypo for the ladies . . .

And no outstanding contracts with competing families to have to honor. They could get their hands into everything.

Yes. Is that even possible?

It's more than possible. It's brilliant. And what better front than an established management company. It makes sense. Fanagin paid attention back in Jersey; learned well how to play on the dark side of the street. And now they're here. Starting from scratch.

Hey, careful . . . Lindsey . . .

She left the room for a second.

Oh. Good. And that's not the worst of it. I think they have someone inside the LAPD.

Of course, they do. That's the first course of action. But I don't think they have a big operation out here yet or we'd have heard of it. There are probably only the Licantes and a few henchmen. It takes time to build a large operation quietly.

We got lost in thought for a second, then Blue spoke again.

So what did McIntyre say?

Hmm?

What did McIntyre say?

I haven't told him.

But you are.

No . . .

Huck. But you are. Going to tell him. Everything you know.

No . . .

Huck?

I could hear Lindsey come back into Blue's room, talking with someone in the background, probably Gables. She laughed. I felt a twang in my chest.

I could picture my brother in the bed, strung up with pulleys, withering away under the crisp white sheets, with Lindsey and Gables gossiping nearby. And then the image changed to how I usually picture Blue when I need him most: on a surfboard. Floating next to me. With the sun baking our shoulders and the undulating sea rocking us back and forth. And sometimes, like now, I go back to one time in particular, when he was coaching me on a certain difficult move, and he said something offhand that has stayed with me forever, carved in granite, embedded just behind my forehead:

We fail only when we waver after *the decision is made.*

His voice on the phone lowered to a whisper.

You're not Pete, Huck. You're better than that. We have rules, you know, society, people, cops . . . us . . . we have rules for a reason.

Ah, but is there reason to the rules?

I'm not Pete, Blue. But I'm not you, either.

I love my brother, but my brother has one massive flaw: He has integrity.

So I said good-bye and called someone who doesn't. Someone like me.

Hi, Pete. Sorry to wake you.

Thought by that little message you left me we'd all be dead by now.

The day is young.

Fuck that mean?

Nothing. I need a little help solving a problem. Chances are whatever we come up with will be illegal and very dangerous.

Now you're talking. I've been bored shitless.

I told him everything about Fanagin and his boys. Pete's witty rejoinders became fewer and fewer as the tale unfolded, until he was stunned into silence, which for Pete is about as rare as a manicure. When I finished he had but one keen observation:

Holy fuck.

We agreed to meet at the biker bar that night after he had a chance to check into a few things.

I dialed McIntyre.

Detective? Sorry about that.

What else would I do with my aimless hours but sit awaiting your gracious call, Mr. Doyle?

You're pissed.

No. I'm a patient man, as you'll see. Now, you were telling me about these two men.

So I told him some of what I knew, leaving out a lot of what I knew. I didn't mention the mob, or Fanagin, or the long list of crimes I'd already committed.

Nor the ones I was about to.

Before we hung up I hesitated, then told him about a certain bloody shirt an assistant medical examiner was testing that might relate to his murder cases.

He really perked up at that.

There's nothing a homicide detective likes more than blood.

CHAPTER TWENTY-SEVEN

Pete's Fat Boy was in the dirt parking lot when I pulled in. The lot was almost empty. The biker joint didn't really get going until after ten.

He was at the bar, keeping a bottle of Budweiser company.

Hi, Pete.

Sport.

You still up for this?

What you think, I got scared?

No. Just smart, maybe.

No chancc of that, is there.

By the time almost every stool was filled and the place was starting to rock we thought we had all the possibilities covered. We'd better. Or we'd both be in jail by tomorrow.

At exactly ten thirty, Pete made the call. He pulled a crumpled piece of paper out of a vest pocket, fished around another pocket for a pen, and jotted down some numbers. He then hung up and made another call, reading off the numbers to whoever was on the other end of the line.

Fifteen minutes later, his phone rang. He found a blank spot on the same piece of scrap paper and wrote down something else. The phone clicked shut. He looked at me and for the first time since I could remember, he smiled. It was not a pretty sight.

Got it. Bel-Air.

Figures. That going to make it harder?

The ultraexclusive gated community of Bel-Air has its own security police. Pete shrugged.

Naw. I know some guys there if we get spotted. Sit back now and relax. Get a drink. We got some waiting to do.

I've got a better idea. Take a drive with me. There's someone I want you to meet.

Pete looked annoyed. He doesn't like any ideas but his own, especially if someone is foolish enough to declare they have a better one. But I could see he was curious. He sucked down the rest of his Bud and belched loudly.

Let's go.

He raised an eyebrow when I opened the passenger-side door of the Chrysler for him but said nothing about it until we were rolling up Mulholland.

That piece-of-shit Jeep finally give out on you or you just decide to go uptown for a change?

Bronco. No. I figured it was hot after I ran from the cops in the Palisades.

Let's see if it is. What's the tag number?

He flipped open his phone and made a call. Listened for a minute. Thanked whoever was helping us out in his inimitably curt way, flipped the phone off, and sucked at his teeth.

No BOLO on your Jeep. Just a report of a routine stop for a busted taillight.

Interesting.

That ain't the most interesting part.

No record of said Bronco evading police in Will Rogers State Park?

Never happened in the eyes of the law.

Hmm.

Yeah. Fuckin' hmm.

We rode for a while in silence.

I parked on the street a few blocks away, punched my spot number into the meter, and fed it a credit card. We stood back in the shadows for a moment, scanning up and down Sunset. The beautiful people were out en force, pretending not to notice one another as they sat under the stars at all the trendy restaurants and gossiped nastily about their best friends. McIntyre's police-issue sedan was nowhere to be seen. Pete seemed a little edgy. Edgier than normal, I should say.

This ain't exactly my 'hood. Who we here to meet?

I want you to see why we're doing this.

Fuck that. I know why *you're* doing it. You're getting paid to. And you actually think the mutt is innocent.

And you still don't? After everything I told you?

Get this, Huckleberry, 'cause it's sort of my whatcha-call-it, *raisin ditto*: I really don't give a shit one way or the other. I'm outta the law-and-order business, in case you hadn't noticed. Those upstanding citizens deserve what they get. Ain't no Roy Rogers white hats and silver spurs in this sewer, but that's what they want.

I stopped walking. Waited until an overdressed couple sashayed past. Then turned and faced him.

If you really don't care whether Joniel is being framed for murder or not, then why are you here? You that bored with life outside a prison?

His eyes narrowed at the mention of prison. Even three years after his release, the subject was well into the no-man's-land of verboten conversational topics. He leaned in close enough for me to smell the Bud on his breath.

No. *You* asked *me* for help. That's all the reason I need.

I wished he'd punched me instead. He stood glaring at me for a moment, letting his perfectly delivered uppercut admonition sink in good and deep, then finished me off with a solid-right homily.

You're still my son.

He started walking. I hurried up behind him and tapped his shoulder.

Dad . . .

'fuck alone.

It's the other way. Hotel Marmont.

The ex-cop, ex-con, always-angry Pete Doyle turned on his heels and headed up the Strip. I followed.

Dad . . .

Fuck off.

Pete . . .

Fuck. Off.

Did you actually just say *raison d'être* before?

Not a word in response.

You know, that's French.

The back of his neck looked a bit red.

French. As in *surrender monkeys* French.

Silence.

And I don't think it means what you think it means.

I think it means shut yer hole.

As we neared the hotel, I called Joniel's cell phone. He answered on the first ring.

'Sup, Huck?

Hi, Joniel. Care for a little company?

Sure. Not doing nothing but playing Madden on the tube. Come on by.

We're here now.

We?

Yep. See you in a sec.

I punched off before he could respond.

We walked into the lobby and past the concierge as if we belonged there. He gave Pete's bad biker dude attire a once-over, but since half the rock stars who stayed there dressed the same way and we obviously weren't seeking his approval, he kept his mouth shut. Attitude can get you into pretty much anywhere.

Nate was standing outside Joniel's hut with his arms crossed. He nodded as we approached and stepped to the side.

I gave the door of Bungalow three a single rap. Joniel opened it a moment later, Xbox controller still in hand. He nodded hello to me, looked Pete up and down, and motioned for us to come in.

Who's your date?

Joniel, this is Pete Doyle.

He raised his eyebrows as if to say, who?

My dad.

Then realization set in, and a half smile of incredulity parted his lips.

No, you did NOT bring that racist, lyin', Rampart framin', Mark Fuhrman, used-to-be an ex-dirty-assed cop into MY hotel room!

Before I could explain, Pete pushed past me and stuck out his hand.

Nice to meet you, too, convict. They let you pick your boyfriend out ahead of time or you gotta wait until the first group shower?

Joniel looked down at the beefy paw in front of him, then his eyes slowly drifted back to mine.

This is unfuckingbelievable.

He sat back down in the chair, pointedly ignoring Pete's hand, which seemed to tickle Pete no end. He began strolling around the bungalow, chuckling, peering into and at everything, seeing how the other half lived, I guess. I picked up the other game controller and pulled a chair up next to Joniel's.

He's helping us out. More than you can ever know.

I lowered my voice to a whisper.

More than I can ever tell you.

Yeah, right. By doing what, exactly? Kicking a few nigga's asses?

That term is offensive and racially divisive. Please refrain from using such language in the future.

That came from Pete, who was somewhere back in the bedroom.

Joniel looked at me without comment, just as his quarterback was tackled in the backfield for a six-yard loss. I paused the game, went into the menu, and changed it to two-player mode.

Who am I, Denver?

Yeah. Fuck you doing, Huck?

Playing football.

He shrugged and got back to business. We played a few downs before Pete came back into the room and plopped down on the couch.

Nice digs. Doesn't look like it's bugged but we can't be too sure. If you know what I mean.

Joniel nodded without looking away from the game.

You mean don't say nothin' that can incriminate us. No shit.

You're pretty smart for a guy with the kind of evidence piled up as you got.

Fuck you, bigot.

Pete got up to leave.

That's it. I'm outta here. Nice knowin' you, asshole.

I put a hand to his chest, which barely slowed him down.

Wait a minute! Pete, wait!

His face was beet red.

No. To hell with this loser, Huckleberry! He's not worth it. You're putting your life, all our lives, on the line and this asshole can only feel sorry for himself!

Hang on, just hold it! Let me explain things to him.

What's he mean, Huck? Your life on the line? What are you doing?

We all had a chance to take a breath. Joniel set the controller down and stood.

What's he mean? Putting your life on the line? Fuck he mean?

Shut up a second, Joniel, and I'll—

I said *our* lives, shitbird! Mine included.

Pete, *shut up*! Look, Joniel, there are some things I can tell you and a lot of things I can't, for your own good. I know you're innocent and I think I've found a way to prove that. But one thing you have to understand is Pete is going to try to help me save your life. And you better goddamn show him some respect and gratitude or we're both going to walk out that door and you can go fuck yourself. He's my father, for chrissakes! You can't talk to him like that!

They both just stared at me. Then they both just sort of sank into the couch.

Then I sank into the chair.

I mean, can't we all just get along?

Neither of them laughed.

CHAPTER TWENTY-EIGHT

So, the thing about right and wrong is this: Sometimes that's a distinction without a difference. Sometimes a wrong can make something right. Sometimes society is best served when its own rules are broken.

Sometimes a sin . . . is a blessing.

We don't want to believe that's true, but deep down, you know it is. We have since the days of Hammurabi set down a list of dos and don'ts to bring order to the chaos that is the natural human condition. Without the rule of law you have only the rule of ruthlessness, and that pretty much sucks for all but the strongest, meanest, or fastest of the species.

But as complicated organisms who lead complicated existences with other complicated organisms, things get . . . well . . . complicated.

Many of the men who risked their lives to wrestle the world back from the brink of brutal global dictatorship in World War II did some things on the battlefield they weren't proud of. Things they could've been prosecuted for, court-martialed for, in some cases, executed for, even though they did them in the horrible, terrifying heat of war. Do those things make them any less heroic?

No.

Because sometimes you do what you have to do.

And sometimes it's the more courageous act that takes you away from the safety net of law and rules and acceptable behavior. A bad, for the greater good.

Or, I could be full of shit and just trying to justify my own moral ambiguities.

And . . . those of my father.

Pete Doyle was, in truth, a dirty cop. He would be the first to admit it. He did so in court, in front of a judge, a jury, a prosecutorial team, and an audience of tens of millions of television viewers. They took him from the courtroom and sent him to live for two years in zip code 94964, which happens to be that, and only that, of San Quentin State Prison.

Pete had been part of a small team of cops who were tired of catching violent gangbangers, robbers, drug dealers, assaulters, rapists, bullies, thieves, and other bad guys, and having them walk out of jail before the cops even finished doing the paperwork. Yes, it's a cliché. Yes, we've heard it all before.

But Pete and his buddies worked in an especially tough part of Los Angeles, so controlled by competing gangs that crossing south of the 101 Freeway into certain neighborhoods was like entering an alternative universe. All the John Jay theories of criminology and all the high-tech crime-plotting, computer-graphing, video-monitoring gadgetry couldn't take away from the fact that those with evil in their hearts and guns in their waistbands outnumbered the cops a thousand to one. The populace lived in fear.

Almost every time the police made a good bust, caught some dealers or a robber red-handed, they were either out on bail and had managed to disappear by the time of their first court date, or the witnesses would simply change their minds, not testify, not be found. The gangs hired the very best attorneys, and the beleaguered L.A. County court system had a hard time matching up. They were playing a zone defense against a team of evil Michael Jordans, and the good guys were losing big-time.

Something had to be done.

Pete and his cop buddies did it.

For a period of about four years, they made busts that stuck. Successful prosecutions were at a record high. The crime rate fell. The gangs in that area had their backs broken as leader after leader was led off to prison.

The chief of police took credit. The mayor took credit. Even the governor took credit.

But it really all came down to one little thing: overwhelming evidence that juries couldn't ignore and prosecutors didn't have to plea down for.

Shame it had to come crashing down when someone in Internal Affairs leaked news of an investigation to the *L.A. Times,* about how the golden boys of the LAPD antigang unit were suspected of planting evidence and extorting false witness testimony.

Suddenly, convicted criminals began screaming from their various cells about being set up by dirty cops. The American Civil Liberties Union sprang into action.

Suddenly, every cable news channel on the planet had reporters in front of the Supreme Court building, speculating about "another Rampart."

Suddenly, the governor and the mayor and the chief wouldn't comment until *the investigation was complete.* It was, after all, an election year.

On the basis of the testimony of twenty-three convicted criminals, whose combined rap sheet numbered more than two hundred felony offenses from A to Z, a grand jury leapfrogged the I.A. investigation and handed down seven indictments, one of which contained the name Peter Armagh Doyle.

Six of the cops pled not guilty and their cases were eventually dismissed for lack of evidence, to considerable public outcry and impassioned demonstrations. Those men were quietly transferred to nonpatrol functions and received generous early-retirement packages.

My dad stood in front of the world and said, yes, he did it. Yes, he broke the law he was sworn to uphold in order to save the people he was sworn to protect. In his angry Irish cop prose, my dad told the world that if you expect to win a wrestling match with pigs, you're going to get muddy.

And then he went to prison.

I've never been more ashamed in my life. Nor . . . more proud.

The interior of Bungalow three was lit by the television screen, on which an animated quarterback was frozen in midpass. Joniel and Pete were looking off into opposite directions: Joniel, I'm pretty sure, lost in thought about my saying I could prove he was innocent and Pete, I'm pretty sure, lost in thought about my defending his honor.

> Joniel, listen, man, Pete has some contacts and some abilities that are absolutely crucial. No matter what you think of him, or what you think you know about him, he's here to help you now. You can trust him.

Joniel didn't answer.

I got up and fished a little bottle of Grey Goose out of the fridge.

> Anyone want anything?

Neither man answered.

> I sat back down and picked up the game controller. After a beat, Joniel did the same. My team scored on a thirty-five-yard bootleg pass.

> Pity you weren't that good in real life.

That from my dad, who I'm pretty sure never attended one of my games of any sport.

He's doing all right for himself. Don't see nobody paying you to hit a ball.

That from Joniel, who could pretty much wipe the floor with me in any and every sport *except* golf.

Don't see nobody paying him to do that lately, do you? Fuck you know about him, anyway? He coulda been a helluva prosecutor, I mean this kid is *smart,* but instead he chases a little white ball around and hopes it goes in the hole sometimes. A complete fuckin' waste of time.

Pete stretched his arms over his head and arched his back. The couch groaned mightily under his mass.

Let me ask you something, Joniqua. Who was the best at *your* game? Baseball. Best ever. Who do you wish you could play like if you could?

Joniel moved his fullback through the gap and rambled him for a six-yard game. I thought he was going to ignore the question, but after a moment he spoke up.

Best ever?

Best ever.

Okay. I'll play. Easy. Babe Ruth. Guy was a hall-of-fame pitcher who gave that up just to get to hit every day. For the team. 'Cause he figured runs was more important than pitching every three or four days. Then I'd have to say Ted Williams. Say Hey Willie Mays. Ty Cobb. Hank Aaron. Mickey Mantle. A-Rod, maybe, if he keeps it up. Dude that died from that disease . . .

Lou Gehrig.

Yeah, right. Gehrig.

My turn . . .

Josh Gibson. Hit over sixty-nine home runs in at least three seasons, eighty-four in 1936. He was the only man who ever hit a home run completely out of Yankee Stadium. Lots of statistics weren't even kept by the Negro Leagues, so who knows what he really did? Then there's Cool Papa Bell and Oscar Charleston. Maybe the best player ever to pick up a bat—.357 lifetime average. What's yours right now, Joniel? .305?

Yeah, somewhere around that. Three fifty-seven *lifetime*? Damn. But you gotta include Jackie Robinson. Jackie's the man.

Pete snorted. I flinched. *Here it comes. Heard it a thousand times before.*

Not even close, kid. Robinson isn't even in the top twenty.

Yeah, cracker. Whatever you say. He just led the league in steals and won Rookie of the Year while racists like you were spitting on him and yelling shit at every single game.

Back off. I didn't say he wasn't a great ballplayer. But he was not one of the greatest of all time. You even know why he was the first black guy chosen to play on a white team, which by the way he wasn't because they'd been using black guys for years who pretended they were Latinos, but anyway, know why?

Joniel rolled his eyes.

Naw. Educate the black man about his own people.

Well, that's exactly what I'll do. Branch Rickey, the owner of the Brooklyn Dodgers, wanted a black player from the Negro Leagues who wouldn't be threatening to the white fans. So he chose a good-looking kid who could play well enough but who had one key thing in his favor. He was married. Back then, white men were scared shitless

254

that the blacks were trying to get to their women, don't ask me why. But that's a fact.

Oh? That why you didn't bring Mrs. Bigot along with you today?

Okay, really bad subject. I started to move between them before Pete put him through the wall but I didn't have to; amazingly, Pete let it slide. He didn't even get red; just kept talking.

That fuckin' genius made Robinson agree to two years of absolute silence. It was in his contract he couldn't talk back to the assholes Rickey knew, he *knew,* would be at all the games. Jackie didn't want to, but he agreed and to his goddamn credit he honored that agreement.

Pete leaned forward and put his big knobby forearms on his knees.

Branch Rickey said he wanted a man with guts enough *not* to fight back. In my book, that's a helluva lot more impressive than just hitting or running or throwing better than anyone else. Jackie Robinson wasn't one of the greatest ballplayers ever. But he *was* a great fuckin' *man.*

He stood and started toward the door.

He was bigger than the game. What the fuck are *you* doing with *your* life?

Pete glanced back at me.

Time to get.

I nodded and stood. Thought about taking a drink along for the road. Rejected the idea. I'd need a clear head if we were going to live through this night. Joniel looked up and slowly shook his head.

You grew up under that?

I nodded.

Man . . . it's a miracle you ain't crazy or dead.

I thought about what we were about to do, and to whom we were about to do it.

What makes you think I'm not?

Both . . .

We turned right off Sunset into the west entrance of Bel-Air and began making our way up the winding streets. Bel-Air is a real mixed bag of real estate: in the higher reaches of the community you can see split-levels and ranch houses that would look normal on any suburban street in America. But then here and there are those massive estates hidden behind twenty-foot-tall hedges, with enough bedrooms and bathrooms to house the Lakers but where only two or three people actually live.

Pete and I were looking for one such place in particular.

We got lost three times before finding the right street and the right address. I began to pull over but Pete motioned me on.

Park in the next block. Find a house with some cars in the driveway and park there. If they're not out by now, they're in for the night.

We found a driveway with a black Mercedes sedan and slipped in behind it.

Pete reached into the backseat and rummaged around for the duffel bag we'd put there earlier. From it he retrieved a black windbreaker and a smaller canvas bag.

We stepped out of the car. As he was zipping up his windbreaker, I noticed the butt of a revolver sticking out from a holster under his arm. He saw me looking.

Never know.

Okay.

I stepped around to the back of the Chrysler and got my Sig Sauer out of the trunk. I wedged it into the back of my jeans and pulled my shirttail out over it.

Ten minutes later we were looking across the street at Pierce Fanagin's house on Stradella Road. Not much of a front yard but it was pretty apparent he had spectacular views of the Los Angeles basin from the back. It was a large place of stone and big timbers, sort of along the lines of a French chateau. All the lights were on. All the windows were obscured by lacy curtains.

Pete touched my arm to tell me to keep walking. We stopped at the end of the street, still within sight of Pierce's place, and pushed into some hedges just as a Bel-Air security patrol cruised by. Pete held a finger to his lips. A few seconds later, a man walking a decrepit beagle approached from the other direction, the dog sniffling and shuffling along on arthritic limbs, not even noticing us as he passed by within two feet. Or maybe he was just used to men hiding in bushes around here.

When they were far enough away, Pete spoke *sotto voce*.

All these fuckin' McMansions are alarmed but most people never bother to set them, especially if they're home. I'm thinking our Mr. Fanagin there is a different case, though. I'm thinking he keeps lots of money and guns and shit in the house, so he doesn't mind taking the time to punch in the numbers when he comes and goes.

He had a gun in his office desk.

Oh? How you know that?

He pointed it at me.

Well, if that ever happens again you can be sure there'll be a hot little piece of metal coming out the end headed right for you. So don't give him the fuckin' chance next time.

I'm hoping it won't come to that.

He just grunted.

We crossed the street and moved up to the shadows next to Fanagin's three-car garage. The garage was connected to the house, but there was a side door visible on the other side of a three-foot-high cast-iron fence. We hopped the fence and squatted next to the door, out of sight from the street.

Pete pulled on some gloves, then tested the doorknob.

He mouthed, *locked.*

He opened the little canvas case, rummaged around, and pulled out a handful of what looked like ordinary house keys for different kinds of locks and a rubber mallet. He tested a few of the keys, found one that fit, turned it slightly, and popped it with the mallet. Something clicked. Pete pulled out the bump key, straightened up, and whispered . . .

Moment of truth.

. . . and opened the door. We immediately heard a steady beeping sound coming from an alarm keypad somewhere inside the garage. Pete reached around and pushed the lock button on the doorknob, then closed the door again. We jumped over the fence and started down the street, walking at a steady but unhurried, and therefore unsuspicious, pace. Pete was breathing heavily from exertion, not that there'd been much yet. Both of our adrenaline counts were sky-high. He had to space out his words.

Standard is thirty seconds . . . for the code to be entered . . . before the alarm goes off. Let's get back to our bush . . . watch what happens.

Seems like a waste of money to have an alarm in the garage but a lock you can open that easily.

People are fuckin' naïve. They think a lock's a lock. And this is just a garage. Probably didn't think it needed anything more. Listen, whadaya expect when half of the burglaries in this city happen when crooks just walk in the front or back door that's not even locked?

I was anticipating the wail of an alarm siren would start screaming bloody hell before we could duck back into the hedge, but the night remained silent. It only took another minute for the front door to open, however, and Pierce Fanagin to emerge with what looked at that distance to be shotgun at the ready. All three garage doors opened simultaneously. Fanagin was peering around and under his fleet of expensive cars when the Bel-Air private police showed up. Some kind of discussion followed and the two rent-a-cops took their turns poking around the garage. All three men checked the side door and presumably saw it was still locked. One of the security officers held out a clipboard for Fanagin to sign, and they left. Fanagin walked back inside his house and the garage doors closed.

We waited a few moments, then returned to the garage and repeated the exercise.

And again.

And again.

By the fourth visit, the Bel-Air cops weren't even bothering to look around and Fanagin was visibly agitated. When they had him sign the clipboard yet again I could hear him say, *fucking ADT piece of shit!* from all the way down the street.

Fanagin stormed back into the house and the security guys drove away. Ten minutes passed before Pete turned to me and slapped my back.

Time to commit a felony.

This time, the alarm keypad didn't start beeping when we opened the door. Fanagin had obviously turned the system off, presumably chalking it up to a malfunctioning sensor.

The other interesting thing about people with expensive houses and expensive alarm systems and private security firms at their beck and call: They never lock their expensive cars when they're parked inside their expensive garages.

The yellow Ferrari dozed in the middle stall between a Hummer and a Benz. Pete popped the trunk and we looked inside. There was a little bag with the automaker's logo on it, the *cavallino rampante,* which held a reflective warning triangle and a few tools, as if anyone who drives one of those cars would bother getting their hands dirty changing a tire. Pete opened the little canvas bag he'd brought and transferred a few items into the Ferrari bag, then quietly closed the trunk. He then took out his pistol, wrapped it in the canvas bag, and gave the right taillight of the exotic car a firm whack. It shattered. Pete stooped to pick up the broken pieces of red plastic.

We locked the door on our way out of the garage.

I didn't notice until I fished out the keys for the Chrysler that my hands were shaking.

CHAPTER TWENTY-NINE

The Super Street race at Irwindale wouldn't start until seven the next evening, which meant we had about twenty hours to kill. I dropped Pete back at the biker bar. He had a few gentle words of advice.

Don't you get second thoughts about this. What's done is done. You know that fuck Fanagin would never get indicted, much less convicted, for what he did to those girls and God knows what else. Not to mention what he'll eventually do to all of us. Don't chicken out. See it through.

Hey, it was my idea wasn't it?

But he knew I was struggling with it. The only thing that put my mind at ease was thinking about two young women whose lives were ended on the whim of one man. And that he'd threatened the people I cared about most.

I went back to the Best Western and got a few restless hours of sleep. I turned on the TV. I flipped through a week-old newsmagazine. I doodled on the room-service menu.

Sitting around waiting was going to drive me insane. I had to do something to get my mind off everything. I called Kenny at seven A.M.

Feel like getting in some practice today?

Glad to know you're still alive, Huckleberry. How's my wife's car doing for you?

Good. Thanks again for that. I'll need it one more day if that's okay. Say, in thirty?

No worries.

I stopped at a Taco Bell and got some highly nutritious breakfast burritos for us both.

What a lot of people don't realize about professional golfers is they have to practice and practice and practice constantly in order to keep everything flowing smoothly and with reliable consistency. The golf swing is not a natural movement, and in order to know exactly where the ball is going to go when you hit it, you have to be exact in every aspect of that swing. If the take-back is off by a few centimeters, for instance, that can change the flight of the ball in a radical way, a geometric way, and absolutely ruin your chances of scoring well.

So we spend a lot of time just hitting golf balls. Hundreds a day.

But for many, maybe even for most of us, all this practice, all this hitting of golf balls, is among the most relaxing, enjoyable, rewarding parts of our profession. There's no leader board to keep an eye on. There's no pressure. It's just you and the ball. Swing and hit. Swing and hit. Watch it fly. Hear the smack and whirr as it shoots into the blue. Make an adjustment. Swing and hit. Try to shape it. Try a cut shot. Punch shot. Three-quarter. Work on that fade that comes in so handy.

Swing and hit. Swing and hit.

Kenny and I didn't say a word for three hours on the driving range. He'd move around, watching my motion from various angles, but he wouldn't say a thing, knowing I could tell when something wasn't quite right, and

I could make the correction. Kenny isn't my coach; he's my partner. He's my supporter. He's my friend.

I finished up by putting about three dozen balls and we called it a morning. As he parked in his garage, he turned off the ignition and looked at me with concern in his eyes.

This thing you're mixed up in. It's gotten bad, eh?

It wasn't really a question. I nodded.

Is it the sort of thing you can just let just blow over?

Not really. It won't go away. I'm just having a hard time doing what needs to be done to clear it all up.

Right.

I reached for the door handle but out of the corner of my eye I saw Kenny settle back into his seat. He was looking out the windshield at the shelves filled with shoe boxes and sleeves of golf balls. I took that to mean the conversation wasn't over, so I sat back, too, and just waited. The silence lasted five minutes.

Doral, last year. Remember your second on the twelfth?

Translation: my second shot on the twelfth hole. Kenny was talking about the Ford Championship of last March. After a strong front nine I was four under par but had stumbled a bit with back-to-back bogeys. On the twelfth I drove the ball into the woods and was faced with a perpendicular chip-out that would've gotten me back on the fairway but eliminated any chance of birdie, or a near-impossible thread-the-needle shot through a narrow gap in the trees. I chose the latter.

I try not to. Remember it.

You should. You should picture that moment every time you pick up a golf club.

I'll bite. Why?

Because that shot is who you are.

The ball was resting against a tree root. I swung an easy four-iron that made a solid impact on the Titleist before the club head smacked into the root. A pain shot through my left wrist; the little white pill shot through the gap in the trees, headed like an arrow toward the pin.

It was a windy day. Just before the ball cleared the trees, a wispy little branch with, oh, maybe two or three leaves clinging to it, swept into its path, deflecting it just enough to send it flying deeper into the woods, never to be found again.

He started to climb out of the car.

Gutsy play.

Yeah, right. We made double-bogey.

Kenny stood, his back to me, and stretched his arms above his head before looking back over his shoulder.

Gutsy play.

I got into the Chrysler and headed back toward the Best Western.

When I turned my cell back on there were three messages. Detective McIntyre wanted to talk, immediately. Judith wanted to talk, immediately. Pete just wanted to make sure I wasn't pussying out.

I called Doc first. She answered on the first ring.

Hello, my dear Huck. You were right about the blood, it's a match with the mystery semen. That's all I can say now. Detective McIntyre says we're jeopardizing his case and threatened to make a formal complaint against me for breach of procedure. He says you have to deal only with him and that I have to stop all contact with you.

Right. Care to have dinner this weekend?

Sure! Call me later.

McIntyre's voice mail picked up, meaning he was probably on the other line, so I left a message:

Detective, this is Huck Doyle. You have no case without me. You would have no evidence without that which I turned over to the highly competent and professional assistant M.E., so quit bullying her or this miraculous gift I keep giving you will quickly dry up. We're all on the same team. Have a nice day.

I hadn't gone two miles before McIntyre was calling me back.

Good day, Mr. Doyle. I got your message. I am not bullying anyone, merely requiring they, meaning our friend the assistant medical examiner, follow correct protocol. I don't usually respond well to threats, but you do seem to be finding out some things my people haven't been able to, so I will exercise compassion for the time being. You are officially on a short leash, however, and from now on, any evidence you find you will call me immediately, you will not touch it, and you will certainly not carry it around with you and hand it over to the lovely M.E., thus putting any future prosecution in jeopardy. Understood?

Understood.

And incidentally, where were you this morning between the approximate hours of eight and eleven this morning?

The Rancho Golf Center driving range.

Are there people who can attest to that?

Yes, including my caddie and the club pro, about six others I can name. Why?

Because the bodies of two rather large, rather dead individuals were pushed out of a nondescript black van in front of one Miss Holly Ann Cramer's condominium at exactly ten A.M.

Okay.

One of the deceased had a leg in a cast, the other a neck brace.

Uh-huh.

They had both been shot in the head with a small-caliber weapon.

That's bad, right?

Both showed signs of torture.

Wow. Yuck.

The victim with the neck brace had a driver's license inserted into his mouth identifying him as one Peter DiCarmelo. Ring a bell?

Maybe.

I thought it might. He happens to be AB-negative. Same type as that on the bloody shirt you handed over to Dr. Filipiano.

Hmm. That was fast.

Blood-typing's easy. DNA takes longer. They're doing that test on him right now.

Of course.

To see if that's his blood on your shirt.

Right.

The lab has graciously made this a priority case. Having a celebrity as a suspect does have its privileges. We should know something soon. If it is a match, I'll need you to come down for a formal chat. You understand. Police procedure and all that.

Hey, if I gotta, I gotta.

Exactly.

We hung up. I didn't want my cell-phone records to implicate her any further, so I found a pay phone and called Judith right back.

Hello?

It's Huck.

Hi! Twice in an hour! This is looking more and more like a relationship!

Ha ha. Listen, the typing being done on the shirt, you have to slow it down a little.

Silence.

Just a little. Just today. It's important. If McIntyre hauls me in for questioning, it could really screw things up on the case.

You realize this could cost me my job. Not to mention jail time.

I'm not asking you to do anything illegal, just slow down the results enough to let me wrap up things. Take the tech out for a long lunch or something. Then it will all make more sense, the shirt and everything. Trust me.

Silence again.

I gave her some time to think about it. All of about ten seconds.

Doc, I know I'm asking a lot, but I am so close to being able to prove Joniel is being framed, and who is doing the framing, but I need the rest of the day to do it. If McIntyre brings me in, the opportunity might be lost.

And I might be dead, I didn't add.

She sighed. I had a sudden, incongruous, ridiculously inappropriate fantasy about hearing that sigh under radically different circumstances someday.

Okay, okay. It shouldn't be a problem. We're so backed up, anyway.

You're the best. Really.

And hey, so what if I get fired, you know? I've been thinking about opening a nail salon, anyway.

Tired of seeing dead people?

No. But judging from your cuticles it's the last place I'd have to worry about running into a certain professional golfer.

You don't mean that. You like me.

I do. But I also like the smell of formaldehyde, so what does that tell you?

I'll make it worthwhile, I promise.

Oh, yeah? Pray tell how, Mr. Doyle.

Well, how about an all-expenses-paid trip, first-class accommodations, and a front-row seat at the tournament at Pebble Beach next week.

Hmm. Watching *with* you, or watching *you*?

Watching me.

If I make the cut. If I'm still breathing. If I'm not in jail. If, if, if.

Sounds lovely.

Any chance you can you take the week off?

I'm feeling a nasty cold coming on.

There's a lot of that going around.

CHAPTER THIRTY

Pete and I were back in Fanagin's neighborhood by three, sitting half a block away in the Chrysler. A Bel-Air patrol drove by twice, eyeing us. Pete pulled out his phone and called someone.

> Johnny-boy. Doyle. Yeah, me too. Naw, doin' all right. How're the kids? Oh? That's great. Got him a Softail? No shit! Nice. Sweet bike. Why I called, I'm on a little surveillance gig and I'm in the area. If you get a report about a black Chrysler 300, ignore it, okay?

He listened then cast his eyes over to me.

> Yeah, Homeland Security gig. Pays like shit but whatthefuck, right? Sure, let's do that for sure. I haven't done that ride in years. Thanks, Johnny. See ya.

Then we waited.

At a quarter to four, a black Mercedes-Benz pulled into the driveway at the faux chateau and then into the garage. Thirty minutes later, the garage door opened again and the bright yellow Ferrari Maranello lumbered out, made a tire-squealing turn onto the street, and roared off in the direction the Benz had come from.

We followed at a discreet distance. Pete flipped open his phone.

It's Doyle. On his way. Just turned onto Sepulveda headed to the 405. I'll call you back when we get on the 101.

Traffic was heavy, but traffic is always heavy around L.A. Fanagin drove like he was already in the race. It became a challenge to keep up with Ferrari as it darted and maneuvered between the other cars, a disdainful god among lesser beings. The Chrysler did all right, but I found myself missing the horsepower of my Bronco.

We were on the 405 Freeway for about five miles. The sign for the 101 loomed ahead, and Pete hit the redial button on his phone.

Getting on the 101 now.

That's when I pulled out my phone and dialed a number I now knew by heart. He seemed sincerely happy to hear from me.

Nice of you to call, Mr. Doyle. I was just going to call you. Seems the DNA results took a little longer than promised, in fact I had to lose my temper a bit with a few people, but the blood in the cold, dead veins of Mr. DiCarmelo did indeed match that on your shirt. I need you to come in as soon as possible, preferably within the hour.

Yes, well, listen. DiCarmelo and the other dead guy committed the murders of both girls, but the man they worked for, the man who ordered the killings, is at this moment getting on the 101 Freeway headed east. He's in a bright yellow Ferrari, you can't miss him.

I see. And what is this gentleman's name?

Pierce Fanagin.

Pierce Fanagin . . .

I spelled it for him. He chewed on that for a moment.

I'll be back in touch. This afternoon, Mr. Doyle, at police headquarters.

Sure. See you there. You better hurry; he's driving pretty fast.

I then dialed another number.

Yeah?

So, what do you think is the absolute hardest shot in golf?

He didn't answer right away, but I could hear the throaty growl of the big engine over the phone.

I gotta hand it to you, you're one brave sonofabitch. I'd be halfway to China by now if I was you. Where exactly *have* you been, by the way?

The toughest shot. What is it?

I don't fucking know, you dumb shit! What the fuck does that have to do with anything?

Careful, Gino. You're letting your Jersey accent slip in.

Fuck you! You're so fucking dead!

Yeah, so you've said. The toughest shot, Mr. Licante, in all of golf isn't the long drive over a hazard or the tricky bunker play. It's not the punch under trees. It's not a downhill lie. It's not two-thirty over water into a wind.

The Ferrari had slowed noticeably, as is usually the case when a driver's engaged in a conversation. I let him stew for a second, knowing he'd never in a million years hang up before getting the answer.

You ready, Pierce? I'm sorry, Gino? You ready?

Yeah, asshole. I'm ready. Thrill me with your fucking wisdom.

A three-foot putt.

Beat . . . two . . . three . . . four . . .

A three-foot putt? What the fuck? Why is that the hardest fucking shot?

Because you're so goddamn sure you can't miss—until, that is, you're standing over the ball, and everything's on the line.

Yeah?

Yeah. And that's where you are right now, Pierce. You think you got it all wrapped up nice and neat, but you're about to lip it out. You're caught, buddy. I'm giving it all to the cops, everything. You're not only going to jail for the rest of your life, but your whole family is about to be exposed for who they are. How's that feel?

That so? Well, *Fuck y*—

I turned off the phone and set it in the cup holder between the seats.

The police cruiser was on the shoulder of the road just before the Universal City exit. We watched as it moved smoothly through the traffic and in behind the Ferrari, a shark stalking a swordfish through a school of grouper.

Blue lights went on.

Fanagin took his sweet time pulling over. I wondered if he was even then contemplating making a run for it. The cop car positioned itself behind the Ferrari.

I drifted over to the left-hand lane and pulled onto the shoulder across from them, about a hundred feet back. Pete glanced over at me with that ugly grin on his face.

This is the most fun I've had in years.

Try Disneyland next time. It's healthier.

Between passing cars we could see the cops approach cautiously, each resting a hand on their gun. Fanagin had both of his on the steering wheel and it was obvious he was yelling something at them. Seems he was already nice and worked up before they even pulled him over.

Wonder why.

The officer at the driver's side door was now talking to Pierce. The expression on the sports agent's face turned from anger to surprise, and he got out of the Ferrari, dressed in his nifty Nomex racing suit, and walked with the cop around the back of the car to look at the broken taillight. The other officer stood a short distance away, watching Fanagin closely.

He raised his arms as if to say, *You gotta be kidding me.* But whatever really came out of his mouth must've been a little more descriptive, because both cops began gesturing in that *youbettercalmthefuckdownmister* way they teach at the Academy.

Pierce Fanagin didn't calm down. Pierce Fanagin looked about as pissed as a human being could get.

In response to something one of the cops said, Fanagin glared even more and reached into a small pocket on his chest to produce what probably was a driver's license.

In response to something else the cop said, Fanagin walked to the passenger-side door, reached into the glove compartment, and handed over a couple other little pieces of paper. I'm guessing insurance and registration.

In response to the next thing that was asked of him, Fanagin angrily waved an arm in the general direction of his gorgeous Italian-made supercar . . .

. . . walked over to it . . .

. . . and opened the trunk.

I held my breath.

The officer bent over to inspect the trunk. He then straightened up with the Ferrari's tool bag in hand. He zipped it open and looked inside. He stared for about five seconds, then turned and said something to the cop standing on the other side of Pierce's car.

Pierce was apparently intrigued himself. He, too, peered into the bag. When he looked up the expression on his face ran the gamut of incomprehension, to realization, to a seething rage.

Pete said something under his breath, something that sounded like,

Yeah, there you go, Porter. Give the motherfucker the bait.

The police officer standing at the front of the Ferrari walked over to look at his partner's discovery. As the three of them stood there inspecting the contents of the Ferrari's tool bag, the distant sound of police sirens became apparent over the steady hum of highway traffic. One of the cops turned with a smirk on his face and said something to Fanagin, who glanced in the direction of the sirens, glanced back at the items inside the bag, then did the unbelievable. The insanely stupid.

The inevitable.

In one quick motion he reached down and snatched the officer's weapon out of its holster.

Fanagin backed away, the gun in his hand jerking as he pulled the trigger again and again.

Only, I heard no shots.

The cops were both crouched, and they both somehow had weapons in hand, and they both opened fire simultaneously. Puffs of smoke appeared from their barrels. The sound of gunshots rent the air above the drone of the traffic. Their arms pumped. Fanagin straightened up. And. Well . . .

When people really get shot it doesn't look like it does in the movies, where they whirl around balletlike from the impact of the bullets. It's much more ungraceful than that. Pierce Fanagin collapsed onto the asphalt like a Thanksgiving Day float that suddenly lost all its air. His head lolled over and smacked the ground. I'm pretty sure he didn't feel it.

Pete punched the dashboard in glee. I looked over at him. It felt like all this was happening in a dream.

Goddamn that's beautiful!

Within seconds two unmarked sedans pulled up behind the cruiser. As we watched McIntyre get out of one, Pete waggled a finger toward the flow of traffic.

Better get out of here. Try to merge slowly to not draw any attention.

I eased the car into drive, waited for a gap, and pulled away from the shoulder. My mind was fogged.

Holy shit. Holy shit.

Pete stayed silent, but he was still grinning. I tasted bile and swallowed hard to keep it down.

Shit, Pete. He really did it. Just like you said. Went for the gun. I mean, I didn't really think he would . . .

I wasn't looking at Pete, but I felt his eyes shift to my face.

His voice was a low rumble.

Listen to me, Huckleberry. And listen real close. Don't go getting all regretful now. Don't you dare. When you got a cancer on your lung, do you fuckin' hope someone asks it nicely to stop killing you or do you take it the fuck out? Huh? That's what this was, sport. That's what this fuckin' was. This was surgery.

But how did you know he would? How could you know for sure?

Because I've known guys like him my whole life. Look, it's like this. Some people, they exist in the world, you know? And some people think the world exists for them. That asshole thought everything around is just his for the taking. So fuckin' easy, it all is. So when the tables get turned, they aren't used to that. They don't know how to deal. So they react like the wild fuckin' animals they are, the only way they know how. They lash out, hard.

But to shoot at some cops in front of hundreds of witnesses?

That's just it. They're not thinking about repercussions or legalities or none of that shit. They hit back hard and then figure it out later. When he saw that shit in his trunk, and after your little phone call egging him on, he knew he was up the shit creek. He knew his cover would be blown, and at the very least he'd be doing some time. So he figured, fuck it, I'll shoot it out, run and hide, and go someplace else. Done it before, do it again.

And if he hadn't?

Pete sat back and looked at the roof of the car, not saying anything. I had to repeat the question.

And if he hadn't gone for the gun?

Well, then, Huckleberry, chances are good Mr. Pierce Fanagin would've somehow managed to commit suicide while in jail. Poor guy would've had a sudden case of the guilts and decided to make his amends.

Pete. You're talking murder.

He closed his eyes and reclined the Chrysler's leather seat as far back as it would go.

No, son. I'm talkin' surgery.

CHAPTER THIRTY-ONE

The drive to Pebble Beach usually takes about five and a half hours, but if you leave early enough you can make really good time.

Traffic was thin on the I-5. It was already warm. I had the top down. Aretha Franklin singing on the iPod. A beautiful woman dozing in the seat next to me.

Pierce Fanagin had been dead four days.

My interview with Detective McIntyre was delayed a few hours while he worked out the details of the incident on the 101. He was initially skeptical but eventually bought my explanation that I dug up the goods on Fanagin through a combination of shoe leather and dumb luck. My guess is his instincts were telling him otherwise, but in the end he believed me because he *wanted* to believe me. It tied up a lot of complicated investigations and despite the mess, three bad guys were no longer walking the streets of his city.

That's just a figure of speech, by the way. Nobody walks in Los Angeles.

The Review Board immediately declared it a good shooting, what with about two dozen witnesses who all saw the same thing: Fanagin shooting at the cops, and the cops then returning fire. Turned out the gun Fanagin grabbed from the officer's holster, a standard LAPD-issue 9mm, jammed—

a bit of good fortune for the police officers, as was the fact that that particular officer, an old, close friend of my father's, by the way, always carried an ankle gun. Just in case.

I was pretty sure the automatic was jammed before Fanagin even climbed into his Ferrari that day.

The officers were criticized in the media for poor procedure, letting a suspect get close enough to grab a weapon, but thanks to a series of reports in the *Los Angeles Times* based on information conveniently leaked to them by an anonymous source close to the investigation—also known as *me*—most of the attention centered on Pierce Fanagin, his extracurricular dalliances, and some intriguing items that tied him to two, possibly four murders.

What the police saw in the Ferrari's tool kit that day was the brick of heroin originally intended to put me in prison for a long time, or get me dead for a long time, and the computer hard drive containing the images of one very dead young woman and one very dead Peter Francisco DiCarmelo, both neatly sealed in a quart-size zipper-lock plastic bag. Which happened to contain a complete set of fingerprints. From Pierce Fanagin's fingers.

Police found no significance in the trace quantities of mayonnaise, balona grease, and bread crumbs also present in the Baggie.

A subsequent search of Fanagin's Bel-Air home turned up a .32 caliber handgun inside a trash can next to the garage. It was clean of prints and the serial number had been filed off, but ballistic tests later matched that pistol to the bullets in DiCarmelo's and Dano's brainpans.

Holly's body was finally released to her family, who had it flown back for burial in Terre Haute, where she was once a lovely little girl with lovely big dreams. A lovely little girl who, when she looked to the west, didn't notice the part of the map that said, *here there be monsters.*

Tiffany—Elisabeth—was cremated. Lindsey and I saw Charlie at the service, standing in the back of the church. We caught each other's eye just for a split second, but his face was as implacable as the Sphinx. He was gone by the time the ceremony was over.

Detective McIntyre was booked on all the morning shows. He was eloquent and interesting while describing how a once-respected sports agency had become a front for so many nefarious endeavors. He announced a multi-jurisdictional investigation into the presence of a new crime syndicate in the L.A. basin. Frankie *the Ear* was never found and my sincere hope is he took an early retirement somewhere far, far away.

During a press conference, McIntyre implied the violent death of Pierce Fanagin, while unfortunate, may have ended the mafia's ambitions here before they were firmly planted, and ultimately shined the light on other businesses he was found to be involved in—namely drugs and porn.

Being a very savvy civil servant, the good detective neglected to mention those very same drug and porn businesses catered to, or benefited from, quite a few big-name celebrities.

In the City of Angels, justice is blind. Not stupid.

I had stopped by to check on Lindsey two days earlier. She was in nurse's whites, curled up in bed, snoozing peacefully. Her head on Blue's chest. He was asleep, too, with a big smile on his face. I left them to their dreams.

Pete and I haven't talked since that day. There's nothing much to say. He knows I haven't completely been able to come to grips yet with what we did. We'll get back in touch eventually, when one of us needs the other, but if the subject of that day comes up it'll be like all our conversations about Blue . . . or Mom. Meaning, it won't ever be discussed.

Don't get me wrong: I'm not sorry Fanagin's dead. And by handing Charlie DiCarmelo and Dano's driver's licenses, I'm as guilty of their deaths as whoever pulled that trigger.

I'm not sorry. I don't know what I am yet. When I think about it, I get restless and squirmy and have to take a walk. Usually to the freezer. Via the cupboard.

Maybe my discomfort with the course of events is less about the results and more about seeing it happen in front of my own eyes. Maybe I'm the guy who loves the steak but can't bear to watch the bull get slaughtered.

I was thinking about all that when a semi blasted his air horn almost right next to us because a bozo in a minivan had cut him off. Judith sat bolt upright, then smiled sheepishly at me and stretched.

Was I drooling?

Absolutely. That imported leather seat is soaked.

Oh dear. I'm sorry. And such nice leather, too.

She looked around.

Where are we?

Just passed the exit to Bakersfield.

Judith reached over, settled back, and began shuffling through songs on my iPod. I could tell she was still mulling over things. A few moments later she proved me right.

What you haven't told me yet is what Fanagin's men were looking for at Lindsey's. Hadrich was probably already dead by then.

She was referring to Tiffany.

The drugs. Tiffany was staying with Lindsey for a few days until she found a new place, and near as I can guess she had stolen quite a bit of heroin from Fanagin's outfit at some point, probably while visiting his place. Lindsey didn't know this, but Tiffany had started doing porn for him. They filmed at a little studio inside one of his men's houses. McIntyre has the raw production tapes. I think Fanagin found out he had a substantial amount of H missing, and he and his boys confronted Tiffany. That's when they must have convinced her, or extorted her more probably, to help them frame Joniel. Or more likely she didn't even know what it was for, just that she had to do them a favor to stay alive. Fanagin couldn't let Joniel make a public fuss over the money he was skimming because it would draw too much attention to him, and also cause him to lose most if not all their big-name clients. By framing Joniel and killing Tiffany, he gets rid of two problems at once.

So she saves the condom after sleeping with Joniel.

Right. That's why she asked to stay behind at the hotel when they finished. I don't think there's a chance in hell she knew how it would be used or that Holly would be killed. But still, she must have been terrified.

And then they planted the condom on Holly. But why kill Holly in the first place? Why not just kill Tiffany to frame Joniel? After all, there were all those witnesses who saw him leave the club with her.

I shrugged.

I have no idea. Maybe they figured it would be harder for Joniel to beat two murder raps that had strong evidence. Maybe a struggling actress makes for a more sympathetic victim to a jury than a strung-out stripper. Either way, that was some pretty unimpeachable evidence for sure. But one of the guys, DiCarmelo, wanted to have his fun, too. So he rapes Holly, then tries to destroy the evidence with bleach.

He almost succeeded.

Her tone was regretful.

I can't believe I was so lazy.

Hey, ninety-nine times out of a hundred it's the simple answer. You know that.

Yes, but it's my job to look past the obvious and I didn't this time.

Well, good thing you have a friend like me then, isn't it? You're allowed one screwup in life and you just had yours. Congratulations; you're now perfect in every way.

The smile returned. She found some old Neil Young and turned up the volume.

And young Mr. Baker, he was obviously grateful to have a friend like you.

If anything, the stud-puppy-All-Star Savior of the City was even more popular than before all this happened. It's one thing to be accused of a heinous crime and be acquitted; it's another to be proven completely innocent and the victim of a vicious frame-up.

Joniel was soon to be back in training. He had meetings with potential new sponsors lined up every day for a month, but Nike was pushing for a record-breaking exclusive deal.

Before he left for spring training camp we had a few drinks in his glass-encircled game room, the lights of the Valley stretching out at our feet. We were playing Tiger Woods on the PlayStation, and I was four strokes behind.

Enjoy this, Joniel. It'll never happen in the real world.

Never know. All it takes is practice . . .

Little luck doesn't hurt, either.

Phsssh.

Man, that I got. That I got.

He set down the controller and turned to look out the wall of windows. A line of jets approached Burbank Airport in the distance, looking like a string of Christmas lights.

I gotta tell you something, and I'm not proud of it but you gotta hear it. What you don't know, Huck, day this went down, when Fanagin got popped, I was packed and on my way out of town. In disguise, man. That passport I showed you, it's in a different name. No way I was going to prison. And I couldn't see any way out of this. All the evidence they had said I done it. I killed those two girls. Shit, everybody wanted to believe it, too. Like they took joy in seeing me come down so far. People was betting *against* me, man! Hoping I'd get put away forever!

Not everyone, Joniel. The line at Vegas had it twelve to one you were innocent.

Not innocent, man. The bet was I wouldn't be convicted. Big difference.

Joniel stood up and walked over to the bar.

So, I was heading out to Thailand for a while. I know people there. Had a bunch of cash with me. Figured I'd grow a beard and live off some investments or something. Better than death row, you know? Either way, all this gets left behind.

I nodded, but what I was thinking was if Joniel *had* run before our hand played out, it would've made him look as guilty as the other guys. A fellow murderer instead of the victim of a frame.

I'm glad you didn't go.

Naw, man, you're not hearing me. I *was* gone. When you called and told me Fanagin was dead, I was sitting in a Lear at John Wayne waiting for takeoff. I came that close to ruining my life. Hell, *ending* my life.

He picked up something out of a dish.

So, man, what I want to say is I'm sorry. I shoulda trusted you. Ask a man to do something, give him a chance to do it before you give up on him, you know? Fuck, I should know that more than anyone. So . . . I'm sorry.

He turned and tossed something toward me.

And thanks. Thanks, man. Little token . . . you know . . .

I caught it in the air and looked down at a single car key. The fob attached to it was a silver disk with a bas-relief of a rearing stallion and the letters F430 engraved underneath.

I laughed.

And tossed it back.

Thanks, but no thanks, man. I'm not much of a Ferrari guy.

And as I drove through California's farm country on a cloudless day, with a beautiful, smart woman by my side, on my way to play the game I love, I thought about luck, and how the trick is seeing what you have, not what you don't, and how I really should, as Kenny always says, honor the gift I've been given by enjoying every minute of it.

I don't need a Ferrari to be happy. There are so many better things in life, I thought, as I lowered my gaze from the blacktop, over the long, sweeping expanse of an elegant hood, to admire the outstretched wings of a very British steering wheel logo.

Which just happened to be attached to a sapphire blue Aston Martin.

EPILOGUE

About a hundred and fifty years ago, legend has it, a Scotsman by the name of Robert Louis Stevenson wandered the California coast near present-day Pebble Beach, looking for inspiration for his stories. He wrote about fear, and courage, and the ambiguity of morality.

In his first and most famous novel, *Treasure Island*, there is a key geographic feature: Spyglass Hill, for which the golf course I happened to be standing on was named. In fact, each hole on the course bears a name from that book: *Black Dog, Long John Silver, Billy Bones*. The Professional Golf Association considers Spyglass Hill, or The Glass as it's known to players, one of the most difficult courses on tour. It has fairways as narrow as a pirate ship's plank. Its greens soar and dip and sway like rolling surf. And players can be forgiven for a touch of seasickness as they approach the par-four eighth fairway, which cants hard to starboard while at the same time doglegging to port, or the fourteenth, which tacks back and forth like a schooner running from a hurricane.

You don't play The Glass; you have a knife fight with it, slashing away at the ice plant rough, thrusting between soaring Monterey pines, stabbing at the heart of its infinitesimal greens. And all the while, the ocean breeze blowing off the Pacific brings to your ears the mocking laughter of long-dead buccaneers.

I let my mind meander to those thoughts as I stood on the tee box at the sixteenth, waiting for the group ahead of me to clear.

I found myself here, at this point, at this place, on an overcast Saturday, with concrete-gray clouds plastered low in the sky, threatening yet another rain delay. I found myself here because yesterday I'd made the cut at the AT&T Pebble Beach National Pro-Am.

With Kenny on my bag, and Judith in my modest little tag-along gallery, I was in the next-to-final round.

Furyk and Michelson and Holmes were edging away from the pack, but with two holes left to play, I was six under for the tournament in a three-way tie for fifteenth place. If I could pull away from that clump with another birdie or two going in, I'd be set to make a run at the serious money tomorrow. And the way I was feeling, that was as sure a thing as we get in this profession.

It was John Silver's pet parrot Stevenson chose to give voice to the pirate's true nature, true goals, true God, by screeching, *Pieces of eight! Pieces of eight! Pieces of eight!*

But we aren't pirates, and professional golf isn't just about money, although money is a huge part of professional golf. Professional golf isn't just about winning, although everyone who plays tries to. It's not about sponsorships or endorsements or equipment or fame or television.

All of that is extraneous, distracting, and even somewhat dangerous, because what golf at the elite level is really all about is the antithesis of those things.

It is, at its soul, a game involving a solitary person, standing over a ball, swinging a club, and making that inanimate object do exactly what years of hard work and genetic ability require it do.

Again. And again. And again. Consistently, over a period of four days.

Under sometimes harsh weather conditions.

Against every defense a golf course designer can think up. With idiots hollering, *It's in the hole* when it's obviously not. With opponents like Choi and Woods and Scott hitting unbelievable shots just when you think they're losing the edge.

Four days of elite-level golf under enough stress to push your blood pressure to Spindletop levels.

If you let it.

But I stood on that tee box, on that gloomy day, with driver in hand and not a tinge of tension in my shoulders simply and solely because I hadn't let it.

I felt no stress as I set up to the ball, lightly flexing my grip, a movie of what was about to happen playing pleasantly in my imagination.

I breathed easily as I rechecked my target before settling my gaze on the back of the ProV1.

I brought the big club back and forward in a measured but accelerating pendulum, launching the pill down the right side of the ridiculously constricted fairway, cutting the corner of the dogleg.

I knew from the solid feeling of the impact that the ball was doing exactly what I wanted it to, overflying the tall pine that was invisible from the tee box and landing past the trees, where the fairway opened up nicely, and where a middle-iron to the green would give me every opportunity for a birdie, and every opportunity to continue to make this what it already felt like: the beginning of a career year.

As I pictured my little white Titleist finally coming to rest, out of sight, on the lovely short green *Poa annua* grass, I thought about those who calmed my nerves and stilled my thoughts, who helped me focus on what was important and discard what was not, who showed me the impossible was possible, and brought me to this place of inner peace and balance . . .

. . . and I offered a silent thanks . . .

. . . to Pamela Anderson's breasts.